The Eden Dream

Angela Timms

Copyright © 2019 Angela Timms

All rights reserved.

ISBN: 9781098585549

DEDICATION

For the Interwired Referees Katie, Dave, Alex and Teece and players. A happy memory even though it was a very dark world.

BOOKS BY THE SAME AUTHOR

Phoenix Rising: The Covenant
Phoenix Rising: Broken Vow
Thunder in the Mountains
No Strings Attached

ACKNOWLEDGMENTS

The Interwired Referees for their inspiration.

1

Black sticky rain fell from a thunderous sky. The liquid glistened with an oily sheen on the tired street, caressing the tired faces of tired people who threw their last bit of energy into dashing for another small piece of cover before that cover too became rubble. The odd one or two just stood, face blank in the rain. Defiant? Too tired to care? Too confused to know anymore? Attacker becoming victim, potential victim becoming attacker as survival feral came out of the depths in many.

A small boy, his childhood curiosity compelling him to frame his face with the window he couldn't resist looking out of. In a moment he was caught by a ricochet. The bullet tore into his face as his lifeless body fell back into the blackness where his mother screamed, her hopeless cry lost in the rattle of gunfire and the screams of the street.

Still the rain fell, washing the blood into pools of sticky liquid, turning the earth to mud, running red from the corpses which lay undealt with. It splashed against walls, against the wheels of an armoured vehicle which picked its way through the running people. The revolutions of its wheels, the hum of its engine, the constant slam and thud as the bullets scraped ineffectually at its metal carcass as women and children clawed at the doors and windows. The doors were locked, the driver and passenger stared blankly at the road ahead, not oblivious to the cries of those they must leave behind. The windows reflected back the tired and hungry faces both inside and out.

The bullet riddled vehicle, dented and patched together, most of its paintwork long scratched off by a deluge of bullets which had rained down on it, scored and battered it. Child like it crawled through the streets, baby steps, jolted occasionally by its partly broken track, just one oriental symbol readable if the mind fills in the gaps, the mark of the Yakuza. Those who noticed the mark no longer afraid, all residue of the old fears gone in the face of the current holocaust. It was written on their faces, in the tears that tracked the dirt on the faces of those who had completely given up, many of whom clutched their knees, rocking in the shadows.

Colours faded to a muddy miasma of browns and greys, tribal markings, clothing and face paint which had once to brightly identified the wearers as one gang or another showed up occasionally. Flashes of those who had shone equally bright in their own world mere hours earlier now running like the rest. Some still howled their old cries, animalistic and unsupported now, no longer noble, no longer safety in the strength of numbers, the numbers were now gone. The scavenger gangs who had once struggled for status now struggled for that little bit of shelter or ran wild until that bullet with their name on it found them.

The bodies piled up as those who had initially been scavengers seeking to capitalize on chaos crawled from the safety of the crumbled buildings to snatch what they could of the clothing and equipment of the falling. If they were lucky they also managed to grab guns and ammunition, used immediately on each other in the deadly squabble over scraps. Many were rewarded by their own space on the ever growing piles of bodies. Others crawled back to the shadows with their prize to risk all again to loot those who had just fallen.

Broken buildings clung precariously to the skeleton of their former glory. With a crack another building died, its heart ripped out by shells ~~instantly forgotten~~. The last grip of their ancient beauty and structure lost. Stonework fell in slow motion, hand carved stone just missiles now. What was once admired, once loved now gravity driven projectiles to crush those who had sought refuge in the blasted shell.

The passenger in the van looked blankly at his reflection in the glass. He was staring at a face he knew so well, at the mirror shades, the long black curls and his face, slightly more gaunt now if that was possible, slightly more worried, slightly paler. He lit up a cigarette, pensively taking a long drag, his hands still immaculately manicured, long thin white fingers elegantly clasping, projecting from fingerless black leather gloves. Elegant hands but hands of a killer all the same. A moment to reflect on that, the killer in a box creeping through to safety if it was alright with fate. He smiled to himself but the smile was without warmth. It wasn't directed, nobody could see him through the darkened glass and his mirror shades.

The driver's muscular build was tested to the limit as he constantly adjusted the course to get through the falling masonry and to make the most of chances to speed up to get through the firestorm as quickly as possible. His eyes similarly hidden behind wrap around shades, his neatly groomed hair immaculately swept back off of his broad brow. Despite the chaos his skilfully tailored black suit, pressed to perfection s~~till perfection.~~ The vibrant colours of the intricate artwork of his Yakuza tattoos a contrast to the black and grey of the rotting world. He sat bolt upright, focused, inscrutable, his eyes fixed on the road as he guided the vehicle through streets which were moment by moment becoming less recognizable.

The passenger cast a glance at him, reassured by his expressionless visage. That made him smile. Expressionless as always were the thoughts that crept into his mind, the inscrutable oriental at face value when he knew the irony of that as a bullet skittered across the windshield, slightly chipping the glass, something he barely noted.

The passenger took a long drag on his cigarette, holding it elegantly between forefinger and thumb. He focused on the red grow at its tip as a woman's lifeless body bounced off of the window beside him. He didn't look up as the red flower of her blood splattered across the bullet proof glass. He glanced up momentarily as she slid down and disappeared under the wheels as the van drove on. There was hardly a bump in the van's progress as she slid under the tracks.

The driver cast a sideways glance at his passenger. "Nothing changes Lightningsan."

Lightning sighed. "Guess it doesn't, is this progress Danielsan? Is this wat it was all for?"

"Alternatives, we've been through all this. Don't get sentimental now, there will be time for that later. Remember your training."

Lightning drew a breath slowly, held it for a moment, leaning back against the leather of the seat, feeling its resilience and watching a young girl run across the road and dive for cover. He flicked his ash onto the floor as he breathed out, a plume of smoke spiralling up into the yellow of the ceiling.

The van rocked, a heavy calibre shell sending it sideways but it carried on as Daniel made the adjustments and navigated around a lump of masonry which had fallen into the road.

Lightning momentarily froze. "So this is what we have achieved? After all that."

"Lightning, the time for reminiscing is over. We discussed it, let it go or it will haunt you, concentrate on the task at hand."

"Sure Daniel, like I've got a choice." He rested his head back, staring at the yellow ceiling, watching the small plume of smoke disperse.

Buildings burned, people died but the armoured vehicle crept on.

Lightning sat in the co-pilot chair, legs raised so that his para-boots rested on the dashboard, his long black coat trailing down onto the dusty rubbish strewn floor, his long black curls falling around his shoulders. The passing world reflected back out of the surface of his light focusing mirror shades like some television show as the wheels turned ad they left the city behind. Each bore silent witness to the death and mayhem that now ruled the streets. A laptop rested in pieces on his lap, wires plugged into it in all directions, a mass of different coloured cables and junctions linking it to other pieces of tech and boxes. As he concentrated on what he was doing he shifted in his seat, feeling the reassuring bulk of his weapons pressing against his torso comforting.

"Shit!" He threw the bits of taped together laptop onto the floor. He thumped the dashboard, his voice agitated. "This'll never work man."

Daniel calmly looked over at him when he judged it safe to after casually circumnavigating a large crater in the road. He gave the pile of wires and tech which now lay amidst the rubbish on the floor his typically oriental disdainful look. "What's up?"

"I'm not a tekkie! God knows how to put this damn thing together and make it work."

"Be calm Lightning-san. Do and it will be done." Daniel's voice was monotone and calm.

"Oriental wisdom? You know, it still phases me to hear you address me in an oriental way, even after all this time. Look at you, to anyone who doesn't know."

"I know, I look like your average all American body builder. Then what was as it seemed in the old world. We were all what money could buy. You know the reasoning behind it and I'm not altogether displeased with what I've been able to achieve because of it. No time for what ifs now. It wasn't that long ago that the Ojabund sent his son to rescue one of your number and not too long ago that everything went to hell because of it."

"I know, I didn't exactly have a ride on the park myself over that one."

"It was a hard time of realization for all of us. The Yakuza were good for the Street, that brought a discipline that was needed, financial expertise and most of all people to bring development and new life into the place. We were rewarded with death." He almost hissed out those last few words.

Lightning leant back, staring out of the window at the carnage and remembered. Back to a time when Jared's Bar still stood on Ho Street.

A black sky hung over the city that night like every other night pretty much. Radiant orange sky burn accentuating the dark clouds silhouetted on the horizon. The city below glistened with pinpricks of light from the myriad of sources that illuminated the latticework of roads, buildings and cobbled together permanent and semi-permanent structures. Black rain fell from the sky, powering down from the laden thunderclouds towering above the Street, before slamming into the concrete and mingling with the dirt, gravel and blood, forming streams of tainted water which made its way into the already overworked and decaying drainage and sewer system.

Cutting through the torrent of water, a black car moved silently along an alleyway, glisteningly sleek, reassuringly expensive. Its headlights were out so as not to draw extra unwanted attention to itself.

On the street people moved hurriedly as they always did, doorway to not be bought. Freedom.

The rattle of automatic weaponry echoed through the street and somebody somewhere died. Then nobody took much notice as it was a normal sound on Ho Street.

Ho Street, built as a circular motorway around the old City of London. That was before PLEXification. Now in the chaos it had become home to thousands of exiles and misfits who had no place in the gleaming dome. It was the first port of call, a waystation for some, home to others. It was the promised sanctuary when leaving the sheltered environs of that hallowed turf when that momentous decision had been made or circumstance made it inevitable. People from all walks of life coexisting in the rat-race of the street. Life was harsh and dangerous, the standard of living far down the scale that it could no way be called standard. Still, these people continued with their daily tasks, struggling to live clinging to that spark of life which didn't belong to anyone else.

The street itself was a continuous rain soaked glistening stream of canopies and other cobbled together structures which offered shelter from the rain. A sinuous Ouroboros snake of protection. Beneath its canvas and plastic stalls, bars and clinics lined the carriageways and a sometimes dry walking area made life a little more tolerable. From that hub came food and what little entertainment was possible for the street's denizens. For those with time to listen the bars regurgitated techno-pop which pounded out its pulsating rhythms, forming the soundtrack of the life of the SINless.

The PLEX ran the domes and life within the domes was idyllic in many ways. There was no crime, no danger and the inhabitants could live in blissful ignorance of the fact that there were people exiting outside their pre-packaged environment. Every thought was monitored for their greater good, every action and deed evaluated for credits which could be spent on leisure time and the daily routine a constant path of reassurance. The property of the PLEX which rewarded good citizens and for those who were not up to standard, the Street.

Ho Street, for some it was all they had ever known and all they would ever know.

Lightning smiled to himself at the thought as he remembered. Days when he and his friends had sat in the bar, feet from death, drinking and laughing and toasting the air with that battle cry that they were free. Free? Free to do what? To run, to hide, to starve. Then when had he starved? His friend Crisis had seen that starvation was far from what he had enjoyed. He had been one of the lucky ones. Boy did he realise that now. Meeting others on the Ho, that had brought him down to earth with a very big bump. It was great being the right hand man of the King of the Hill but when you got down into Ho Street, that didn't really count for much. Reputation yes but bullets were bullets. When they were down in the dirt with what he had once thought of as "little people". Well in theory that was how it should have been but was it? Doubts crept in at those quiet times, had he really known, even back then? A shiver ran down his spine, neural sensors racing overtime, synapses crackling with energy as he remembered. The pain was sharp, the memories were sharper. No romance, the Street was deadly and dark. A demon that could not be tamed, could not be reasoned with and if you thought you had got it pinned, hell you were in for a shock. The house always won when the chips were on the table and every day could be that last gamble.

He had mostly been north side, living well on the money that the Urban Hunt Club had gathered in. They specialized in raves, all legal, well as legal as anything could be on the Street. Safe and fun, Crisis always saw to that, a real diamond guy when it came to providing a safe environment and safe recreational drugs. Hey, they were the good guys, no PCP's, no bad acid, you could trust the UHC, you could believe in them. The best bands, the best sounds, good quality clips ensuring good experiences all at a reasonable price. No hype, they were the real deal. They were dark angels with shiny black limos. Yea right, they were hustlers like anyone else, working the street for their cut, their part of the action and when they first hit the streets it was a big cut and a lot of action. Crisis was "the" man, the one to know. The "All American Hero" with an accent that could melt butter. It did the trick on many occasions. He got the deals, he got the contacts and before he knew it, well top of the hill, cool apartment, better than average sound equipment that worked without glitches, nearly new cars and cyber-ware. He paused a moment to consider his immaculate nails, smiling to himself, no manicuring needed there, the nails would not grow, they would not break, they were not real. They were a toughened silicon, hard as steel and as deadly, not retractable rippers like Crisis had chosen. His steel claws shot out to make his hands into deadly weapons. He had chosen something smaller, more discreet, neater but just as deadly when he had trained in how to use them. He clenched his fist as another body hit the windscreen and slid off. He knew how to use them.

Kings of the hill they were. Him, Crisis and Diane. Diane, there was a woman. Crisis' squeeze, just an ordinary girl, no he didn't think so, Diane and Blue, boy if he'd known then what he knew now. Twenty-twenty hindsight, a wonderful thing. Hindsight on the Ho, foresight, peripheral vision and no sentimentality, you needed it all.

The black car pulled to a halt at the end of the alleyway, and the side door swung open into the rain.

A black, leather boot splashed onto the drenched pavement, the hem of his duster coat briefly sweeping over a forming pool. His tall shape detached itself from the interior of the car to stand in the street, the wind whipping long black hair about is smooth face. His hand reached slowly inside the coat, briefly running ultra sensitive fingers over the cold metal of the semi-automatic Beretta 92R pistol, lingering momentarily before moving again. He extracted a mangled pack of cigarettes and a chromed lighter, turned it slowly in his hand, running his thumb over its inscription, 'Victims... Aren't we all.' A half smile crept across his face as he remembered the movie. He slid a cigarette from the pack, and the lighter flared into life, the reflection of the flame glittering brightly in the mirror shades that rested snugly onto the bridge of his nose. He closed the lid of the lighter and returned it to the safety of his back pocket before turning on his heels towards a door in the side of the alley.

He hesitated, took a deep breath, his hand reaching for the handle, savouring the anticipation he opened the door to reveal the bar he knew so well. Cigarette smoke swirled in the chilled air, illuminated by the slightly blue glow of the bar. Almost immediately the tension of the street lifted from his shoulders, he visibly straightened slightly as he stepped into the sanctuary of a place that many called home due to the amount of time they spent there. Groups of people sat in the smoke filled room, cradling their drinks and basking in the neon atmosphere, their faces illuminated eerily by the up-lights from the tubing in the tables. Others sat quietly in corners, conducting business in hushed voices under the background noise of late twentieth century rock music. Some turned as he entered the bar, a healthy habit that could keep them alive if the guest was an intruder. Recognition? Faces he knew, some smiled slightly or was it just relief, others turned unmoved back to their drinks.

A young raven haired woman looked up and he couldn't help smiling, a genuine smile crossed her face. He quickened his pace and crossed the bar to meet her.

She moved to meet him, graceful and cat like, the clientele parting like a sea to let her pass, her black PVC coat billowing behind her and shiny black body suit, chrome encrusted skirt and silver nail polish glimmering in the bar lights. The up-lighting and wall lights accentuating her high cheekbones and gray eyes. The movement was smooth and natural as the two moved together, winding their arms around each other in a greeting that was natural and comfortable, two good friends where friendship was the most valuable commodity you could have. Their eyes met, hesitation, too long a look, they broke away as if guilty, as if someone would notice. She smiled, her red lipstick reflecting the neon light as he watched her lips, her teeth waiting for the words. "Lighting, good to see you." Her accent was local and she was using street speak, the words clearly pronounced, a single inflection on a word could change its meaning to someone who knew the language. No hidden messages tonight though, they were among friends and it was strictly not business.

"You too. Hey Chrystal, how you doing?" He replied with a soft American accent, the tone noticeably gentle. He wound his arms more tightly around her, feeling the smooth warmth and the slight resistance of the material as he slipped his hands over it, lingering momentarily on her shoulder blade before slipping his hand down her back, under her long flowing black coat and running his finger down the small of her back. He felt his tension melt to a comfortable calm. He smiled, he was always calm when she was around, that and feeling the reassuring bulk of her Berretta so carefully concealed in a holster in the small of her back. Running his fingers over the familiar cool metal always reassured him. How often had knowing it was there saved him from a difficult situation when others watched for the gun in his holster or movement from her. She smiled, her eyes bright, her arms around his shoulders be he knew she was watching the room, ever vigilant, the room, the door, one movement out of place and he would know, he would feel her tense. He knew her moves, knew what they meant, no need for words and that was their strength. Taking in faces, their actions and reactions. He felt her tense slightly but not enough to worry about. Any more reaction than that and he would have known to reach for his gun or hers.

From the other side of the bar an older man in a long cream coat shouted over down the bar. "Hey Lighting. The usual?"

"Yeah, thanks Jared."

Crystal relaxed. They slipped apart. He frowned slightly.

Jared, an interesting guy, cop turned android-hunter turned barman. His long coat concealed many weapons, as many as he could possibly carry. He filled a glass with what was nearly beer and slid it across the bar, an invitation for them to come over. Early days in the bar, before the changes.

"So where's Crisis?" Crystal's voice was sharp, she looked worried, but then again, Crisis took a lot of worrying about.

"He'll be here in a while, he's just finishing up on a deal." Lightning took a long drink from the glass, tasting the bitter flavour of the beer and feeling the chill of the cold liquid. He wondered anew why he even bothered drinking, the toxin binders in his blood stream meant he had to drink enough to kill a bull elephant to even feel the slightest hint of intoxication. A small price to pay for the number of times it had saved his life in a not so scrupulous world. He watched Jared, so steady, so reliable, someone who you know can cope with every situation.

Crystal smiled, her eyes were too bright, he knew that look. Smiling on the outside but the eyes told another tale. To him she looked exhausted, the worry lines didn't show but the concern was deep down, he knew that. With her nothing showed on the surface, the woman he had seen change so much over the time he had known her. The woman who stood in front of him was no longer the street kid he'd first met all those years ago. He saw the woman in those dark grey eyes, reflecting back the chrome of his mirror shades, she was a reflection of the Street. The Street did that to you, changed you. No such thing as innocent youth any more. He knew that within the hour she would probably be back on the Street, carrying packages and just picking up information that was of value. She would slip out of the back door into the darkness and that would be it, she'd be back when she wanted to be whether it was a day, two days or longer. That was the thing about the Street, information was power and she traded information. There was more to her little nightly jaunts than that, he knew that was well and speculated on it often. Long nights spent in the upper rooms with Smiling Jared downing coffee with locals and just talking about things, things he was not a party to. Jared was concerned about her too, he knew that. Neither of them would ask her or talk about it. It was like an unwritten rule if they had rules, until she told them and that he doubted she would ever do.

He'd seen her talking to Doc Harley, leader of an environmental group responsible for the resistance against the PLEX and probably behind most of the soup kitchens and suppressant supplies that had appeared on the Street. The Red Plague Virus was virulent and infected pretty much everyone in one form or the other these days. The only way to survive was to take a suppressant as there was no cure. You didn't get it your would bleed out and die. The British Freedom Army (BFA) were the heroes and the good guys in the eyes of those who lived on the Street. That sort of thing did fit Chrystal's philosophy as far as he knew. She had begun to care about things just after he'd hooked her up with the Urban Hunt Club (UHC) and that unnerved him. There was a possible division of loyalties there that could become a problem. That worried him, then again she unnerved him, she always had and that was the problem. Who would have foreseen in those early days that she would be Jared's woman but looking back on it, yes, the body language and chemistry was there. Now in the here and hell-cart they were together and that was somehow right, if indeed they were together or alive.

There he was, back in the present and not somewhere he wanted to be. Looking out of the window, the sun going down, the silhouettes of the broken houses that had once been homes, the sickly orangey-green of the sky, the world of the here and now. He picked up some wires and began trying to work out where to put them that wouldn't cause sparks or damage. He had to have faith that she was out there somewhere, hopefully with her man and their daughter and the others. He sighed, dragging himself back to the past, to the image, all he had to hold onto in what was now a very crazy world.

Chrystal noticed him watching her, stretched cat like and almost purred as he moved a loose strand of hair from her face. He didn't really know why he'd done that but it was one memory that seemed to stick in his mind, even now. She always did that, got your attention but then would feign disinterest. Part of her job perhaps, gaining trust, gathering information but somehow unless you were really stupid you knew you'd never get anywhere. It was that unattainable aspect, that coldness that was Crystal, cold as ice, or she could be. He hesitated, letting his fingers rest on her cheek until his attention was drawn to Jared who had finished pulling another pint. Jared was paying attention to what he was doing. He pulled away from Crystal as Jared lifted another glass onto the bar but somehow he too seemed distracted. Most of the beer was bottled in those days but Jared still preferred the old way and had a supplier somewhere who still provided barrels.

"So, is there much happening tonight?" Jared looked sincere. As always he wanted to know, the barman's prerogative but there was something in his voice, something Lightning could not place.

He never got to answer. The side door swung open, then silence, cigarette smoke billowing into the chill night air, a figure silhouetted, the red glow behind a sea of titanium armour, a yellow number just visible on the right shoulder. The armoured unit stepped into the bar, there was silence. PLEX Cops. The tension was almost visible as they marched in, three of them, carrying pulse rifles, straight to the bar and everyone knew they had not come for a quiet drink.

Jared tensed, his hand involuntarily creeping to easy reach of the shotgun with the special rounds he kept gaffa taped under the bar. Possibly no good against these guys, their armour was clearly top of the range but it made him feel better. Black reflective visors hid their faces. Obviously designed to intimidate and why not, that was their job. One of them stopped in front of Crystal. Lightning put his hand on her back, steadying her as she noticeably swayed and any sign of guilt could bring down trouble. The man towered over her and she was leaning heavily on Lightning as all her senses screamed to run away. Lightning realized that he was holding his breath.

The PLEXcop raised a metal plated glove, hesitated as if he was going to strike and then touched Crystal's coat. Even through the visor she could feel his eyes on her. The moment hung in time. Intimidation, lightning knew she was bright enough not to budge as she kept looking firmly away from the PLEXcop. The cop grabbed her hair and turned her face towards him. Lightning cursed under his breath, retinal scan, the last thing she needed was to be put on record. Safety's clicked off of weapons around the room. But, there was something strikingly wrong. Only he was in a position to see, the PLEXcop wasn't holding her directly looking at the visor, she was slightly at an angle, enough of an angle that there could be no complete scan. The PLEXcop pushed her backwards, Lightning caught her, holding her up as he felt her knees buckle. The PLEXcop turned and moved on.

Lightning exhaled deeply, releasing the breath he had been holding in, put his arm around her and pulled her behind him. Everyone in the bar knew that the PLEXcops could kill for no reason with no comeback whatsoever.

The three PLEXcops moved as a unit, silently, taking in faces, lingering near the ones who were obviously trying not to be noticed. The tension in the bar was building. The last people welcome in Smiling Jared's Bar were the PLEX. All over the bar hands were creeping towards bulging jackets.

The door swung on its hinges, its frame empty, they were gone as quickly as they had arrived. They left a silence and the swirling cigarette smoke in their wake.

Gunfire was heard outside, bullets rattled, digging into the white plaster wall inside the open door. Someone screamed in the night, someone nearby.

Lightning glanced over his shoulder, moving slightly to put himself between Chrystal and the door. "Guess they found who they were looking for."

There was silence. Jared strode to the door and kicked it closed. "Shut the bloody door you cretins." He surveyed the damage, just a few more bullet holes in the already blasted wall. He returned to the bar, pulled himself a pint and drank it down in one.

Crystal stepped away from the bar and turned around, still keeping close to Lightning. She was shaking slightly. Jared looked over, half smiling. Lightning lifted her chin. "Problem?"

Crystal looked into his eyes. "Doubt it, he didn't pull my head direct on for some reason. Not the angle to take a print. He let me not look straight at him. Just Big Brother asserting his manhood perhaps?"

"Just another day on the Ho." Jared smiled and racked up two more pints before there was a rush at the bar and pretty much everyone came up for a refill.

The atmosphere relaxed once more, the reassuring hum of conversation returned and most people had returned to drinking though some still nervously glanced at the door. The music that Jared had chosen was relaxing, melodic, ambient. When the atmosphere had chilled out a bit the rebellious favourite protest music. Everyone knew what it meant. In the words of Pearl Jam "We're still alive". A little bit of quiet defiance which granted they couldn't hear but somehow it made everyone feel a little bit better. Defiance in a world that was closing in on them all too fast.

A group twenty somethings sat crowded together around a tiny table. Through the smoke they could be seen handing out zip lock bags full of multi-coloured computer chips. Jared caught sight of them out of the corner of his eye and then watched them with interest before turning to Lightning. "Seems like only yesterday when that would have been you and Crisis."

Lightning tensed a little.

Jared smiled. "Only recreational, no illegal stuff either, not worth losing the license over."

Lightning turned and carefully watched the group. His enhanced eyesight getting a good look close up at the chips in the bag from behind the safety of his mirrored shades. A rare smile played across his clean-shaven face as he recalled how things had been back in the States. Life was undoubtedly easier then, Crisis did deals, he was the hired muscle. He had only been a kid then, but still faster than most of the others, even without enhancements. Memories flickered into his mind of evenings long ago, visions remembered through the haze brought on by the narcotic abuse that was his life before he had those damned toxin binders implanted. They had been good times then which were just vague memories now.

Like everything else that life had been blown away. He couldn't quite remember how it had all come about. All he could work out was that it was something to do with local politics. They had had a run in with one of the gangs in the area. That did coincide with a very hasty exit with what they could carry. The Urban Hunt Club, as always known then as it was now. The Crisis man had always seen to that. They had been around in those days and their rep was still growing. In comparison of course they had been a much small time then. Even then and when they came to the UK people had always seemed to be pleased to see Crisis and his shadow coming into the bar.

When they left the US there hadn't been many of them left. Just Crisis, Lightning, Blue, Jared and a couple of others who tagged along for the ride before falling by the wayside. That was the way of things. Few had made it as far as the bar but there was a link between those who had. The UHC had rebuilt a rep and had just been on the verge or really making it big. Then of course the Brownout happened. That was the day that the whole computer network went down along with all the power on the street. Not just that, money via technology was gone in one night. That was the night he'd found Crystal but lost Blue. Bitter irony, wasn't there always. The UHC had built up, they had money, connections and were beginning to be a name. They had a flash pad, a flash vehicle and everything at their feet. Then wham, in one night the web was cut off, even the back up power and back up programs were destroyed. Money just disappeared into cyberspace. The little snippets of text flashed out of existence. It still made him shiver and nothing would make him forget Blue. Her face still lingered in his memory. Her playful eyes, short black hair. He put the memory aside, it was all too painful.

Unbidden the memory came back again. Blue, it still left its mark even after all this time. He hadn't realized that he felt so much in those years. He'd never told her, only for her to die so senselessly at the hands of a corporation when they had kidnapped her. He had given up his freedom to try and get her out of there. He'd sold his soul to the Yakuza to get their help. The night they'd lost Blue and pretty damn near lost Crystal in the process. The night he could never forget even though he wasn't there. An old anger began to well up in him. He forced it back into place with a large swig of whisky which Jared had just placed in front of him. As usual Jared's timing was impeccable. That was the night that Chrystal nearly died too, one traded to save the other, the night that the medic had used the combat meds and changed Chrystal's life forever. If he'd been there he wouldn't have let Chrystal walk onto that balcony. She wouldn't have been there, he should have been. That hurt him to the core. Why? Because they wanted something from Crisis, they wanted him to sell them something, something he didn't have. Typical Crisis, his bullshit had got them all into that trouble, then again how often had that same bullshit got them out of trouble too. He' had the story second hand but from what he understood Crisis couldn't pay the ransom so tried to get her out. She was there in a room with guards. They had killed the guards but she was wearing a wedlock collar which was designed to blow her head off if the controller got too close. Somehow that triggering device had got too close to her in the aftermath and blam, her head ended up all over the floor and walls. It was still too much to take in even though it was ancient history.

Lightning looked up at Jared. "Yeah man, that was a long time ago. Bit hazy though, I wasn't quite the dark, dangerous motherfucker you see before you today. I was just some punk kid with a drug problem and a gun." A smile flickered across his lips.

"Well Lightning, we all have to start somewhere. Another?" Jared placed a bottle of Lightning's favourite down on the bar next to him. Chrystal snatched it up and held it behind her back playfully. Sometimes, just sometimes she could be completely irritating.

She smiled. "When you two are quite finished reminiscing I'd like to point out that there are some of us here who are still waiting for one of your famous parties. Whey else do you think I stick around?" she smiled playfully at the two men.

Lightning frowned as his thoughts were dragged back to the present. The history of it all, somehow it seemed important to go over it, like a mantra, set it in order in his mind. I will survive interspersed with facts. A time before now where the main worry was being caught by a gang on the street or pissing off a PLEXcop. Then the Yakuza came to the street. Openly taking over businesses and gradually gaining the trust and valuable business of the people of Ho Street. It was a relationship that worked and although there were initial worries many realized soon enough that as long as the deals were honoured the visitors would keep their end of the bargain. They were getting involved on all levels and gaining power and influence. Then one night a report came in over the net, someone had used a Maass Driver and flattened Japan. They had literally dropped a huge rock on the a country the size of a small planet and just crushed it and all its population. Gone in a terrifying skull crushing moment, gone forever. Culture, civilization, hopes and dreams, all gone in a moment. Not wiped from History but wiped from existence. Just because they were doing well in business and the PLEX wanted sole control. Wiped out because they had kept their personnel back at home with their families rather than spreading them in offices around the world. Worse than that, it didn't take long to find out that the PLEX had sent the employees they wanted to get rid of on a free holiday there just before it happened. He sighed, remembering the night that they had found out. That was what they were up against. That was why. Did anything make any sense anymore?

Lightning picked up the pieces of the computer and continued working on the booster switch he was soldering. "Do you think they'll get the message even if we can get this heap of junk to work?"

"I don't know, but we can only give it a try. They're going to want to know we're still alive down here and we want to know they are alive up there. The way things are going down here there isn't going to be much alive very soon."

After another ten minutes of work, hampered by the vehicle bouncing along the uneven and blasted road Lightning flicked the laptop "on" switch. The screen was black and then words appeared, code running through as the laptop booted up. The operating system worked and there it was, a functional machine.

Daniel looked over momentarily. "Nice work Lightning-san."

"Save the thanks for when they get the message." He began to type, wondering what to say as his fingers flew over the keyboard. A moment's thought then he began on the text.

"Hope this gets to you and you are all safe there on the Orbital. Daniel and I managed to scavenge together enough batteries to power a laptop and jury rig it into the car's power outlet to send messages for now. If the signal is strong enough hopefully it will reach you.

Everything is in chaos down here. After the power went out the whole world seemed to explode and everyone with a weapon was keen to use it. We managed to get loads of supplies together and an AV. We got in a bit of trouble in Spiral territory and missed the meet. So we figured out we were kind of stuck here so we have got together what we can and we're headed back up to Portland Down. The Yak ran up one hell of a credit bill just before everything went down. No idea how that happened but we have an AV full of useful things and food.

We got caught somewhere around Nottingham when the lights went out. It was quite a thing. A silence just descended. It was a couple of hours before people realized that the power down was everything and permanent. Some are probably still in denial. Then it really went to hell. We could hear the sounds of fighting from miles outside the city until the heavy weaponry ran out. Everyone turned on everyone else. We've decided to stay away from the city. We're trundling on in the AV somewhere in the countryside now but even out here in the Oogra the air smells of death.

We've got enough suppressant to last us for a good few months but after that we're fucked. Neither of us know how to make it. So unless you lot have got any better ideas we're on borrowed time down here. Assuming of course that we don't get killed anyway. I think Portland Down is a start. We can hole up there for a few weeks and see what supplies and stuff are about after the PLEX pulled the place apart looking for us. Hope this reaches you and you're all OK. Lightning and Daniel."

The AV pulled to a stop on an empty part of the road. Lightning plugged the laptop into the AV's communication system. Daniel reached over and put his code into the keypad and the system sprang into life. He looked over at Lightning. "Fingers crossed."

Lightning sat back, feeling the reassuring comfort of his chair. "Yeah man." He hit send.

2

In the depths of space on the SAISH Orbit
instruments and screens Crystal sat back on
She swiveled it to look at another screen of te..
another. A young blonde haired man looked on in ho...
the wrist. "No, don't." She glared at him and he let go.

"Vortex, look, there has to be something."

Vortex had been lounging back on a chair, his torn trainers crossed ...
the console. He relaxed and took up his previous comfortable position. He tipped a bottle of cider with his other hand, draining it dry before lifting another from the console and knocking its metal cap off on the edge of the table. "So here we are once more."

"Yep." Chrystal toasted the air with her half empty plastic cup.

"So, how would you carry on Letter to Asha then? How would you make us sound as we sit here and watch the devastation?"

Chrystal downed the cider in her cup, wincing slightly. Vortex shrugged, pouring her some more. "I'm just glad that I don't have to. Well for now. It was OK writing it while we were in the AV on the way here but somehow now, that is another matter. Now there seems little point as she's here with me, Jared's here and she has her parents. Then again we are not all here, not yet."

Vortex nodded. "You mean Lightning and Daniel." Vortex gave her a knowing look. "Go on, how would you put it."

Chrystal looked at him for a moment. "I guess I'd put it something like this. Day one, not a day like any other. It was worked for, dreamed about, some died for it. Was it worth it? Now that it is here. Farewell to technology. Now that is overnight evolution for you. We sit up here in the SAISH Unit like the Gods of Olympus playing games with the lives of mortal men but we are not gods and this is not a game. People are dying, real live people and there is no reboot for them. Here we sit, safe and sound in vessels designed to save the remnants of humanity so that the world could start again after terraforming. We've replaced their idea with ours so nothing much different other than the terraforming which could have provided a clean slate. It was not our plan but one we have stolen off of the PLEX. The idea and their equipment and after dismissing their board with a 9mm pension and voting their Chairman out by virtue of his lack of breath, we have brought a certain lack of democracy to our new world.

So the lights went out on the megacorporation and now we sit watching the so called civilized world fight its way into oblivion. For some reason the feeling remains that we merely pulled the plug on the planet's life support. No, on mankind's life support. The planet will always recover in one form

We based this on facts which were given to us by Danforth, yea
d Matthew's computer sidekick. The Chairman of PLEX's right
ᴊer mind. Who knows if we were the plan all along but as he died I
ıt. Now all we can do is watch as the projected figures of the dead
ᴊme real people who once had real lives. Those are real people down
.ere in the dirt and blood. They are feeling it all. We just sit up here,
comfortable in the knowledge that we are at least safe. The room we are
sitting in, think about it. It is neat, clean and cyber chrome. So different to
the shabbiness of Jared's Bar, so far from the reality of it all. This IS reality,
our reality, creating their reality. Have we become the corporate monster
enjoying the comfort and safety of position and wealth? I have more
materially in the time we've been here than I ever had dirtside. That is what
is so wrong.

I should be down there trying to deal with what I have caused, I and others. What right do I have to live up here in safety? Who decreed that I should be breathing the filtered and conditioned air while so many others suffer in what is left of the atmosphere on the planet. I eat while others are hungry and I live while others are dying.

Vortex looked up from contemplating the top of his bottle. "Asha."

"It is rare that I get to hold her. She hardly seems real sometimes. Jared is terrified of taking her out of that metal cocoon he so carefully built. She is safe, then so were those people in the domes. Safe and innocent, controlled and manipulated into happy comfortable lives as they didn't know anything else. They were untouched until the world came to touch them. There is an irony in that too. Should we have left them to their innocence and worked harder for another way? Were we the snakes of Eden, bringing knowledge to the innocent which inevitably took them from their own form of Eden?

It is against all I believe in to keep Asha encased in metal where she cannot be touched, neither by harm or love. She is a machine, fed with what she needs to survive and the information she needs to develop. It is as if what Jared says is law now and he is so terrified of losing both of us. He means well. I know he would never enforce his will on me, that is why it is so sad, so impossible. I can't be me in this metal cage. I can't think up here. Day and night the place echoes. You must have noticed it. It drones on like some beast's heartbeat that dulls the senses. It is like we don't talk about it."

"Survivor's guilt. Who can't? Not you and Jared, you talk about everything."

"We used to, when we were dirtside, when we lived day to day."

Jared smiled. "Love and bullets."

"A bit like that." Chrystal took a long drink.

"Its more than that though?"

"No." The sound was too harsh to be an answer. Vortex knew that tone of voice, it was the "don't ask me anymore" type of voice. "So what now?"

"We can't really say what we feel. Odd really that we were the ones they could not silence. It is easy to rage against the establishment. Put the boot on the other foot, put us in the position of being the establishment and having to deal with real solutions to real problems and we are as silent as they were. Silence spawned through conscience and a few million deaths on our minds.

I tried talking to Jared. He's tired, his leg hurts, he's been through so much and just wants to be quiet with his family around him. We finally have time to be together. Time which somehow still gets taken up. There has been so much to do over these past few days. We haven't had time to "celebrate" our success. Not that it feels like much of a success. The lack of contact. I felt that when we all had more time. Well I guess I felt wrong. I feel nothing at all at the moment, just a numbness. Something is missing." She looked down into her drink, took a large mouthful, rolled it around with her tongue before swallowing it.

Vortex thought for a moment. "So that is why you hang around in here so much double dutying it. And I thought it was my witty conversation." Chrystal glared at him as he tipped back his light blue baseball cap, it still proclaimed the anti-PLEX slogans, he still had the bag beside him even though his deck was silent now, he was still Vortex.

Chrystal shrugged. "I check in with the one place where we still have contact with the outside world. So what am I waiting for? Certainly not to hear the ever growing statistics of the dead and the dying from people who are for now stuck down dirtside."

"Not tonight, not last night. It is quieter now or we've lost contact with the last pockets of our people with battery power. Look Chrystal, this is my shift, you have been up most of the day and you took my shift last night. I don't think you've slept properly since Day 1. Don't you think that might be having an effect on your ability for clear thinking? It is quiet and I promise that I'll come and get you if he calls."

Chrystal glared at Vortex but she couldn't be angry. Too much time had been spent in situations where they could both have got their heads shot off. He could say thing others wouldn't dare to say. She stood up, swayed a bit and went to the door. One hand on the metal frame she looked back. She didn't need to speak, he smiled and turned back to the console. "I promise, go to bed Chrystal."

"OK but…"

Vortex watched her go, smiled and went back to watching the screen and taking the odd swig from his bottle.

The message from Lightning and Daniel came in at about 3am. Vortex swung his legs around, feet hit the floor and the message had his complete attention fractions of a second later. He saved the location and the incoming relayed message knowing there was no chance of an immediate response. He read the message, noted it in the Activity Log File and went to the door. He looked long and hard at the console. "Fuck procedure." He went down the corridor and stopped outside Chrystal and Jared's room. Gently he tapped on the door.

Inside Chrystal looked up from staring at the wall, got up and wrapped a gown around her black satin nightdress. She slipped out into the corridor where Vortex was waiting for her. She could see by the look on hi face, blue eyes gleaming and the real and genuine smile that something had happened.

"Hey Chrys, I thought you'd want to know. Is..?" He cast a look over her shoulder as she pulled the door almost closed.

"He's asleep. What is it?" She looked worried, her brow furrowed, her eyes too bright and alert. It was like the old days with the gnawing hunger for information.

"Message". He handed it over and walked off. "I think it is what we've all been hoping for."

She opened the door and went back into the room. Gently she woke Jared up and they read the message together. The baby in the machine in the corner gently gurgling and playing with the lights which kept her amused.

Jared, Chrystal and Vortex sat in the Comms room. There had been such a buzz of excitement around the SAISH when the news got out.

Vortex was typing a message back.

"Hey Guys!!!

Good to know you are okay. It all went to shit up here, a one shot deal, shut it all down or get blown to bits. Well, guess we finally made a quick decision. No time for that now. We'll send a shuttle to Portland Down when you get there as we have no way of locating you on the road.

The catch up is in a letter I wrote to Asha when it was all hell in a handcart. It might amuse you on the way.

Chrystal, Jared and Vortex"

It was done. Vortex attached the file and hit send as he gasped a little. Fear, excitement, blood pulsing through their veins. The nervousness of not knowing if they were going to see someone again. Just like being back on Ho Street.

3

"My dear Asha,

Is it that the sky weeps endless tears that fall on a dying earth. Silently they cascade from a grey and lifeless sky, sinuous shades of black and silver. Sticky, a disease ridden travesty of the purity that must once have fallen from the heavens. Is there still a God up there? How can there be? Endless rain washes the cracked and broken pavements, swirling in eddies into the gutters, running into rubbish clogged drains, down into the concrete encased earth.

It is like you can feel it, sticky, dirty, corrupting all that was once beautiful. Well I suppose it was, they say it was, how would I know? All I've ever seen is this concrete jungle. I was born here and I thought I'd die here. Now it is rubble and everyone I knew is either here in this van or probably dead. This is what they call progress.

The sky weeps on the red wounded earth as the fires burn. A flaming circle around a central dome which sits serene in the eye of the storm that rages all around it. A haven where the SINful live. They don't see the street burn, that would not be correct. They have to be shielded from the truth, even now. The powers that look after them would not allow them such pain, such knowledge. Perhaps some see a red glow through the rain soaked dome. Perhaps they had a slightly red sunset. After all, why should they care about us, the dispossessed, those who don't fit into their plan? It makes you wonder. What will the reports in the Dome say? What will the news reporters report? Riots? Gangs? It will of course be our fault, they kills us, they destroy our homes and it will be our fault.

A quiet voice cries in the wind, drifting, would be in the moonlight if the moon wasn't shrouded in dark thunderous clouds. It is as if I can feel it, it is as if mother nature weeps for her unruly children even though they ripped out her heart. Ancient claws are encased in concrete now. Ineffectual, leaving her a disembodied wraith, her screams lost in the cacophony of death as she screams in desperation at the Dome. They think that she will give up, not a chance, with ethereal arms she reaches out, again and again, ancient sinuous emotions as old as the earth or perhaps older. No synthetic barrier can hold back her power as it stretches through the reinforced wrapping. She will reach out to touch her children, like any mother who really cares. Touching her children even if they no longer listen. In a way that is her victory, he still touches them in the quiet moments and some can still feel her touch, some who have not sunk too deep into Consumer-packed oblivion. What does it feel like to touch sterile trapped infants? What does she feel for those kept from her and protected from the freedom she would give?

Does she gain strength that some of her children have chosen to live free? Do we matter to her? How often has she rejoiced to be able to sweep that dark driving rain around us? How many nights have I spent in the storm? It might be corrupted by pollution but she can still feel us, still, despite the heavy cloying chemicals that mix with what she would give us. Tonight we who live free, die free. The fires burn to ash and the ash is carried in the swirling rain. Her tears cannot drown out our sorrows or put out the fire. She cannot save her children, she just cries as she feels us slip away one by one, as we find the peace that perhaps we could never find here. The question screams, why are we still here? Why are we alive? Why do we still breathe when all we have known and cared about gradually crumbles to nothing? Is it some great purpose or just mere luck? I don't know but I hope all this makes sense to someone sometime. We, the people of Ho Street, those who have managed to find our way into an Armoured Vehicle (AV) and head north to safety. Nothing romantic about it, we leave all we have ever known and the people we have known to die and to burn. People I wish you could have known, people who made me who I am. OK so they were rough, most would kill you for precious little. Burnt out junkies, jack-heads, some more tech than human and most of that not working anymore. Sounds wonderful doesn't it but they were just like me. I'm nothing special and they sure as hell were not but none of them asked to die. None of them had done anything tot hat bastard who chose to blow them to kingdom come.

So it came to pass that the wrath of the Mega-Corporation fell on the dispossessed of the street. Ho Street, a fungal growth of streets and alleyways called home by so many. So, the fires rage through the damp wood, centuries of dust and dirt which fuels the fires of hell. Wiping the SINless from the face of the earth. Don't worry, I'll explain later.

A voice in the darkness, an old woman crouching in the burning doorway of a building, its very soul is burning in her eyes as everything around her burns. I could hardly see her through the tiny window I was looking out of.

I have heard it said that while we have dreams we have hope. There is one woman who has just realized what it is like to have no hope and no time to dream. As the fires rage and the place we once knew and loved turns to ash and the sound of gunfire echoes in the night, how can we stand? Why have we been spared? Is it just to suffer that little bit more? If there is a God up there, why?

What has happened to us? Did it have to come to this? I really hope you never have to deal with the crazy world we are seeing tonight. No hero can survive out there tonight. They are all dying, turning to blood and ash. Congratulations, there are a lot of heroes in heaven tonight. The sky is fire and the streets run with blood. Couldn't someone have seen this coming?

I can hear the engine roar, and another, and another close by but I can't see. Tiny vehicles in the grand scheme of things, leaving behind the labyrinth and the dying. The tired and the dispossessed, huddling in the iron shod bellies, skeletal land locked leviathans, those inside praying if they still have gods. Clinging together for comfort, for a little peace. What peace can we find when we know what we are leaving behind, and what is happening here and having no idea where we are going other than it is probably going to be a little better than this. Is the only peace to be standing on the Ho Street, our home and dying with it? Is there some great purpose or is this just one more road to the same pain and death that we feel now? This is the night the Ho died. If we are the only hope this world has then I pity the world. Guess all those writers who envisioned the heroes that once were and will be again just didn't get the picture. Look at us. No return of King Arthur, no second coming, just ordinary people. We are just ordinary guys and gals, most of us have lied and cheated all our lives. Now they expect us to come up with a plan. Look at us, then again, who the hell is still out there alive anyway? When it comes to it, who is more likely to survive? Rock on mother, guess you at least chose the kids that are going to get out of the initial hell. I just hope that somehow what we do can make a difference. This is not the time for a moral high ground and love and peace. This is the time for being careful, watching your back and dare I say it, your mate's back as well. Somewhere in the fires the hate and the selfishness has died too. If we don't stand together now, well I don't think I have to write it.

We can expect no support from the media and the reports that will be available to those interested enough to listen will be highly edited and will favour freedom's nemesis, the PLEX. Somehow the truth gets lost when reported. Even this letter can only be from my point of view. I am going to write it as I saw it and as I lived through it all, that's the only view I have.

This may be the only opportunity I get to let you know who your father was and who I am.

OK, so how do I start. A bit of history I suppose. Fine. I never knew my parents, I was left in a box on the steps of a bar, oddly enough Jared's Bar though it was called something else then of course. I got lucky, someone found the box. So I got a name, Chrystal, because that was the name on the box. I was small, guess I must have been sort of cute because I got taken in and looked after. Then again children are worth something. With the pollution the chances of carrying a child to full term on the street was minimal even then. Everything has a price. As to whether I was sold or given or taken, what does it matter? All I remember is being passed from family to family until I struck out on my own. Work on the streets is easy for a kid. Simple rules, don't shoot at a kid. Gives us the edge and a bit of a chance. So I started running information. Bits and pieces to start with, then I got to hear the more interesting stuff. I just remembered it and when it fitted in with what someone was saying I would sell it on. Got a name, got a rep, got a life. The information was contacts, I'd know how could do what, where they were and what they knew. Not secrets, I kept everyone's secrets, I just put them in touch with who needed to know who could do what.

To know why things are as they are you need to know about the street. No sentimentality here. The street was a bitch of a place, dark, corrupt and polluted. Urban decay on acid. It may have been a good place once. The buildings towered around the main circular motorway but the vehicles crawled in a constant stream, slowly, outer lanes stopping and parking on occasion, inner lanes a madness of armoured vehicles and drug-crazed nutters. Lights, as the sun went down and the eerie red filled the sky after the grey black of the day, well the neon. Headlights and HOLOimages cutting into the night sky. The streets were paved with neon and dreams danced in the puddles. In the dirt and darkness there were sparkling colours. I always marvelled at the street in the rain, it had a beauty, it had a scent, not always rotting garbage. Sometimes you could smell something else, something metallic, the old stone buildings, age, reliability, home.

Then there were the people, time worn out, most looked worried but then in the latter days everyone had some version of the plague and precious little hope. What hope was there, you were born on the street or you ended up there with no way to progress unless you wanted to sell out. Just breathing for one more day. Just living to cut a deal, just one more day was an achievement. The City of the Damned.

Dark, somehow it was always dark, even in the day. Thunder clouds shrouded the sun, the moon, the stars. Slightly tinged in red since they nuked Mexico. I hear that was green. I've seen trees now, not long ago but I know they are as tall and as real as they look in the pictures. Well Mexico was supposed to be the last open land and wham, don't know why but someone let off a nuclear bomb there and blammo, it's all gone and the winds bring its death to a dying world. Sorry, bit melodramatic but there you go. So now what do we have? Inky black skies dripping sticky rain that sticks to everything, drying to an oily powder. Black was the colour of the street, black and gunmetal grey. And still it rains…

This was home, this was Ho Street. Touched by Angels, fallen ones, drifting into oblivion in the year of our lord 2089. Broken tenements, burnt out shops and on every corner there was someone trying to sell something. On the street everything has a price and I mean everything. Life having the cheapest price of all, the cost of a bullet. In some cases not even that.

It wasn't always like that. Even I know that. I've seen the magazines, seen the pictures. There were forests once, everywhere. Green places where children played. People had safe jobs then. They drove to work, they came home, they watched TV and they had rights and views. They talked about a world and ecological matters. So, what happened? What did they do to preserve that dream? Quite simply they were out of place, outnumbered and out of time. They couldn't have seen it coming or if they did well they just talked about it. They were well meaning perhaps, the Flower Power of the Sixties, the New Age of the year 2000, boy did they have hope but did they have reason? Did the Millennium bring them brotherhood and unity? I don't think so, well it couldn't have done. Oh there were the good intentioned, there always are but were they listened to? I doubt it, no doubt the asylums of the time were full of the well-meaning people and the therapists pocketed the cash as those who "cared" went home to build their lives to care more for themselves and less for everyone else. Love themselves, wasn't that what humanity had been doing since its creation? So he who must be the servant of all becomes he who must love himself first. So much for unconditional love. What did they say love others but don't hate yourself. I think someone lost the plot or at least misunderstood the message. Did sitting in peace and thinking change anything? Or did it bring more of a false calm than any recreational drug? Did they have the answers? I think they did, I think in the silence, in the images they were given the answers. Reading some of the books, all strictly black market of course, I really think that they did and how many of them were ignored. The prophecies, the thoughts, things known as channelled works, it was as if someone was trying to give us a message. Then again we don't listen now. How could we be expected to listen then? I wasn't there so I wouldn't know. I guess my parents would have been. I cannot even begin to speculate as to who they were, what they were like and quite honestly I don't really care. What difference would it make to me? History, now that does matter. We are supposed to listen to the mistakes of the past, so why were most of the books destroyed? Quite simple, there was a man, he had a dream and the dream was PLEX. The man, well he was a lunatic and he took over the asylum and boy did we all know about it. All before my time but it is important so I'll try to explain it, just so you know.

It ended with the torching of the place we called home but why begin at the end or is it the beginning? Ho Street, what had once been the M25 Motorway but which had become built up when the traffic stopped on the creation of the London Dome, only local traffic now. It became the first settlement place of the refugees who chose not to live in the Dome. So it became a shanty town, no resources for proper buildings, just tenements built from what could be found by dodgy building contractors put out of business by the PLEX. So they built death traps which soon fell into decay. Then Jared Matthew, Chairman of PLEX UK had a dream. He would bury those without SIN and create a better future for his minions, those who followed him mindlessly and kept the heart of the beast pounding. The name of the beast was PLEX and it had no number. The beast created SIN, Single Identification Number so that everyone had a number and the beast looked around with hungry eyes. It looked from its UV Filtered Dome and it saw a land out there, stretching into the distance, but land it could not control. So it taught us the first lesson. 2032 PLEXification of Britain was complete. The land was no longer Great, welcome to PLEX UK.

So that left the rest of us on the street, hustling for just one more break, one more deal or that deal that would cut it enough to give us the edge. No big ideals, no big dreams, just survival in the ever changing maelstrom. You soon learn, no number, no credit, no hope. Oh yea right so we had dreams, we had hopes but when living from breakfast to lunch and finding something worth eating is top of the list, well kinda puts your life in perspective. So, you cut a deal with one dude, the next day he's gone, deader than deadski and there you go. Simple lessons of the Ho, don't hand over anything unless it is an immediate deal. What is there today will be gone tomorrow. Live for the moment and wait for that bullet, you know its out there, it all depends on when it catches up with you. Wear the right street kit, walk tall and learn attitude fast, that and peripheral vision. No point being a geek because geeks get very dead very fast, unless they are real smart. Get what you want and need and try not to piss anybody off on the way, that is my advice. It is easy to play hard and be a bully, that is no way to get respect though. No respect means no deals, no way out but a wooden box, but only if you can afford it because nothing comes for free. That was how it developed, the area outside the reach of the PLEX. They concentrated on the cities, the rest, well for a while they just forgot about it and hoped it would go away. Unfortunately we did not go away but worse, they remembered us.

Rain on the streets, swirls of green and purple oil, surface scum. The water splashes, somewhere there is a gunshot, another and another as bodies collide, looking for cover, but there is no cover as a howl sends the bodies running. Automatic gunfire and the bodies fall, cut down like corn, muzzle-flash highlighting the almost demonic face of a boy, the boy is only a child. The boy laughs, the laugh is mindless. Paper falls from his hand, neon imagery on white oiled paper fluttering into pooled water, the crack of another gun, the boy falls, the boy dies, blood mixing with the white powder residue clinging to the paper. Another death on Ho Street, another voice silenced forever. The people scream, the people run. A PLEXcop pulls out his radio, he dies in a hail of gunfire. Two PLEX Armoured Vehicles descend on he area, engines screaming, like birds of prey into the crowd. The flash of more gunfire from the A.V.s and there is silence. Silence as blood mingles with rain and with the dirt of the street. More statistics. We would give the statistics a voice and the statistics scream, until they too are silenced. Their numbers are not convenient, their voice is not politically correct, their cause too radical. Street chaos and combat drugs, sign of the times some say. An excuse, the theory had been bandied about, the supply, had to be a PLEX supplier. One hit and death roams the street. God for a moment but it ends the same way. One less punk on the street, but the dealer laughs, pockets his money and walks away, hands in pockets, collar pulled up against the rain. Names and faces, if you are not a name you are a nobody and there are so many nobodies out there.

 I can't say I was exactly a faceless nobody, moving around without being noticed was my trade but being known got you business so I got myself known. Me, and many others like me. Unnoticeable when we wanted to be, free to gather what can be the most important crop on Ho Street, information. It wasn't much of a trade but when you can't read or write, have no skills of any measurable worth and no money it is a good option. I was building a rep, not a big one but a reliable one, getting trusted and a list of names and faces I could count on to give me work. It was fair to say I had a working knowledge of the streets, knew where to go and where not to go. I suppose I was a courier, packages, ammunition, you name it, I moved it around, small valuable stuff, the essentials.

 I mainly worked North Ho Street, Clan Territory. Easy money if you are in with them. I'd given them no reason to turf me out so I could go pretty much were I wanted.

 Once upon a time I could lose myself in the anonymity of the streets. Once upon a time I loved nothing, believed in nothing, I was nothing and I liked it that way. A life of hanging out in bars, digging in for evenings of loud music. A lot of the bars off the main street play late 90s stuff. Music before it became completely computer generated, so Consumer-packaged. The music is as good I suppose, in my humble opinion but it's the lyrics. How many pro-PLEX messages can they get into one track these days. It is easier to listen to the music of the 90s and some earlier stuff, revolutionary for its time no doubt.

 We weren't on the Ho when it happened and all we have are the reports. I'll set out things as they happened but for now I write out of pain, as the fires burn, I want this emotion to be on paper as I feel it. It is my way of remembering those people. Most of them were nobodies, most of them I'd never spoken to but I never will now. Some were my friends. Places I have been, things I have touched, all gone. I can't believe it, it doesn't seem real but it is, so very, very real and it isn't going to get better. I'm not going to wake up tomorrow and walk down the street. I'm not going to walk into the bar and see the familiar faces and smell the familiar smells because it is gone.

We have a small CD unit in this AV with us so we drive to the sounds of Pearl Jam, something about beginning life again. "I'm Still Alive", damn straight we are. It's a pure act of defiance, PLEX hasn't wiped us out yet. We might be a tiny convoy of survivors but we carry with us hope. A vague hope but when you've lost everything then what does it matter if you risk even the spark of life for something so very important. That sounds very melodramatic but we have been given a chance. Way, way back four executives had a flash of insight, well okay they realized that one of their number was a madman and they did something about it. By some stroke of good luck they decided to put in a back door to a superior Artificial Intelligence he was creating just to give their children a chance at a future should the worst happen. Well, good on them because the worse did happen and here we are. The madman who was their partner was Jared Matthews and from those humble times he ousted them and made himself the sole ruler of the megacorporation known as the PLEX and he and his computer AI Danforth pretty much rule the world now. Very Manga I know but there he is in his ivory tower, with his computer side kick planning the demise of his opposition to give himself absolute rule. There he is, pushing buttons and giving orders but as in all good plots, he now has a fatal flaw that the intrepid heroes can find and destroy him. Just one problem, they wrote in the wrong guys, we aren't heroes. OK so someone has a plan and they've given us the information and it started with balls. Well it didn't actually but it sounded better than a key, which led to a safety deposit box or something which led to finding some lottery balls. We also have a commode and various other things and the way they fit together actually escapes me other than they give us an access code to be able to gain a back door and get part of Danforth the AI to work with us. I'm no tekkie, they could explain it to you but it seems that an AI is multifunctional and part of it is sort of acting as a double agent and working with us. I know it sounds ridiculous probably.

How will history record all this? Guess it depends on who wins and how this all ends. Will we be sinners or saints? It all depends on your point of view and as Jared Matthews controls the media it doesn't take much to guess. PLEX credit (currency) truth, synthetically engineered to reflect and image. Why not, they are rebuilding everything else.

The vehicle jerked and then we were thrown into darkness. I leant back against the cold metal. No room to move, we are laying side by side across the floor of a ten by five foot space that is full of stale air and the smell of metal and gun oil. Around us is dark, there are tiny windows near the roof but nobody has the energy now to stand up and look out anymore. It is a bit quieter and it is darker out there so either the fires have died down or we are in more open land. We've seen enough death. We piled into the back of this armoured transit van and are now languishing in the belly of this struggling beast, just waiting as we move on. All that was available at the time I'm afraid. No chance to pick and choose.

Silence at last. For the past few miles all we have heard is the regular plink, plink of shells against the outer metal hull. The sort of sound you have to get used to and be grateful for the solid outer shell. Alright so occasionally something heavier hit us. About a mile back, a dull thud of impact and the van rocked to about a forty five degree angle. Had to be heavy calibre weaponry. Don't ask me why, someone had to be mad to try it. Then again there are some really strange dudes out there. I'm just glad I'm in here, with your father and still breathing.

It is nearly dark in here. I'm laying underneath a security light, a hazy red glow is just enough to write by. Your father is beside me. Time I told you about him. Jared, tall, red haired, good looking, heavy built, the sort of guy you don't mess with unless you want him to try out some heavy weaponry on you. If I could put a smile on paper. He's the most gentle man I've met under all of that. Then again I'm not exactly the perfect mother figure so between us I guess we make a very strange couple. That is what we are though. In the middle of this hell and mayhem we have stayed together and we have something that is just so rare. We sincerely care for each other. Not in some stupid romantic way but in that way that overcomes the really serious problems in life. I'm not going to go into it all here but read on. He's had to go through hell with me and he's done it. Without question and without complaining. That is some man I have laying here beside me and something even better, I know he is happy with me. I can only hope and pray that you find someone as understanding of you as he has been to me through all I've put him through.

The intercom crackled into life again. "Hold on tight, we're going to bust through a roadblock. I don't like the look of the gangers hanging around." Right, that was Daniel. Daniel was one of the Yakuza, a man of great honour and someone I had come to respect. When he first came to the street I was not only suspicious, I was downright resentful. What right had they had to come to our part of town and take over. They strutted around with strange foreign ways and expected us to know how to treat them. Well I knew how to treat them OK, with complete disrespect until they earned it. Strange thing was that they did. They might have been crime lords but they did a lot for the street. They gave it back some respect when it was losing it. They brought a discipline and a code that it had lost through death and chaos. We did business with them, they were fair. We welcomed them, they didn't expect more than we could give but they took, boy did they take and they owned. They pretty much ended up owning everything and that was not the way of the street. You got to feel sorry for them though, they stood against the PLEX and boy did they pay for it. Particularly Daniel, he bore it with honour but he lost family, friends and everything when the PLEX fought back. He was left one of the few Yakuza still on the streets after the PLEX dropped a rock on his home. I'm not kidding here. They literally flattened Japan. They dropped a chunk of earth on it and drove it into the sea, killing everyone there. Daniel, good looking too, he chose a body sculpt so that he could look more European and it suited him. A good friend I think, I'd have trusted him with anything.

I guess I feel stronger because your father is here. I need him, like I needed the street once and it was him to took me from the street, brought me inside, but that was a long way into all this.

I guess that doesn't make much sense. I lived most of my life on my own and I looked after number one. That meant having a very cheap bed sit in an apartment building where the walls were paper thin and the neighbours' arguments were as entertaining as the TV set I had until it blew up. Screaming, shouting and the sound of gunfire, damp cracking walls and a boiler that was desperately in need of a service. Add a cooker that was a death trap and you have home sweet home. Truth is that I didn't have the money to call someone in to repair anything. Not that I would have admitted that one to anyone but my nearest and dearest and as I didn't have any of them. That was my life, that and living free in the world. I owed nobody, I was free. Free but very lonely. It was great on the street at times, the money came in, the people were friendly and the beer flowed. It was that moment when you came home though and you closed the door. Then those walls closed in.

In the beginning there was the world and the world was without SIN. In those days the children played in the parks for in those days there were parks and the air was clear and it was good. So it came to pass that with the progress of time there came the Day of Judgment as it had long been foretold. The years rolled by and the Millennium got closer, spurring on every religious groups of every nation and giving them the meaning in life they had been looking for. So it came to pass that apocalyptic hysteria gripped the consumer led world. New Age Groups grew up all over and it was "hip" to be spiritual. Trouble was that every street magician started selling courses to the uninitiated and the people needed something to believe in. They didn't look and they didn't think until it was too late. Every cult, every lunatic with a good voice and something to say started to get followers. Somewhere in the confusion God and all the other deities got lost and mankind tipped itself over the edge. I'm not saying that there weren't those who started bringing people together. You could say we had all the clues, we just chose to ignore them. As always, it was easier to buy into the dream than take that long walk to enlightenment. There was a growing market for all manner of beliefs and there were people waiting to exploit the lost and the lonely. Mass marketing in the media and religious fervour, the churches and cults never had it so good and the congregation's money rolled in. Someone will always make the most of a situation like that and terrorists of every political or religious persuasion found their calling and their reason to be.

Was it the start of the insanity or just a natural human progression towards its own destruction? Flying on the wings of fanaticism the wild crazes fanned the fires. The news reflected the age, carrying the fanaticism to every home, bringing the discussion to every dinner table where there were still families. Not that families were encouraged, the word was individualism, that and self-belief was the mantra. Free speech meant that the Governments could not or would not curb the ever growing publicity for fanaticism until the excessive became the norm. One faction bred another, the names read like some crazy roll call to arms. It was the new religion, all you needed was a list of beliefs and enough Semtex™ to get noticed. Privatisation increased, even though the government had promised to keep some control. This culminated in the privatization of the police force and the licensing of private protection.

The new craze, the bodyguard army and every home had to have one. Well for the rich anyway and it did make a big hole in the lists of the unemployed. It cut the crime rate to almost nothing, well it did after the government made it clear that they weren't going to prosecute anyone for shooting a burglar. It was good in its ideals but not too difficult to abuse. Invite your enemy round and then blammo, then make out he's a burglar, simple. Of course that was about the time that they privatized the Post Office and our friendly local postman started delivering your post from an armoured vehicle by grenade launcher. Then of course technology moved on and nobody sent letters anymore.

The rise in terrorism and development of technology had far reaching effects on business and international travel. Transatlantic flights all but ceased and Virgin Airlines went under. British Airways survived purely by some careful dealing and maintaining core internal government flights within Mainland Britain. Then came the big break for Virgin, suing the US and British Government. It all came down to money and the British economy was left bankrupt. So it came to pass that a deal was struck and Virgin got hold of the BBC, so it was that Branson Broadcasting was born. No problem there in principle, by what I've read he seemed to be doing practical things and putting a reasonable price tag on them.

Apparently it was a sign of the times that every fringe group was on the streets demonstrating in their own special way just how their demands should be met and governments throughout the world were seriously under threat.

September 2003 brought matters to a head when a terrorist organization known as the Klan took possession of the Empire State Building claiming doorway, always keeping an eye around them for fear of receiving that last searing kiss, that one bullet destined to end their existence and take the one thing they truly owned on what everyone was all too aware was a dying planet.

Flickering neon projections, dancing on the streets and projected onto hoardings pounded out their messages of escapism to anyone who had the time or luxury to glance up at the adverts for the Sim-Stim parlours. The only release and escape in an escapeless world. Those darkened smoky places so popular in a world of pain. A coin in the slot and for a while you can forget your dismal existence an fulfil your heart's desire or be who you want to be. Once your neural network is interfaced with a terminal your virtual reality of it all will stimulate, sight, sound, vision, taste and feeling. Your every desire catered for, extracted from your mind after an initial sweep and fed back to you for instant gratification. Processed and more than likely recorded, your inner thoughts adding to the collective consciousness of the mainframe. Your inner secrets known. Whatever was your passion or need. Everything you could desire, fleetingly, until the coin ran out. Something, anything that wasn't merely struggling for survival day after day. Your greatest desire without the risk of actual death or infection. Nights of unreality which somehow managed to take away the pain. Tiny islands of oblivion in the cold harshness of life or so the adverts would lead you to believe.

In truth the dark and shadowy parlours mostly catered for pornography and all the perversions of a twisted time while identifying the trouble causers and giving them a dose of urban pacification and a need to return for their regular dose.

There were still some that offered the dream but most of the legitimate ones had closed down or were clinging to an existence of outdated machinery which broke down regularly but remained free from control. Second hand equipment. The fodder of the SINless, those without SIN, the Single Identification Number which identified the individual as part of the whole being in PLEX, the Megacorporation's new world, the number that proved you were owned by them. Reject that number of the beast and you walk the streets a nobody, free but living on the castoffs of the consumer society. Free to think, even though your thoughts were irrelevant. Free to feel though that was mostly anger at what was going on. Free to act in an ineffectual way in the outskirts of "where it was at". Free to die. That bit was truly free and dished out on a regular basis on the semi lawless streets. Either by birth or by choice if you didn't have SIN you had no rights to all the things like medicine, clothing and adequate housing. For these things you had to make do, scavenge and do the best you could. If you didn't conform you didn't or couldn't "get". Without credit you are nothing, well that was the propaganda. The reality was very real. Crumbling buildings, faulty electrical equipment but something else, something that had no monetary value because it could rights for single white landowning males. They threatened to explode a home made nuclear device and this got them noticed but not believed. So most of the US exploded in a nuclear holocaust of fire and death.

This all but crippled the American Government, they were seen to be incapable of dealing with the onslaught of terrorism. Other governments feared the precedent had been set and so endeth the age of sanity and began tighter laws and control to try to stamp out the fanaticism. The seeming oppression fuelled the fires of dissent. There were repercussions throughout the United States with every fanatical religious cult believing it was the end of the world and every redneck out there with a gun keen to prove his manhood. The result was inevitable, within a year the US was left with a glowing nuclear wasteland. A chain reaction being set off that sent shockwaves throughout the isle. There was nothing anyone could do. God Bless America.

The world had limped on after the Millennium with all its foretold destruction. How our families saw it I do not know. I don't think anyone I have ever spoken to remembers anyone hearing what the people said. All we have are old news reports and what the history discs say and they will be biased depending on who had control over them. The world was still here on the morning of 1st January 2000. No Angels, no end of the world, just another day.

None of the destruction that had been foretold but destruction had come all the same. It was years later and a creeping desolation but it swept on silent wings. Firstly an increase in skin cancer and sterility. Then mankind noticed what had happened to the ozone layer as Global Warming increased. Sea levels rose, yet still nothing was done to stop the exploitation for profit and gain. Everyone jumped on the band wagon, from real estate agents to record companies. Eager to please whoever had the power at the time, eager to make that last buck until ashes to ashes, dust to dust, they were gone. RIP. They wouldn't give up while there was a profit to be made, not while there was a chance it could be someone else's problem. By 2043 85% of the rainforests that had been our lifeline at the turn of the century had gone. That was the apocalypse, not fire and thunder, a creeping death as the world began to slip beneath the ever rising seas and concrete. There was nothing left to repair the damage, so as it had been prophesied the seas rose, there were storms and floods and this left us with what we have now, a situation where there is one Corporation, PLEX, one person in charge, namely Jared Matthews and everything is owned, except for us of course, which was why the order to destroy the Street was given. We don't need to be on the board of directors to work that one out.

I don't understand a lot about politics. I got most of this from new videos and the British Environmentalists (BFA) sort of filled in the gaps. I had the honour of meeting Doc Harley, the leader of the BFA. I guess the best way of describing them would be to call them freedom fighters. More survival specialists, they were what came between us and the forces of the PLEX for many years. It was difficult to say whether they were an undercover force or not. Lets face it after the initial confusion what did it matter. Most of us were on the Corporation's hit list just for breathing, what difference did it really make if you fought back? These guys certainly did that, in any way they could. I don't know when Harley hitched up with them but he was a born leader, probably because he had no care whether he lived or died. That was well known. He had hitched himself up to a rock star in his younger days, a beautiful woman by the name of Aztech. Anyway, as I heard it she had blown out Jared Matthews to hitch up with him. This was after Matthews had given her parts of Mexico. It must have really upset him as she and the land got nuked in some corporate argument or jealous lashing out. The details are a bit sketchy and I don't know the truth of it. Apparently since then Doc had been far from his normal self. Guess that is what love does for you. So his SIMstim star is missing and all we have to guess her location is a huge glowing hole in Mexico. You can hope though, who knows.

Anyway, back to the history as I know it. By what I have heard that was a time for desperate measures politically. There were still political parties, they got together to form what is known as a coalition. It was all they could do to make a stand against the growing Green, Anarchist and Luddite Movements. The land was dying then, they weren't going to listen so the people were rising up against them. This was the time for emergency measures, and it didn't stop with shooting a fair proportion of the population just for turning up on marches. If you want to know when they built hell then you need look no further. They closed the London Flood Barrier and flooded Kent and what was then known as the Home Counties. The details are still a bit sketchy, they claim there were accidents but if you look really deeply into the statistics you will find that most of the farmers and locals had precious little warning and those who resisted leaving their homes were either shot or left to drown. Then they threw the bulk of their finances into building a huge UV proof Dome over London stretching out almost as far as the M25 which was by then a slow moving roadway ringed by ramshackle structures inhabited by refugees and laughingly renamed Ho Street.

This was a time of major trade upsets and much political manoeuvring. I've had it explained to me and no doubt the history clips are full of it but it means precious little to me other than in 1999 PLEX Limited was formed from smaller global enterprises, under the chairmanship of Jared Matthews.

I read this somewhere. 'Jared Matthews, a company chairman, was a remarkable man. Gifted with an unique ability – to find a new slant on things, to get around problems, to innovate laterally and to eliminate all problems that stand in his way. PLEX decided that the best way to win and keep dominance in a market was to own it, and in the entertainment and real world, that meant you had to own the consumers'.

It involved loaning money to a government that was seriously licking its wounds after funding the London Dome. Next move, infiltrate the government with PLEX employees and Britain gets privatized. By 2076 PLEXification of Britain was complete. The royal family remained, but only as some sort of real life soap opera.

So the world was born to SIN. If you were SINless then you were outside the system and there was no place for you in the controlled environment of the domes. Simple and uncomplicated. If anything can be. So that was how we fell from grace. The rest is how do they say, history.

We live with it every day, eat, sleep and drink it. It rules our lives but even though the street may sound like a living hell of death, insane people and poverty it has the one thing that the Dome does not have. It's people are free, free to think, free to care about what is happening. They can have opinions of their own, thoughts that are their own and they are free to do what they believe is right, not what they are told is right. That's the choice. It could be a tainted view of history, but those who conform to the ideals of the consumer culture always follow a pattern. It seems that to have the corporate way of life, or any money at all, and I mean serious money here, it seems essential to conform, to be owned. The more money you have the more image and labels become important and the less people seem to matter. Credit purchased respectability without the basis of truth, justice and a simple compassion for others and a respect for the world. I'm not being very clear but then history isn't either. What I means is that those that "have" seem to lose their free will in the scramble to comply with the most up to date fashion and to get more. I don't just mean clothes either, ideals seem to go the same way. I guess its always been the same though.

We spend so long fighting for our beliefs I guess we don't really get time to talk about what they are any more. We want the right to think but we spend so much time fighting and dying for it that we don't have time to really think what it is all about. It is different for each one of us I suppose.

It takes a bit of understanding at first. I didn't think about it but we have all lost so much and we are all from such different cultures. Take Yali, she is basically a Tribal Shaman. I've heard her talking about Voodoo and those things, of Loa, of spirits, of all kinds of things I'd have liked to have found out more about. Her tribal beliefs were deeply ingrained and survived and worked with her training and technological skills. The individuality of the street, a child of the Houn 4, a Clan of Tribal Warriors who live on the North of Ho Street and still practice all their old religions which originated in the Pacific. I should probably say lived now. I don't know a lot about the religion itself but I've spent some time on their turf, a religion based on fear and the idea of spirits, their Loa, by what I have seen but I could be wrong. Effective and very dangerous. She was not someone I would want to annoy. Well, any of her clan anyway, she always seemed friendly enough but then she, like many others got turned by the street and street culture. What I mean is that she could have her moments. She could have such flashes of inspiration and come up with the best of ideas but then, at other times forget everything while ranting and raving and then it is best just to leave her if you know what I mean. Then is it just that emotion is dead in me. Who knows. Tonight I can see her point.

    It is getting late and I'm really beginning to get fed up with the constant drone of the engine and the movement of the van. We have no privacy. I would love to be able to talk to your father and spend some time alone with him but we don't seem to get a chance for that, haven't for a while, even before now. Strange really, I guess now I really regret all the time I spent on the streets. I know I was fighting for a cause but part of me really wishes I had spent more time with him while we had a home, even though it was a beat up drinking establishment. Strange really, this is probably the longest we have spent together and we have hardly spoken, nobody has, stunned silence, we are too shocked and dealing with everything in our own way.

    I never thought I would miss Ho Street's darkness, rain soaked, screams echoing in the night, mingling in the neon glow with gunfire ringing in the ears of those who no longer listen, hurrying to safety between dilapidated buildings that in the years gone by would have been condemned long ago. One more voice that cries out to be suddenly silenced but even that silence disappears into the drone of the constant stream of traffic on the four lane wide road. Well even the traffic is silenced now. Each life lost was one less life to litter the overcrowded streets as the darkness closed in, velvety black on the rubbish strewn alleyways, but even the alleyways are gone now. Rubbish that was never collected as what was of use was taken from it, what was edible was eaten by rats and what was left melted into the general detritus, discarded metal, paper, the lot. Some of it was used to patch up buildings, to become walls of back street shelters. So many with the street as their bed. Someone's rubbish, another man's home, or somewhere to hide when the PLEXcops come round.

    Darkness, the occasional flashing light, the gentle hum of the engine, the music and the occasional burst of gunfire. Yes, we are still alive. I don't know how or why. All I do know is that by living just one more day we defy the PLEX. In some small way you are the greatest defying gesture we could all make. You are the symbol for Smiling Jared and myself that if we do not survive all this then perhaps you might. I suppose that life has been broken down to basic levels for your father and me. It makes even the smallest success seem so much more beautiful. Just the touch in the dark of someone you truly love, knowing that tomorrow the memory of that touch may be all you have. It makes everything so much more real so much more necessary. No time to argue, no time for petty squabbles. It puts such a value on the life we have that each moment is precious, each goodbye could be the last. There is a kind of purity in that. A wild savage beauty that pulls us together in despair, in hope and in knowing that if we don't stand together its likely we won't be breathing, let alone standing. I can feel the others around me, in the dull neon light from the end of the AV they are silhouetted. Tired and torn, grabbing what rest they can as our world falls apart.

I'm trying so hard to cling to the memories. To remember those faces and carry them with me. It is as if by remembering them they are still here. We are all that is left. We have to look to the future, try to carry on. If I had transport I would go back. I want you to know that but I know your father would not let me. I know he loves me, I know he understands me and for once I think it is his time to dictate what this family does, for a family is what we are, somehow, in this crazy world. This is so strange for me that I know I must be scared. I just want to cling to your father so tightly and for once in my life I really don't know what to do. I need his steady practicality, his strength, his love, without that I would never have made it this far. I wish I could tell him as easily as I can write it here, then he can read this too.

It is hard to concentrate on this. An explosion rocked the AV just then, could have been another landmine. The locals are obviously terrified of strangers picking their way through their roads, probably as scared as we are. You can feel the fear in here, we're trapped like cattle and the walls are beginning to close in. All we can do is rely on the armoured wall and cling to what faith we have left, be it religion or just Daniel to keep this hunk of metal on the road and moving. I can feel the warmth of you father next to me. He watched me for a while but he's so tired. He needs to sleep. We don't know what we are going to meet further along the road. I will sleep soon too. I'm tired enough but this is important to me at the moment. I don't know what is important to tell you and what is useless ramblings of a tired mind. Should I tell you about the last year or so? If I do, will it change your life? I know I would have liked to have known about my parents and what they believed in. I would like you to know about some of the people who lived and died to bring a future, however it may end up. I write this in the hope that you are living the Eden Dream so I will start with that dream as written by Doc Harley and others.

A man and a woman sit in a forest, Everything around them is green
The earth provides their food and they are not hungry
They drink from the stream beside them and do not grow sick because of it
They have no guns, because no one wishes to kill them
They are not judged because of the way they are born, because of past actions
Or because of what they own or whom they are owned by
They are judged by what they do now, by how they have lived
and how they love

And the judgement is – that they shall be absolutely FREE…
One day they may choose to have children, to care for and to love
These children shall not be taken from them
When they are grown they will make their own choices
And together with all the other people they will build a world
where only truth and justice will rule
This is not the past, this is the future, THIS IS OUR EDEN DREAM
For which we fight, for which we are prepared to die
And it shall set us free.

I saw it so often, cut into the crumbling plaster in bullet blasted buildings. I had no idea what it said until someone read it to me. It meant nothing to me until now, it was just a set of words that didn't relate to the sprawling fungus of alleyways, buildings, shacks, pieces of material and wood bound together as shelters, to the bars, trade ins, all manner of sleaze and every perversion you could wish for. Everything had a price on Ho Street, the most valuable commodity being knowing someone who could do something.

Crowds milled along the pavements, plying their trade, invisibly except to the initiated. A haven for crime and all the dark corners of the human mind. It was hell on earth at times but it was our hell, how could the Dream relate to all that? It was a vague memory and if you clung to sentimentality like that. It is a hard world, you have got to be hard with it. It takes something very special to show you otherwise, or some very special people. It takes faith.

I need to rest. The walls are closing in and my eyes sting from staring at the white paper in such dim light. Let the darkness close in, let me forget about all this just for a while, slip into dreams and perhaps there I will find what I'm looking for, that little bit of peace, that moment when I can just relax. That place where nobody is trying to kill me and where my spirit can be free.

4

So here we are, the second day. The engine drones on, it has all night and it will all day. Add to that the vibration from the engine and the wheels up and down over potholes and the steady rhythm of rain on the roof and you have one annoying cocktail. Rain, some things never change. I used to think it was just condensation off the dome. That was one theory. No, it is just that the atmosphere is dying and the earth cries. Dark black thunderclouds are all we deserve now. The blue skies and fluffy white clouds somehow imply a sort of innocence, the innocence we have destroyed. So who is innocent now, certainly not us. There is too much blood on our hands already. Just by living. I know, that probably sounds melodramatic but hearing the radio messages, I have to ask why I'm still alive. Listening to people dying and not being able to do anything about it. Am I hoping too much? Should I just take my gun, put it in my mouth and forget about all this? Are we being punished by surviving or is this a reward? Are we sinners or saints? To be honest I don't know. Is it that some insane deity has sent his angels to destroy his Sodom and Gomorra as a mockery of God? The fires burn and all are dead. Did we deserve it? I don't know so I'm going to write what I saw. Nothing much makes any sense anymore.

Unceasing rain, no longer drowned out by the gunfire. Unending water torture. The air is also getting stale. I turned the ventilator to full. It leapt into life with a dull drone. As always I realise all too late how much nose it is going to make in this tin can. There were people sleeping. Gunshots are one thing, we are all so used to that, we can sleep through it. This strange drone spewing metallic smelling air somewhere above my head was a completely alien sound.

Bill stirred, he dragged himself from under his blanket, steadied himself as he stretched his cramped limbs and stood up. I've always liked Bill, he's probably as dodgy as they come, having so many corporate connections, but who knows? I've pulled a few stunts on him before and he doesn't really seem to cut me out for that. If I could choose people to be here wit hme, he'd be one of them. I hope you'll meet him one day. If I'm not around to tell you, he's on the wiry one who's strong (mentally and physically) and the one who can cope. He's the one who usually ends up sorting things out for everyone else and then they don't appreciate him but he still does it. One of he unsung heroes. I thought I'd blown it once by trusting him but he proved me right or wrong, whichever way you want to put it. Right to trust him, wrong to doubt him. Guess the guy turned to our side. He wouldn't be here if he hadn't. Then again, who do you trust? You'll know better than me as you'll know what will happen in the future when all this is sorted out.

Hot black coffee from a small machine taped to the worktop at the front end of the small area we now call home gurgled slightly in invitation. Bill seems to be the only one who woke up so that wasn't too bad. He came and sat back down after pouring a couple of mugs and handed me one full of the black sticky liquid and swearing as he bumped his head as the van jerked. The road is still pretty uneven, I don't have to see it to know that and I can imagine how blasted it is. Not just the Ho Street was attacked then. Craters and holes. Testimony to too many explosions. It takes a lot to stay standing with the number of bumps and dips. Bill is on the next shift to drive anyway and Daniel must be exhausted. I don't know who is co-piloting. He's driven us about eleven hours straight after the night we have just had. Of course he'd never admit that he's tired. Still, he only has another hour to go and we must be getting clear of the worst of the hostility by now.

Trouble is that we don't know the rules around here we are now completely out of our territory. We don't have a rep and we certainly don't have contacts here. I had one or two contacts in Manchester but they went by the by when the man by the name of Gamer lost his position in the area. He was acting as go between while doing the PLEX for all he could get. It is fine being a Corporate Netrunner when there is corporate interest in you. Then it is the good housing, the good food, medical insurance and all the perks. Then one day, when the bottom falls out of your field or someone younger and sharper comes along the good life melts away and it is back to the streets with no home and no contacts as your old ones sure as hell won't want to know a corporate sell out. Don't try telling me that they don't know its going to happen. The guys in charge I mean, you can't sell the idea to me that they don't set these guys up and then watch them crash and burn. Take a really cool tekkie and a good one can get into every system. So if you employ them, pay them, feed them, get them dependent and get the best of their knowledge then you have to do something with them when you don't need them anymore. I hate to write it but the young rule the waves when it comes to the web. Its reaction time that counts, particularly when you are up against serious opposition. Hit that key a fraction of a second too late and your brain ort of flows out of your ears. Not physically but it might as well. Where are the corporation benefits then?

Basically the most you will get is a stretcher to carry you out of the building. Trouble is then that same Netrunner that they have so carefully trained is going to use those same skills to survive. On the street or non-domeside those skills usually mean something illegal in the minds of the PLEXcops. Probably why so few actually make it to retirement.

News travels fast but we've got no way of knowing if what happened on the Ho was isolated. Most of the major cities are part or fully domed. I've never thought about it but there must be places like the Ho around all of the major cities. It's a chilling thought that the fire and death we experienced could have been a country wide thing.

The wheels keep turning. My coffee has gone cold. Smiling Jared moved and pinned me down for a while. I didn't have the strength of the inclination to move him. I need time to think, time to work out what to tell you. We are getting closer to our destination and its really strange. It's like adrenaline rushing as I think about the hopes and fears.

Well, it is like when all hope has died and you think this is the end. I felt like that. I had settled down to the fact that I might have a couple of months on the block with Jared then I'd get what was coming then whatever comes after. I'll take you back to the beginning, the time when I hitched up with these guys.

So, back in time, back to a bar on the Ho Street, Wombat Territory. I'd got nowhere to sleep there, I was planning to cut out of the bar early and get back to my bedsit before dawn and crash out there. Just one more beer and I'd be gone. The bar was warm, sort of trashy but comfortable. I'd got myself a comfortable armchair, the seating was quite a mix of old car seats, stools and old sofas. Whatever the management had got hold of, dining tables, coffee tables, tea chests, palettes on boxes, whatever the could get. The next fight and half of them would be matchwood anyway. No health and safety here, no complying with the regulations.

I relaxed back into the comfortable decay of the armchair, smelling the old sawdust it was stuffed with, musty, add the cigarette smoke, body odour and gun oil common to all bars and there you have it. A rickety table was within reach, a tiny tray ashtray I was working on filling up and a chipped glass tankard held the amber liquid that was one of the better brews. I was honoured, I'd go there early before the glassware had run out. I really hate those plastic beakers that seem to be all we can get these days. Especially that they have PLEX stamped into the plastic. Can we ever forget, even for a moment, that they pretty much own everything?

The bar wasn't particularly crowded. There had been a drive by earlier and that tends to keep some of the less determined in whatever hole they call home. It is why I had turned in early. I'd got three packages through, mostly bootleg tapes for a couple of clubs run from a dealer in one of the ever dwindling arcologies. One private package, didn't take long to work out it was extra shells for a very old gun that guy loves so much. Guns and ammunition are my usual cargoes, it's the specialist stuff that there is the greatest need for, the old stuff, sort of collector's items I suppose you could call them. There's a man I know, but then there usually is. Anyway, all packages safely delivered, one more pick up, in Wardog Territory, if I can get there but that was unlikely. The "border" was looking very dodgy earlier, there was a running street fight and I didn't much feel like travelling roofside. The package could wait where it was tonight, I'd pick it up in the morning. It was a non-urgent one anyway. Stal just wanted it to get off his hands once I got him a contact. Nonperishable by what I heard. Yep, I'd do that one in the morning.

Then this dude walks into the bar, into my life. The door sort of swings open, like one of those old Western Films I managed to get my hands on once, and he strolls in sort of cool like. The Man In Black, describes us all pretty much. Anyway, he looks cool, walks cool and as he puts NewYen on the table he acts cool as well. Tall, thin, expensive suit. Got to be rock hard to wear a suit on the street and not be taken for corporate cannon fodder. Long black curly hair and reactolight mirror shades. I'd seen those things domeside, yea, I've been there, I'll tell you later. They are chipped, reacted to the light while keeping the mirrored face to the world. Other functions too no doubt, like they magnify, enhance and filter, analyse light and give the wearer a little black readout in the bottom right hand corner. The top of the range ones have a motion sensor as well. Enhanced peripheral vision with an audio chip to magnify sound if you need to and a recording function which is rarely used on the street. Real nice and real expensive. Everything about him was expensive, from the cut of his suit to the cut of his hair. Quality and he'd got my interest and I didn't just mean the cyberware.

I was too far away to hear what he was saying to the barman but I saw the barman look over to where I was sitting. I looked away, keeping him just in my field of vision. I felt cold, like water falling inside me, I tried real hard not to react. I watched him, he was coming over and I felt like making a break for it. This could be trouble, by his cut he could be an Eurosolo and they were hard, rock hard, instant death for street slime like me. My mind was racing, had I annoyed someone bit, was that package more important than I knew? No amount of experience makes up for their training and the amount of wiring those guys can afford. They can draw and shoot you before you even know they are there. If he wanted me dead that was it, kerblammie! My only calming thought was that I was too insignificant for anyone to bother to send anything as expensive as that after me. He moved with the grace of a dancer, he had to be wired. He stood over me and I was caught in the spotlight like a frightened animal. I heard the click as he took off his shades, folded them and slipped them into a top pocket.

He indicated an empty seat opposite, it backed the door, that guy had to be confident. I had to play it cool, see what he wanted. I shrugged and nodded. He sat down, pulling the knees of his trousers so they didn't crease. I was too laid back, it didn't help my tenseness. I straightened in my chair, feeling the springs in my back as I slid up to meet him eye to eye, then he spoke. His voice quiet, so reassuring, yep, just like a cat about to pounce on a mouse I thought.

"You're Chrystal?" His accent had an indication of something American, soft, questioning.

"That's about right." I didn't know what to say. Some say its hard to shut me up sometimes, not that night though. I was in a state of shock.

"Word on the street is that you are good. We need good people." He was so relaxed, so off beat it put me at ease and that worried me. "I need some courier work done around the North Ho Street. We're getting a lot of gigs together and we need the equipment moved. Not the big stuff, that's going AV, but the other stuff. The sounds from some of those wire-head junkies down on South. Are you up for it? The credit's good."

"How good?"

"The Crisis man delivers. None of us go short." He smiled that enigmatic smile, realizing I had no idea who he was and trying to hide his disappointment. " I should have introduced myself. I'm too used to being known." I could feel myself blushing, I'd offended him, that was a great start. "Guess you put me in my place there. I'm Lightning, Crisis' right hand man." He held out an immaculately manicured hand.

As I shook his hand and felt his firm grip I couldn't help wondering how much of it was real, how much titanium plates and armour. There was something else, a stirring, fear or excitement, I couldn't tell which. As I said, he cut a very impressive image.

"Just music? I'll tell you now, I don't run anything other than basics and recreational."

He smiled again, those eyes, so clear, so blue. I couldn't help hoping they were real but there wasn't a chance that they weren't enhanced, the image they gave him magnified in some way. "Sister, you must have been living under a stone. We don't run bad shit. Ask anybody. Crisis sees it all straight, just recreationals and good quality hardware. Look, there's a bar opening tonight. I've got to meet up with Crisis and Diane soon. Up for a night out? On the Club?"

I weighted it up, a night in the dark brown decay of my bedsit and watch the paint peel off the walls or a night out at someone else's expense. Girls like me don't get offers like that every day. "Sure."

"Let's move out then." He indicated over his shoulder and I saw what he was meaning. Three Wombats were taking far too much interest. Their black and white tartan tribal colours standing out from the greys and blacks of the other locals. On the street here you respected the tribes or you were dead. I'd worked up a rep, he obviously had just walked in cold. That was then I got the angle on it and why they needed me. I had the ability to move about the whole of the Ho without being questioned. Get yourself a rep and a name for money and you are a target wherever. Somebody always thinks they are hard enough to take you, and let's face it, how have half of the guys got their reps? Getting lucky with a guy that would on average have wiped the floor with them. The deal had to be straight, perhaps I was onto something.

I downed what was left of my pint, picked up Lightning's now empty glass, walked over, next to the tree who had been paying far too much attention and put the glasses on the bar. I met them eye to eye. It was a tense moment, I could feel Lightning behind me, could almost sense him summing them up, evaluating how to take them down quickly and effectively. I smiled while keeping eye contact. This was one piece of turf I wanted to keep access to. They relaxed. The nearest one turning to lean on the bar. "Night Chrystal, see you again real soon."

"Yea, damn straight." I relaxed a little.

"Look Weavil, down on the Shiners has a gun I want. Deal's done and I need it picked up. Can't go into that patch. I put one of theirs in the cooler last week. Letting it die down a bit. Chrystal, I can't pay much."

"Give me access to Gweeb's Shack and an intro and I'll run it for fifty."

His face brightened up. That collectors hunger would be fed. "Cool, suits me."

"Manyana or the next?"

"Cool, no hurry." He handed me a slip of paper with his mobile number. Weird really, you sort of start thinking of the Clans as being tribal basics but most of them have mobiles. Communication, that is the key and where its at. Networks of people, talking to people who talk to people. Not that anything is safe, there is no such thing as a safe line.

We left the bar. I was about to turn right to a short cut I know when Lightning hailed a combat cab. Life was on the up. I tried to make out that I had been moving to check something out as Lightning opened the door and stood back. Natural nervousness, I wondered why, but went with it. I stepped into the dark interior, he put a hand on my back to help me in. It felt so strange, so sort of gentle. Sometimes you forget you are a woman. Oh I've seen the vids of the Domeside Tarts, painted and pampered. Paint yourself like that on the Ho and you'll get offers a plenty. Vanity can get you dead, image is power, image is survival. Black, the colour of the street, everything practical, tied down, to hand. That and the respirators and goggles necessary in the "fresh" air these days. What is the point of make-up which takes ages to put on when it is going to end up all over the facemask that is inevitably going to be necessary if any length of time is spent outside? Lightning, he obviously had no need, no doubt air filters had been built into the wiring and hardware he'd had implanted. It confirmed my suspicion about those eyes, had to have UV filters built in as well for those rare times that the sun did break through the almost never ending thunder clouds.

I relaxed in the cab. The drivers, mostly retired ex-military knew how to handle their vehicles and their weaponry.

The neon signs and milling crowds flew by, a couple of shots bounced off the armour plating but nothing the cab couldn't handle. The riot in the Wardog Territory still raged so we took a cut down side streets. A tenement fire cut us back onto the Ho somewhere in Wardog Territory but it was relatively calm. We circled the Ho and came to the relatively well-off area where the new bar was opening.

Lightning was very quiet, like he had a lot on his mind. I wasn't going to ask, it wasn't healthy. Private is private, those are the basic rules of the street, except of course if you come on some information that is worth money. Crazy double standards but hell this is life, not some twee soap opera.

The cab slid to a stop on the far side of the highway. Lightning handed over credits and got out, holding the door for me. I could see him watching, taking everything in. The pavement was empty, that was usually a bad sign. The cab drew away into the stream of traffic and Lightning unbuttoned his jacket. "Third doorway on the right. Two punks, one armed, heavy weaponry, they're watching." He slipped his arm around my waist and turned me round, pushing us back into the empty doorway behind us as naturally as we could manage.

I heard the footsteps. Lightning pushed me behind him and pulled out his Berretta, clicking off the safety. I held my breath. Metal shod boots on stone. Closer, ten feet, five feet, I could hear them, silence on the street, that was rare. A head appeared around the corner, a Berretta muzzle under the chin and the punk backed off, hands in the air, rifle hanging from a strap over his arm, his companion doing likewise. He spluttered, his accent strongly local. "Look man, I was only taking a look. This is our territory like, oh Christ, look don't kill me man. Hey, don't I know you? Look sorry man, it's Lightning isn't it? I'm so sorry man. Should have recognized you. You, Crisis, the UHC, look man like I wasn't expecting a big name to be here."

Lightning clicked on the safety and left the two punks to watch him go. I followed but I know he was keeping them in sight, even though it didn't much look like it.

We wove our way through the traffic then took a left up the Ho to the forecourt of a café. It had once been one of those places where you say out at tables in warm weather and watched the world go by. Now it was a park for hover-bikes and rubbish. The café had closed hours ago, its last greasy meal served about five. A skinny waitress moved about in the dimly lit room between the tables, clearing away the rubbish and broken furniture. Cracked and broken music drifted from their ancient PA System. It was not designed to play music so its quality was lousy and I could see Lightning visibly cringing.

A more up market combat cab smoothly glided to a halt outside the café and the driver got out and opened the back passenger door. A man in a black suit got out, slightly shorter than Lightning, shoulder length straight black hair, heavy set brow and a slightly hawkish nose were distinctive and he carried himself with confidence. By the way he walked, by the way he wore that jacket with too much comfort I placed him as being Crisis. The cab drew away and Crisis strolled over. He and Lightning hugged each other, slapping each other on the back and then he turned to look me over.

"So I guess this is Chrystal." I tried to look cool but there was something in the slow and deliberate way he spoke. That deep American drawl that melts like butter and the way he stood just close enough that you could feel him there, but far enough away that he didn't crowd you. "Like the name, very UHC. Lightning has said good things about you, welcome to the Club."

The Club, Urban Hunt Club, like THE Club to belong to. They were Big and I mean very big, I didn't know the specifics but I'd heard of the UHC.

Lightning looked worried. "Crisis man, where's Diane and Blue?" I could feel my brow furrowing. I didn't know but it seemed somehow important, something in his tone of voice as he said the names.

"Bitches struck out earlier. Something about stop 'till they drop. Hell I don't know. Some cooky old idea of actually going and looking at the stuff for real. Can't see why they didn't just buy on line. Broads, hey, who can fathom them?"

"Yea right." He was hearing it but he sure wasn't buying it. There was one unnerved man.

Crisis shrugged but even he looked a little worried. I didn't know who these two women were, I sort of assumed, but then assumptions can be wrong. "Well kiddies, never mind the broads now, let's blow this place and get down to the bar. I want to see what that old dog Smiling has come up with this time." He reached into his pocket and pulled out a tape. " I know the old boy's taste, here we have some real sounds." He looked at me and smiled.

Lightning offered his arm, I slipped my hand through it and we strolled down the Ho and I have to say I was feeling pretty pleased with myself.

After a while you don't notice the rain. Certainly on the part of the Ho running up to Smiling Jared's. Canopies strung to the street outside the glowing neon and amber glow of the shop fronts. Punters on the street could stop in the relative comfort of being sheltered from the rain, except when one of the drains blocked or a canopy collapsed which did happen when they filled with too much rain and someone was careless enough to leave them too long.

It was a busy night. The street was crawling with people. Girls in strappy PVC, a seedy elegance of black shiny minimalist clothing carefully cut to show them at their best. The light on the street was dim, the claustrophobic closeness of the seething mass and they didn't have to worry too much about how they looked. Nobody was going to get a close look, not until they had paid their credits and taken that walk up the stairway. Fixers on every corner, selling a powder or a pill for every occasion. There was no legal or illegal, the main dispute being whose patch it was and whether the stuff was lethal. Most were one hit addictive, some one hit lethal if you got a bad batch and that depended on who was doing the cutting. Names on the street got the best pitches and even the locals defended that, even if they didn't approve of the merchandise. Less likelihood then of some crack-head getting a bad trip and going on a spree. In the public interest so to speak. Public awareness, especially since Free Love of America dumped a load of LSD into the water system in the States years back. Free love alright, free death in the riots that followed. The street sort of has its own controls now. Sell bad goods and the street doesn't ask you to move on politely.

This had been home turf for me once. I knew most of these faces and they were established. A couple of new ones but nothing I'd worry about. They were social alright giving me the nod still, in their own sweet ways. You get used to it after a while.

I saw the building the fuss was about. It had been a bar for years, too right, could say I was born there, almost, found there, just like coming home. Now the purple piped light in the window spelling "Smiling Jared's" and the broken glass and burnt out interior had been painted and replaced. By the size of the panels of glass out front they had to be UV filtered and bullet proof. This Smiling Jared had spent a bit on the old place, the shape was the same but that was about as far as it went in comparison.

We stepped down a side alley, the side door was always popular, even in the old days. I knew that old door, embedded with years of shells, painted over again and again until they had formed a bullet proof layer themselves. Painted over again now a deep blue but already there were new shells embedded there and scratches where stray shots had gouged out the paint to show the metal cases underneath. All the fun of the Ho Street.

The alley was fairly wide, more like a side street opening into a courtyard where a couple of dumpsters were parked, two small alleyways leading off of the main and piles of rubbish that had failed to make it into the dumpster decorated the floor. The alleys were empty, well as far as we could see. The outside brickwork of the bar riddled with gunshot, dried blood and layers of graffiti. A pool of blood just outside the door was still fresh. We looked at each other and stepped into the smoky brightness of the bar.

Jared's Bar, crowded with all forms of life known to man, some sentient, some making an attempt to be so. What strikes you on first entering is that the place is clean. Scrubbed clean. Chrome tables and chairs reflecting the blue glow of UV lighting, a creamy blueness that has an atmosphere of its own. A surreal light-headedness helped along by the amount of recreationals that were in the air. Nothing to do with the management, purely a gift from some of the more relaxed of the customers. Even the shadows crawled with life, street life from the cybered up jack-head trying to find a comfortable way to balance a pint and keep far too heavy weaponry balanced against the wall yet handy to the obvious netrunners clutching bags which they were trying to make out were unimportant. Trying to make out that their whole lives in the form of a cyber deck wasn't in there and really wasn't valuable and worth nicking.

The plastic sheeting on the floor and walls was a little unnerving to start. It gave the walls a silvery glow that added to the surreal atmosphere. The floor being non slip was reassuring. The gentle hum of conversation filled the air, rising cigarette smile and music drifting from what sounded like an expensive system. The bar was packed, seriously packed. Full of people trying to keep space between themselves and other people trying to do likewise. Street Warriors nursing bandaged limbs, trying to hold a pint or open a can. Some had companions who would help, others well they just stood around on the periphery and looked lonely but everyone was lonely on the street.

The bar was backed by a huge chrome plate, plastic shelves crossing it with all manner of cans. I couldn't help thinking that it made the whole thing look like a shooting gallery. A silvery white backing for the long up-lit chrome bar.

Lightning whispered in my ear. "Chrystal, we've got a job tonight. We're keeping an eye on some bitch with some cash. Crisis and I are going to swing round the bar and get hold of her. Hang about here a while."

Couldn't argue with that. I thought I'd just take a look around.

The bar had a rectangular design. The front, street facing wall was a half wall with a door in the middle, large glass windows looking out onto the Ho with blinds that could be shuttered to shut out the night. The door was open and led out onto a glass encased veranda with half mock wood walls and a door out onto the front. Then there was a wide area out front before the pavement. There had been another building in front once I remember that much but it got wasted when an AV crashed into it and hasn't been built up again since.

Chrome tables spaced by natural suspicion and a need for space, leaving a central gangway from the front door to the bar. The bar filled most of the back wall. Of the two door in this wall one was behind the bar, the other was to the left of the bar. On the left hand wall int eh back corner was the door where we had come in and a second door which led to a room which cut into the main rectangle. The bar was packed, spilling out onto the veranda but people were leaving, nine thirty, a good time for business.

Lightning and Crisis had got to the bar and Crisis waved me over. They were deep in conversation with the barman, his long duster coat obviously hiding heavy weaponry, longish red hair, a care worn face, sort of lived in good looking, over thirty at least. There was something of the burnt out cop about him, sort of off duty casual but not too casual. Black suede waistcoat, white shirt and tie, almost corporate. There was something about him, something comfortable but something else. Something I didn't see initially but I felt it. I must have been staring. Lightning leaned over, whispering in my ear. "Ex-cop, ex-Android Hunter."

Great combination and I made a mental note not to cause any trouble when he was around and concentrated on the bottles on the shelves behind the bar. There were choices then, beers from all over, even some local to the Ho. It is amazing what could be made into beer. Not just PLEX brand beer in those days.

Lightning caught the barman's attention. "Jared, this is Chrystal, she's UHC."

He looked up from knocking the top off of a bottle. "Chrystal." Flat monotone, disinterested tone of a barman who met so many people every day. Smiling Jared, that name had to be ironic. Wat that a smile he cracked? The chilled glass against my hand brought me back to planet Ho Street. It was chilled in contrast to the warm mugginess of the air. I took a long cold swig, watching Jared as he watched me, no money changed hands. The alcohol burned a little in my throat, this was the real stuff, not the watered down pints I'd been getting on Wombat turf. It was like I ought to say something but I couldn't think what. Oh well, basic rule, if you can't think of anything cool to say at a moment like that, keep your mouth shut and smile. I caught Lightning's eye at that point and somehow felt better. Couldn't place it really, I knew Lightning would be dangerous, but this other guy, something else, I shrugged it off.

It is the small things you remember the most, the scents that bring back memories. The bar would never again smell like that. It is the first time you go there, where it is all fresh and new. I ran my finger along the chrome piping, blocking out momentarily a small patch on the long blue strip light. The chill of the metal on my fingertips, the dull murmur of whispered deals going on all around me. The faces in the crowd that were strangers then, faces that would become so much a part of my life. Care worn faces, there was something in the air.

Jared and Lightning were deep in conversation about Uranium Ammunition, I knew where to get some but somehow I felt awkward for once in my life. Crisis must have seen someone as he slipped away. I lost myself in taking in he faces in the bar. Then I was aware of Lightning, so close, I could smell the heady aroma of his after-shave mixed with eau de gun oil. My concentration was drawn, it was as if he was the only person in the room. That annoyed me. Life on the streets, don't you just love it, one simple distraction could mean that you miss those vital few seconds that get you out of the way of a bullet. Simple rule, notice everyone, react to nobody. But, I had reacted to him. I could feel the warmth of his body, so close, almost touching me but not quite, in my personal space. I felt his breath on my hair, warm as he whispered. "Crisis has gone to get her over." He stepped away, but not too far. I was used to keeping everyone at a safe distance, if they can't touch you then can't get you. He was too close but somehow I didn't mind. "Come on." The words shook me out of my thoughts and we moved through the crowd to at table by the door that led to the veranda. He sat back and took a long swig from his bottle. Stopping to toast the air. "Here's to the UHC, flying high."

We toasted the UHC, our bottles clinking together.

Gunfire outside. Crisis looked a little uneasy. "What's up Lightning?"

"Diane and Blue are out there."

I thought I'd better try to help. "Do they often disappear?"

Lightning still looked worried. "Not generally. There's something wrong, I can feel it."

There was a shout outside, as if on cue. Lightning was on his feet, gun in hand, safety off. People were moving into the bar off of the veranda, half carrying a woman who staggered, her long brown hair falling around her face. Up market street clothes shredded and muddy. I was left in no doubt as Crisis leapt from nowhere to take her in his arms and help her to a chair that she was one of the missing women. Lightning looked confused. All he could say over and over again was "Where's Blue?" So, it had to be Diane by the way Crisis was all over her and the obvious fact that Blue was missing. I felt a bit out of it and I'd already worked out that they were a tactile lot, bad choice of a group to join for a tactophobe. Lightning had moved even closer than he had been, before he crouched to hug Diane. She said something to him and he was out of the door onto the veranda. I followed.

He turned and caught my arm. "Chrystal, go back, its.."

"Dangerous on the street..." I finished his sentence and there was a sarcasm in my voice as I raised an eyebrow. I pulled out my Berretta, he looked at the matching guns, smiled and we stepped out onto Ho Street. Crisis was behind us on the balcony but he didn't follow out onto the street.

"Thanks Chrystal, not much of an introduction to the Club." His expression was serious and I could tell he wanted to get back inside to Diane but equally wanted to find Blue.

"Hey, you owe me one quiet night out on the Club." I turned and followed Lightning out into the night.

The streets were milling with night-crawlers. Both women and men, selling their talents, hanging about almost casually, trying to get all too close. Let them get too close and you will lose something. They were the niftiest pickpockets on the Ho. Follow them upstairs and more than likely you will leave with more than you came with, more business for the clinics. Seeing we had guns drawn they gave us space. It was necessary, sort of a calling card for getting along the street quickly, a universal sign.

There were endless alleyways out there.

"Chrys, do you know a road with the "Blue Willow Nightclub" at its corner?"

I did, relief, I could be useful. "Follow me."

He stopped, looked at me and then we headed down a side street. I knew exactly where he meant. This was all so quick, first I was in the bar then I was off running down back alleys and this was not what I was being paid for. This was for free and I couldn't work out why. A PayCop car skidded into the alley and we backed into a doorway, surprising a drunk who was sleeping there. He saw the lights as the car drove past as well and kept quiet. He saw Lightning in silhouette and kept quieter still. We left him to his half bottle of something foul smelling and ran down the alley. Two right and a left next and we came to the alley Diane had apparently mentioned. The Club had long since gone out of business, the charring around the door streaking the brickwork. I nearly stepped on a body. There were two. I kept an eye out for more PayCops as Lightning searched them. It was quiet, all too quiet. That was never a good sign. As he searched he spoke, a little out of breath. "Diane said they were caught on the street and ran down here. Diane fought these two off but Blue got bundled not their car and they drove off. I just want to get something off of them, some ID, something that will give us a clue, then we get out of here, fast."

"Fine by me, keep searching."

He stopped, looking at something.

"What have you got?"

"These guys were wearing street clothes but they have matching T-Shirts underneath. No logo but we have labels and I don't think they are street made."

"Straight up, well you better get done with searching pretty sharp. I'm not dealing with PLEXCops int his alley, there's no easy way out but to run and those guys have long range weaponry, got it?"

"Not much more to find here. Their clothes aren't their own. No personal stuff in the pockets. They just wanted to look like they are street punks. Another thing, too well groomed, these guys have been taking time to grow stubble and grime."

"Lovely, if you've done investigating their personal habits let's get out of here. I'm beginning to get edgy."

"Yea, me too Chrys. Come on, let's get back to the bar."

The streets were fairly clear, well the back alleys were. There was a riot going on around the Ho so we kept to the back streets and swept up behind the bar. I was feeling mighty pleased with myself. It had been a long time since I had walked this turf and I still remembered it. A lot had changed, a lot of the more useful stuff had gone, like back street vendors, all burnt out. Either there was one hell of an arsonist on the prowl or. Ask no questions I suppose, that was my philosophy at that time. Just get my tail back in the warmth of the bar, get a beer inside me and see what the guys wanted to do.

Getting back to the bar wasn't too difficult. Lightning looked threatening enough that I didn't take the usual round-about route, we just strolled on in there. There were a lot of PayCops on the street but they were heading for the riot. They weren't looking for street trouble so we got back really easily.

The blood had dried outside the bar. Somewhere in the darkness someone stumbled into a can and swore. It was drunk night on the streets. Lightning stopped, reflexes working before he thought he pulled out his gun and released the safety. Hearing the can he flicked the safety on ruffled my hair and opened the door to the bar. I stood there a moment. What gave him the right to get so touchy feely? I liked it though, I'd let it pass.

The bar had thinned out a lot. The riot had taken most of the clientele, there was always good pickings to be made from riots, particularly when it was invaders on a home turf. The bar was almost half empty, and more were looking like they were just finishing up their beers before calling it a night.

Jared looked up as I came in, he was the sort of who took in faces. That unnerved me a little, but hell, it was his bar. Lightning was over whispering to Crisis and I went over to join them. Diane was looking a bit better now. She had a chair and a beer and that seemed to make all the difference. She coughed slightly and looked up. There was something very gentle about her and I couldn't help wondering what she was doing on the street. She seemed too refined. I checked the hands, manicured, she was no street woman. There was something dome bred about her. She smiled, an uncomplicated smile, like it didn't mean something or nothing. It was a genuine smile. What the hell was she doing here on the street? Then I saw the way she looked at Crisis and I knew why. I had to feel sorry for her. The bitch obviously had it bad. I think she saw my hesitation.

"So you are Chrystal. Hi, I'm Diane." Her voice was deep, like she was going to say something really important, sort of made me listen. I'm used to getting the handle on someone as soon as I met them. She was just so "ordinary". I don't mean it in a derogatory way, just like the girl next door in the domes but something wise, an experience she carried without arrogance. Not in our world though, she was out of place and if she wasn't careful she'd be out of time.

"Hi, bad night?" I didn't really know what to say.

"About right, welcome to the UHC." Her smile was sarcastic, but then it suited the moment as heavy music drifted over the music system and smoke swirled around us. Backlit by blue neon, her long brown wavy hair flowing around her shoulders and Crisis clinging to her. Like some tableau from a historic romantic SlushVid. Kinda made you feel a bit warm though. Crisis was saying something to her and her attention was completely drawn to him.

"See you in a while." I slipped out onto the veranda and left them to it. I needed a cigarette and a bit of space. So I leant against the wall and watched the traffic rolling slowly along the Ho and the crowds milling about from the safety of behind the reinforced glass.

I wasn't alone. About five feet away I had company. I liked the jacket straight off, brown suede with some suede cut to fringes. I think they call it a Western Jacket, that and his hat was very cowboy. He looked like he had the troubles of the world on his shoulders. Bowed over his clasped hands just looking out into the night. Well you don't ask do you, you just wait and see. He looked up. His face a mask of thoughts that seemed to be flashing past him too swiftly for him to comprehend. He was slightly taller than me, his short dark hair neatly cut under his hat. His eyes were so sad. He looked at me for a moment and held out his hand. "Hi, I'm Chuckles."

Yea, a bundle of laughs. I smiled and shook his hand. This was all getting far too weird for me, too close. What was it with that place that made strangers talk. We talked, we talked for a very long time, just watching the Ho life go by. He had his troubles, but then those who have seen active service usually do. The drugs they pump into them, the flashbacks where gentle people are forced to kill. I'd sat through it all with Max, Max was a burnt out alcoholic I'd found in a bar and taken home. Not something I'd usually do but he crashed on my sofa until he got his act together then he sort of moved off. That's also what they become, they hang around until they get their act together an then their off after fortune and glory again. Well that was my belief until I met Chuckles. The problems that Chuckles described, the voices, classic flashback. I tried to reassure him and well, I guess we got to know each other a bit. He had a partner or something, marriage wasn't common on the Ho, name of Runt, I knew her. Good kid, ran this neck of the Ho and successfully by what I heard, well no great bullet holes in her lately and that is success on the Ho.

Then the lights went out. I kid you not, like the whole world went dark, the bar, the street, everywhere. Only the headlamp of cars were left blazing which was the point when we got back into the main building. I grabbed my phone and made a call. Snifter was down the other end of our "zone" and I knew he would be out and about.

The line crackled into life. "Yo!"

"Snifter, its Chrystal."

"Like the whole world's gone to shit down here. Sorry kid, can't be pally, the PLEXCops are really shaking our tails. Word is that it's a power cut and a big on. Gotta fly." I heard a shot ricochet. "Shit." Click, connection lost.

Someone shouted from the other side of the bar, the Net's gone down. I heard Crisis swear, like with a passion.

Lightning had moved over to stand with me. He looked down and he looked worried. "Chrys, you know what that means?" I think he had got the angle already that I knew jack shit about the net. "Take out the power source and money just sort of drifts away when its electronically stored. He's looking at a wipe out here. He doesn't keep it in hard cash."

I didn't know what to say. My mind was flailing about with what I'd heard. Simple logic, why were the PLEXCops on the streets so quick. We could expect trouble. The first round hit the glass as I thought it, cracking it. Jared was in the middle of the room, he let out a long moan.

"Fucking ballistic rounds." Crisis was on his feet and the comment had come from him. He had a handful of white pills in his hand which he flipped into his mouth. He washed them down with someone's beer. He grabbed a gun, opened the door to the veranda and stepped outside, like he was mega pissed off. Off his head more like as three PLEXCops stepped out from a side street and he blew one of them away. Lightning was out there in a flash dragging him back inside. We were back from the main street, somehow I can't help feeling that they might just have left us alone without that. But then they had already fired on the glass. The cops returned fire, Lightning jolted, his head flew back in pain but he kept dragging Crisis back onto the veranda and shut the door. A second ballistic round hit the glass spider webbing it. A third sent it smashing inwards in a shower of shards. Lightning was in the bar, laying under a table, his head on my lap and I have no idea of the actions that got us there. Forget my non-contact, don't give a shit attitude, I was just trying to stop him losing blood.

Someone came over, said his name was Slater, dressed the wound and told me to keep the pressure on. I held Lightning across my knees. I could smell the blood as bullets rattled along the outside of the building. He reached up and stroked my hair. "Thanks Chrystal." He didn't have to thank me. I looked down at him, his long hair matted with blood, his face twisted with pain.

Crisis skittered across the floor, avoiding a volley of gunfire that bounced off the back wall of the bar. "Here mate, take this, it'll help."

I saw the white pills. So did Lightning and he grabbed them. "Cheers pal."

It had all gone crazy. I pulled Lightning fully under the table as bullets flew around the bar, answered by a loud explosion of many guns out on the veranda. Then relative calm. There were still noises out on the street but not close.

We were dead in the water, without the net connection we were cut off. Landlines were down, only mobile phones were working. I tried a couple of numbers but no reply. I left messages but somehow I just knew they wouldn't be calling me back, ever. It was a wild night, there was a scream and all hell broke loose, not for long. An explosion of gunfire and silence. Lightning said it first. "Spirals." A vicious clan of dust-heads that eat Grievous Angel (a highly addictive, eventually lethal drug) for breakfast and lived the rest of the day on the effect. Unstoppable, that was what the drug did for them, they could have their legs shot to bits and they'd still keep running. Great, and they were running on the streets and this was their idea of heaven. No fear of death, no pain, the drug would kill them if the bullets didn't first, today, tomorrow, they didn't know when.

"Incoming." I recognized Chuckles' voice. "Friendlies."

How did he know? It was just so dark out there. Bodies bundled into the bar, three of them, carrying a lot of equipment and I could just about make out camouflage green in the darkness. Crisis swore. "Bloody Doc Harley and the BFA, all we need." I don't think they heard as they moved into the bar and threw down their equipment.

The tallest of them, the one they called Doc Harley, towered over me as I held onto Lightning under the table, turned. His voice was deep, resonating. "A carrier went down on the far side of the highway. There's something out there. We saw it leap off a building. It's hell on the streets." In silhouette he looked like the classic soldier, off of those old ad boards that sometimes turn up as walls down back alleys. Big gun strapped across his back, camouflage gear and a smoke marked face in the light from the car headlights out in the street. The fire had begun to smoke, its grey sinuous tendrils weaving around everyone adding to the darkness. Lightning moved. Someone had put an automatic weapon in his hand and he looked like he was about to get up. I tried to stop him but he was drugged up to the eyeballs and stronger than I was anyway. All I could do was follow him so we swapped the relative comfort of the bar for the veranda where various dark shapes crouched, waiting. Movement alley side, muzzle-flash cut the night, illuminated tense fences. That bright light just before someone dies, falling in pain, their blood so red, so bright. It's the grey black of everything else. It was a boy, hardly more than a child. He leapt over the veranda wall, his eyes were so wild and I'd seen that drug crazed look too often. A world without hope and for the duration the quick fix lasts, without fear.

It is the children that always reflect how bad things have got. No hope, no education, just taking their breaks where they can. No doubt they do in the domes as well but they stand more chance of the drugs being cut with something that isn't going to rot their brain. It was his eyes, that wild uncontrolled look, the look of someone off their head on Grievous Angel. A bitch of a hit, addictive first go. A human being reduced to no more than a rabid animal. All it took was an accurate shot, one bullet from Lightning, straight through the temple. The boy stopped in his tracks, eyes staring at something that just wasn't there. He fell to the ground, a trickle of blood ran down his face. As he fells to his knees he touched the hole in his head, looked at the blood on his fingers, then at us and fell forwards onto the veranda.

That look, that accusing look, we had no choice. It was standing over the body, just starting down, in full view of anyone who wanted to soot me. It was Lightning who dragged me from my thoughts and down out of sight. His bandage had come loose, his blood was soaking through making the matt black of his suit shiny. I crouched beside him and as carefully as I could I wound it back into place, feeling the comfort of another human being. This was beginning to worry me. I never needed anyone and after Max had walked out I'd put even more distance between myself and anyone.

Anarchy on the streets, sirens and gunfire. We were off the main street but we caught the gangers coming up the alley. Target practice mostly for those who hung about on the veranda just wondering where it was going to end. Just wondering how it had started, why it had started.

Then the power came back on and an almost unnatural calm descended on the street and the bar.

5

"Right Lightning, so they were in the AVs heading for Portland Down. We know that somehow there had been some long term plan that meant we had control over Danforth, the semi-independent AI. Has she put in more detail about that?" Daniel looked serious, half watching the road ahead, mostly trying to catch glimpses of text.

"Yea, I've been skim reading and I think this bit helps."

This is where Azrael suddenly became very important. He'd been around and to be quite honest I'd not taken much notice of him. Other than the odd greeting he had just been another guy on the streets. Anyway, I get a message from Shade that Azrael has got some great lead to something. His inheritance is what he calls it. I heard about the lottery balls first. I think Vortex was trying to do something about investigating what they meant as well. Anyway, we didn't work it out immediately and I sort of got tied up with other things. Then I hear that they have solved the problem. Apparently after visiting the Camelot Theme Park after hours where the balls were kept they sort of left with them. I don't know exactly who was on the recovery mission but it was pretty successful. Then came the working out of what exactly we were going to do with them.

Once the jokes had died down we could manage to think about it rationally of course. According to Vortex, our friendly neighbourhood genius netrunner, certain of the balls felt different. On further investigation they gave clues and soon enough there were two or three parties breaking into official buildings and causing a bit of mayhem and destruction to get the articles back that were needed. In our usual fashion there was a lot of mess to clear up in our wake. Still, I got to wear a corporate suit and it didn't feel too bad. Not that I'd do it again you have to understand.

Anyway, back on the streets we get to put the information together and we get a map location which took us to a place called Portland Down, an old nuclear site back in the 80s. The place has been decommissioned but there are now people living there.

Well, then all hell breaks loose. We're at this place just trying to get a grip on some new information we have come across. This is the biggest thing you could imagine, this is a chance. It seems that years back, when Jared Matthews was just a corporate puppy but climbing ever higher his colleagues began to get very worried about his mental state and the power he was getting under his control. So, in good corporate fashion they expected him to do something to gain complete control. This was unacceptable to them and although they could do nothing then they decided to leave a legacy for their children, just in case.

When Jared Matthews created an AI to help him in his plots and schemes these people created a back door. In all good spy traditions they left a trail to lead their children to finding their way to Portland Down where they had hidden the technology that would open up that back door. This would give the operators control over part of the AI. Something we now have control over! Of all people to get hold of something useful! Not that I believe for one minute that this isn't going to be discovered by Jared Matthews and that he doesn't know about it. Let's face it, the man is brilliant, a mad man but brilliant all the same, or so I've heard. Lateral thinking is quite a skill go have. Give us what we want and we go running to a strange place, gather together and splat, he drops a rock on us. He did it to Japan, he could easily do it to us.

Now we have the use of the back door and the most powerful AI. We have to plan now what to do with it. We have a plan alright.

Through talking to Danforth we have found out about the ALKAHERA project which in short is that there has been a plan to blast off an orbital, known as a SAISH Unit to Mars and terraform it. Terraforming, well that is creating an atmosphere and the physical needs that mankind needs to live on a planet. Danforth actually had a plan, all on his own, to save the species. That sort of makes you think when all mankind has done is wreck this planet and an AI with no physical form as such actually does something about saving it. Anyway, we have a variation on his plan. We take people up into the orbitals and then shut down power and manufacturing on the planet. That should stop the cascade and cut down pollution almost overnight.

I guess we have all expected that there was some likelihood that the planet had been irreparably damaged. This was the cascade. I think there was something like four years at the rate we were damaging the ecosystem before we rendered it unfit for human habitation. We decided to do this and then it was time to consider the downside. We have just decided to cause the death of several billion people. Not directly you have to understand but they rely on power and they have no idea how to survive in a world without it. The planet cannot actually support all those people either. They have only been maintained by synthetic means, the means we are just about to take away. Not bad for a pacifist.

The plan sounds like it will work on the surface but to do that will throw everyone back into the dark ages. We are going to have to cut out our main communication system as well just to give us a chance. Not that there are many people left and if what has happened on the Ho is common then what does it really matter. We are firmly of the belief that the earth needs a chance to start again. We can't see any other way forward. I suppose in one way I feel that I'm just not important enough to make a difference but in another I know that somehow with something as important as this it is only right that the people with the least say have a chance to put this right. I'm not saying that we are saints, that we are not. Read on and learn a little about the group that you are reading about and perhaps you will see why I worry.

Lightning stopped reading and looked up.

"What's up?" Daniel kept his eyes on the road.

"She's writing something here but its lacking something, you know."

"No I don't, what do you mean?" Daniel cast a glance across but it was a difficult part of the road so he kept his concentration on the road ahead.

"She's writing a history how she wants it seen. I know, I was with her at Portland Down."

"What do you actually mean?"

"I mean she's trying to set down the facts as she sees them but she's writing a story for her daughter, not relating the facts as they were."

"Are you saying she is lying or embellishing them?"

"No, but she's skipping some pretty major stuff."

"Like what?"

"Like how close were all were and the."

"Lightning, it is a letter to her daughter, a memorial to us if we don't make it. What do you expect her to write?"

"I don't know."

"So what do you feel is missing?"

"The reality of the situation." Lightning's voice was agitated.

"Which is? You should listen to what she is saying."

"Doesn't matter, I'll go on."

You know it's really strange but everyone has an image that is "home". I know I guess for me it will always be Jared's Bar. It was my first real home but it's the people I remember. Like the Vid-news seller on the corner. He was there day after day, same place, same time, nobody noticed him. They hardly spoke to him when they got their news but he was there. It was as if he had no life to them other than that but when he went home he was a real person, he did real things, and now he's gone.

Bill broke into my thoughts.

"Has the bar gone?" There was a hesitation in his voice.

A question I guess I knew the answer to but an answer I didn't want to acknowledge. I don't know, perhaps I felt that if I didn't say it then there was still hope. "Bill, I don't know. Jared called, the lines dead."

Bill looked down. So perhaps he did care a little. It gets to everyone after a while. I've seen the dark side of Ho Street, its dirt, its decay. It was in intensive care, it didn't need putting down. One thing cannot be denied about the domes though, the "Domers" do have a good quality of life. Clean air and good food. Not a choice I'd take. This is something you will probably have to come to terms with. I cannot say sorry enough but I am totally responsible for your poor health. I was given a choice to move into the domes before you were born. It was our choice that you would be born on the streets. If you are suffering for it then I find it difficult to justify other than it was for an ideal. Ideals don't seem to count for much at the moment as the dead and the dying lay piled high on Ho Street. You were a symbol of hope, that is what Asha means apparently, in Sanskrit. Why should I name you in some ancient and dead language I don't know. Perhaps its symbolic. I just don't know anything anymore.

Back in the bar that night of the blackout I had pulled a chair up to the fire and Lightning was propped up under a table. He looked comfortable and he had a beer. The chrome elegance of the place transformed into a pile of chairs and tables that were now just that little bit more dented. Lightning too, that sharp exterior was gone. I saw the man that night, not the wired up enhanced sidekick. This could be the pain of the loss of everyone I know or something else. Itis the advice a mother can give to her child. When you feel something, don't deny it. I know how I felt when he lay there after being shot. I hope you don't live in such circumstances. It's an electricity, a power that grips you. This is just the loss of all that I know talking but what the heck, I want you to know me. I didn't know your father well then, there will possibly be others you will know before you find your life's mate. I know how I felt for Lightning and that was what kept me at the bar in those early days, that link, that power. We were inseparable but I know now it was just that we worked well together and I found out later, too late that he loved another. I found out shortly afterwards how much your father cared. That was the most valuable gift on earth. There is no value in loving someone, they have to return that love. If they don't then it becomes destructive. I learnt that, our father loved me, that was what mattered. We came together and you were born, the verification that this was right. I hope and pray that you find someone as worthy as him. There are different types of love. My love for Jared is the real kind, the partner, the friend kind.

Oh well, back to the bar. It was reasonably quiet though. Crisis sat hugging Diane, around the bar groups were bandaging wounds and generally looking stunned. The power was back on and there was movement in one corner. The netrunners, couldn't miss them, in moments they were linked in together wired into cyberdecks and off into their own rather huge world. Fanatics but so very, very useful. Strange to think that in the latter part of the 1900s they were considered to be "geeks" and "anoraks". Then getting hold of a waterproof anorak in a world of rain, perhaps they saw that one coming as well.

Jared kicked the music system back on line and everyone relaxed a little. The effect of music on the masses. How the world turns, information is power and information in abundance lays in the net. The night I met Shade and Yali, and the others. Doch had jacked in as well and they sat in a little circle communing with the spirits in the net.

Lightning thumped the dashboard.

"What is the matter Lightningsan?"

"I thought, no, I didn't think. It was later on, at the co-op, you know, in Bordertown. I'd just heard that Blue had died. Chrystal was my friend, I told her how much I'd loved Blue. It was just that I didn't realise until she got up and walked off. Then I felt it, then I knew. She became distant. I told her. Guess it was just like saying lets be friends but that wasn't what I meant, I just meant… Next time I went into the bar it was after she'd been off to Wales, then it was her and Jared. Look I've no place to get between them."

"It's a crazy time. Is what you are saying real? Or just a reaction to the then and now?" Daniel didn't look sideways, he was watching a group of cars which hung together just a little way ahead and didn't lose focus until he was past them.

The past hour or so had made something so evident, how vulnerable we really were. That's the way it goes I suppose, a limiting factor, the more advanced you get, the more limitations you bring on yourself. But, from that you find your strengths. If you are not tested, you are not strong. Or your strength is wasted.

A jolt and the netrunners "jacked" out. They looked really out of it. Stunned. "Total chaos". The deep voice of Doc Harley. "Millions has been wiped off of the NewYen, might as well use it as toilet paper. Major banks were kept off line long enough to really interfere with transfers. Any transfers being done just got lost on the way. The money just fell into cyberspace."

Silence and everyone looked at everyone else. Life was harsh enough. This would hit hard. Perhaps I had better explain as no doubt things are different for you. The NewYen and old cash were the currencies of the street. PLEX Credits were used in the dome. The Yen was the currency of the grey and black markets, our markets.

Doc threw his jack plug onto the table and stalked out onto the balcony.

I was warm, I was comfortable and I wasn't moving for a while. Crisis had moved with Diane to sit in the corner nearby and pretty much everyone else had come in to sit around. It had been a long night.

Doc came in. "Look, we have a cell coming in off the upper sector. I want to bring them in here. Aztech might be with them. We've got to bring them in."

Crisis scowled. "Well you cannot."

I spoke without thinking. "Why not?"

Doc turned to face me and I felt really awkward. He smiled, it was a reassuring smile. "Right enough." That deep voice like velvet. "They've been out there in all that and they need somewhere to go."

It got heated. Crisis arguing that there wasn't space. Doc arguing they had to go somewhere. Then the report came in that they had been wiped. Doc went white, muttering something about Aztech. I didn't catch what he said. Then pieces started to fall into place. Her ecological connections just before her trailer went up in a fireball. The rumours on the street and then wham, Mexico gets wiped off the map. Not just that, mainly the land owned by her. I didn't know enough to put anything together before.

What I did know was that by speaking out against Crisis I had put my foot in it over being UHC. I had a dilemma as well. I wandered out onto the balcony and Doc was out there. He didn't look so "toy soldier" out there, more the troubled freedom fighter. He spun round. "Get inside, its dangerous out here."

I leaned against the wall. "It's a dangerous world."

"Too right."

"And you are doing all you can to save it?"

"Someone's got to. I'm Doc Harley by the way."

"Hi, I'm Chrystal."

"Nice name, are you that breakable?"

"Don't know yet."

"Look, what you said, are you interested?"

"I guess I must be. Look this is really hard. I'm UHC."

"Then you have a problem."

"Look, I'll see them through the troubles they are in then can I contact you?"

"Catch me before you leave, I'll give you a contact number. Keep your head down tonight."

I felt so torn. No loyalty for most of my life then two in one evening. That sort of leaves you spinning. The world was closing in and getting very, very involved in my life.

The hours slipped by and it was still quiet. Jared had offered sleeping space at the bar. I decided to hang around. The cockroaches would have to live without me again. Bodies crawled off to bed one by one until I was left with Doc Harley, Lobo, one of the shapes that had come in with Doc. A dog man who didn't stop moaning and I think Lightning was there as well. We had the music system on real quiet and Doc was talking about some of the problems in the world.

I have no idea how history is going to record him, if it mentions him at all. Jared Matthews' favourite scapegoat but then I suppose by what I heard that night it was probably a vengeance thing. As Mr Matthews was so obsessed with the Sim-Stim queen and she sort of made off with Doc it is hardly surprising. Mr Matthews could rule the world but he can't have the one thing he truly wants. Live is like that. She was gone but her memory lingered. Not that there weren't rumours of Aztech CPO on the streets and enough bodysculpts to start their own nation. CPO, that was the night I first heard about that stuff as well. Take a brain, liquidize it and make it into a pill. Whoever takes the pill becomes the person whose brain was liquidized. Needs a pump to keep it flowing round the system though or something. Complicated and unpleasant, doesn't last either, then the old personality is so lost there is no way back. Some things are probably better not discovered but there you go.

We stopped about a mile back at a trading post. It used to be something called a motorway café. Then nobody really uses motorways now. There's better ways to travel if you really want to. Why risk getting shot up on the road when you can fly or communicate through conference TV or the net? Sort of put these places out of business after the family unit broke up and there was no need to visit relatives either. They have become small pockets of life in the wasteland, suppressant distribution centres and trading posts. They have their own laws and are usually almost tribal in their outlook with a patriarch or matriarch in complete control. Razor wire was their first defence, then as much security as they had managed to get hold of. Not that they don't welcome visitors, when they have been checked out and they know they can let the rare small bands of travellers into an outside compound. Well, then they are quite hospitable. I'd heard about these places. Then there was nowhere else as safe to stop so it was hardly surprising. Prices are high and they prefer to barter but they are generally fair by what I heard.

I woke your father, it's the last break we are going to get for a while. He looked better for sleeping but it can't take away what is in his eyes. He just held onto me like he was never going to let go. I could feel the tears welling up, I don't want to cry in front of him, it makes it all worse for him. When will this end? I suppose the worst part is knowing there is no way back whatever happens.

Once the side door opened the chilled air blew over the sleeping people, clearing out the stale air. In came the crisp post-dawn air that bits the throat but without the grime and dust I was so used to. Then came the chaos of movement and the flash of cigarette lighters. Tiny wisps of grey smoke in the morning air, little defiant messages that we are still alive, signals to the heavens or a cry for help.

Daniel now Ojabund without a City, a tall muscular example of breeding and tradition, stood by the doorway, cradling his sword. It was all he had left of what he had been building on Ho Street. His dark hair still immaculately swept back, strong features expressionless. Reliable, unbending, uncompromising. Even his suit had defied the situation and was immaculate in spite of the evening and the drive. Perhaps just by force of will.

Memories, images ingrained, a scrapbook of bits and pieces. Information is power. I'd watched the Yakuza move onto the Ho Street. Watched and waited. The street was always very cosmopolitan. Little pockets of different cultures, reflected in the buildings and the local trade. This group were different though. They sort of moved in all over, integrating and buying into the life. I don't know exactly where they came from. I mean which company, they came from Japan. The name on the street was Onosendai, something o do with decks or cyberware or something. They were criminal families. Yea right, and we weren't all criminals in the eyes of the PLEX?

People come, they go, it is if they stick around they make a difference. It looked like these guys had a future. Play ball with them and there was no hassle. It was easy to work for them. They mostly used their own people but when they asked you to do something you knew that at least you would get paid. They hung out in bars, upholding their honour and drinking their shots of Saki. I got hold of some for Jareds, available on a know and request basis. PLEX don't approve of free trade like we do.

I don't know if it was the crash of the NewYen that brought them to the street. They had an interest in Crisis that was certain. Then a lot of people had an interest in him. Crisis was playing it all pretty close at the time. Lightning was out on the street constantly trying to come up with something. As was I but it was like every path we took ended in a dead end. We had a name, roads were leading to Genoa Genetics. As I've said before, little things, we traced it through the T-Shirts. Pretty much every transaction that isn't street side goes through the net in some way or the other. Payments, orders, deliveries, it's all there if you have the patience and the know-how to look.

So Genoa wanted Crisis, the big question was why did a corporation as large as Genoa want a street fixer and DJ? I wasn't going to buy any ideas of him running their next office party. They wanted him bad enough to snatch his sister and she seemed to be expecting a ransom. Information was sketchy and I was pretty much working in the dark over this one. I'd taken to hanging around Jared's Bar when I wasn't working but since the blackout business had been dead so I spent more and more time there. The aftermath, finding out who had survived and who still had cash to do deals, that was the order of the day.

I got the general impression that this wasn't going to end with a trade so it was time to get out on the streets and get digging. I guess only now it makes sense. To start with it was a bit mercenary on my part. The UHC had a rep and a real hard hold on your hard cash. Doc and the BFA were a good crew to mix with. I don't really understand it. I know they touched a nerve, opened up something in me but most importantly it was that these guys really did give a shit.

It was just another rainy night, the oily shiny blackness that glimmers on everything, reflecting the neon signs. I lit up, pulled my collar around my neck and watched the bar. I could see people I knew through the bullet proof glass. The blue white glow, and I could almost hear the hum of conversation but there were just times you don't want anyone close time to think. The street wasn't the place to do it. Lights from a passing AV flashed in my face, blinding me. I heard a yell from my right and stepped back into a doorway of an abandoned shop. There's a lot of them, shops I mean, something to do with having nothing to sell.

Spirals, I recognized that yell. Images of the night before came flooding back. I moved as far back into the doorway as I could, put the cigarette out on the blackened glass and waited, listening. The sound of running metal shod boots and gunfire. Gunfire? Unfair, Zoners have clubs, they didn't use firearms. A line of automatic fire from an AV ran along the front of the shop, glass shards flying everywhere as I crouched in the rubbish and the windows around me exploded.

Pretty heavy weaponry to be using against gangers. The two gangers who fell outside my shelter were a pulp. Blood everywhere, bone and what was left of their thrown together clothing. Not Spirals though, these were Wombats, I could tell by their colours. The bolted on pieces of metal were no protection against that kind of firepower. I kept my head down.

About half an hour and a very painful stiff leg later I stumbled out of the doorway and thought about crossing the street.

The crowd in the bar was thinning out, groups wandering off to their part of the street. The bar made a lot of sense at that point so I pulled up what little protection I had against the rain, ran across the street, dodging traffic and slipped into the bar through the side door.

A few people clustered around a table looked dodgy, like more than normal, they were taking far too much interest, you know what I mean. Jared wasn't about so I slipped out the side door. Looking back I suppose it was him I had gone there to see. There was something in his look, his voice. Something I needed. His company. He always had time. Not that what was said was important but he had my attention and somehow I felt I had his. I'd half turned into an alley when I saw Diane, stalking down the street, head bowed. A very stupid way to be on that part of Ho Street. She just hadn't got the angle on peripheral vision. I was going to follow her into the bar but melted back into the alley. Crisis slipped silently down the street, standing in full view of the Bar. Just standing in the rain, staring at the window. Over his shoulder I could see Diane in the bar. Jared had turned up so I watched for a while and she looked really upset. I saw her sit, talk and shotgun five beers. Jared didn't look much happier. Private moments. Don't know why but I sort of felt like this wasn't a place for me. You know, like I shouldn't be there. They felt like family but all that emotional stuff, wasn't really my sort of thing. It's the sort of thing that gets you a bullet in your brain, not always by someone else.

I must have stood there for about an hour, the rain just running down my face, watching Crisis, watching Diane. Then she makes to leave. Crisis moved. I'd sort of drifted off into thoughts, trying to sort the whole mess out. So, Crisis slips behind a dumpster, about ten feet from where I Was. I saw his face as he turned, it didn't look like he'd slept for a month. Greying skin, greased up hair, he looked like he was seeing a ghost, a death mask with a twisted grin. Diane had stepped out of the bar by then and was walking back the way she had come. Crisis moved off behind her.

My thoughts were racing, trying to put it all together, why, where what? Why come to the bar individually? Why didn't Crisis go in? What had she been saying to Jared? I didn't know then and to be quite honest I never asked since.

I let them both get clear of the alley then slipped back into the bar. Jared looked up, he seemed pleased to see me, like he brightened up a bit. I was just glad for the shelter. Of, I as glad to see him too.

I hadn't felt tired until I sat down. I'd been running on adrenaline for the past day or so since we'd lost Blue. I just needed answers and they were slow in coming. Crisis was holed up with Diane, no chance to pick up even a lead, or direction, there by what I had just seen. Genoa were just too big to get more than the basics on them from my usual sources and to be quiet honest, I had hit a brick wall and needed time to think. Said it all when I sat down and Jared put a bottle in front of me. "You need it kid."

Too right I did. He served some Wombat Zoners who were hanging around the other end of the bar. None of the usual crowd were in so he came and sat with me.

"So Chrys, how's it going?" His voice was deep and steady.

"Had better ones." I had to be honest with him.

"You and me both kid." His voice sounded tired.

That was how the conversation started, the night drifted away, the bar emptied out until we were the last two there. Jared walked to the door and pulled the bolt across. "There's a place to crash out back. Give the streets a rest tonight." I can't say that I thought that he was up to something, that didn't cross my mind. This was Jared, he didn't do things like that.

We talked, and talked and we drank some more and we travelled further down that spiral until we hit rock bottom about dawn. That magical hour when the sun comes up, crawling its way over the rooftops, driving out the shadows, shrouded by heavy clouds, the sun making momentary guest appearances. It has a feeling about it, like something really creeps into your consciousness if you watch it. Jared saw it too I think. It is only at that lowest point that things like that really start to matter. Like the world is falling apart round your ears and you can stop a minute, just watch and listen. It keeps you sane.

A moment to treasure, a moment of peace after the constant stream of bars and faces where I had been trying to find out all I could on Genoa, the Urban Hunt Club, Crisis and the links between them. This was in the hope that what I found out might just tip the balance in our favour. Not that I expected any thanks. It was just something I had to do.

Well I'd got the handle on some of what was going on. I'd found out more about the UHC. I had to have been living under a stone for the past year to have missed it. The street was full of Raveheads desperate for a fix. The Club had been putting on Raves every month or so for a while, so they'd just got bigger and bigger. The sounds were on the street, pirated of course. I got that info from a slime ball DJ by the name of Trash. Then wipe out. The rumours were many and varied about what had happened after the Blackout. Those didn't really concern me. Facts, Crisis was off the street, the Raves were off the calendar and myths abounded.

Crisis, the name on the lips of the populous of SINlesstown. Word was he had had one and they were probably right. Still, at least his rep was clean. I couldn't find anyone who had been stiffed on a deal by him. It was not like the raves cost like the could either and the drugs he sold, really clean and only basic street legal recreational. The dude came over as a regular Prince Charming. He used to hang around with a girl called Blue, who said she was his sister. Rumour was that was doubtful, you know what I mean? Handy in the net, rarely seen without her deck. They all lived happily in a really cool apartment, way up on Ho Street, almost dome living. Real friendly like and then Crisis got himself a woman.

Diane, the word was that you could smell the corporate on that one. Nobody seemed to know where she came from. Then overnight she was with Crisis, joined at the hip. Depending on who you spoke to. A man with his rep, well the word was that he could have had anyone he wanted, why had he gone for a SINtart? Makes you laugh, what they were really saying, well the women anyway and possibly some of the men was why didn't he go for me? Written all over them. That's hormones for you, that and the money that turned up with her of course. I knew a guy who had a guy that kept an eye on PLEX Bounty Lists. A few weeks back he'd dropped me a print. "Wanted for Armed Robbery DOA" and it was her! Swear to gods, strange old world. There had been rumours about that but what the hell. We all have some sort of a past. Get a rep and you buy into the big wheel of intrigue.

The word on Lightning was that he was not as close as he had been with Crisis. Understandable considering we were chasing our tails to get some word. No point hanging out together. Word is he's hanging out with the psycho florist, goes by the name of Domino. Hadn't met him at that point, so couldn't fit a face with the rep.

Silicon Avatar, tall, blonde, thing and hyper was mentioned too. Three was a real headcase who had got that way by too much time in the net. Not dangerous but a chemical personality no doubt about it. Word is when contacted and questioned by anyone he would come up with some kind of Zen shit. Weird, he's gotta be hot to jack in when he's tripping by what I've heard.

There were just so many questions that need answers. This was personal. The finances were running down and the work just wasn't out there anymore. Speculation abounded and conspiracy theories seemed personal to every bar which was no real help.

No blinding revelations seemed to be coming my way so I had to resort to hard graft and asking the right people at the wrong time. I find that usually works, not that information is free, it costs, usually. One lead moves to the next and it always amazes me how something so completely minor turns out to be really important. It's the little things, the tiny bits of information that get slipped in. Just a word, a name, a place and you were on your way.

The big news on the street at the time was the Red Plague. There had been diseases that had spread before but this time this was something big. I don't remember when I saw my first plague victim. Once you've seen one you'll never want to see another. Anyway, I thought I had better try to get an angle on it. It had crawled into my life, word was everyone was carrying it and if it was there, hell I might as well know about it. There are several clinics working out of the back of bars and shops distributing stuff. Word was that they only gave supplies to those who came in actually showing the symptoms. Note I say give here. Seems that in a world where everything has a price, well, there were places giving the most valuable commodity away. So I sit down all cosy like with one of the guys down on the north side and he explains to me in straight talk where it is coming from. It is not that the vaccine is any sort of a cure, but it drastically increases the timescale of the disease. Take the vaccine and nobody dies but it has to be taken daily. That was Helix Luna. So they don't sell it and it only has a shelf life of a month. They don't hand it out to just anybody and were trying to stop people stockpiling it as that stopped others from getting it which was all pretty much fair enough. They were also scared that someone might be stupid enough to start treatments before they got the symptoms. He said that they weren't sure what it would do, but it was likely it would start the active phase of the disease.

This was north side and I'd had to move through the streets to get there. Weird thing was there were no BFA slogans. Somehow I got the general idea that this guy wasn't BFA either. Large biker type, long brown hair, greasy, black T-Shirt with the slogan "Be Fucking Angry" on it. Then there were a lot of gangs and groups on the streets then. Then there were a lot of gangs and groups on the streets then, he was probably one of the Stormtroopers I had heard about. I settled for getting hold of information, and an empty canister I found in the rubbish. After I pocketed it I moved back to the area around the bar to a side street where a girl I know had a place. Nice girl, bright, knows when to help and when to keep her mouth shut. I gave her the canister and she got real excited. I sat for nearly an hour watching her move carefully around the forest of glass tubing and rubber pipes that was her laboratory. Small and large bottles were grabbed and their contents poured, stirred and looked at. Electronic equipment, scanners and much muttering of "this is way above my head". So she came and sat down, bringing two cups of steaming coffee she had pulled out of the microwave. The information from the clinic checked out. From what she knew she could tell me that the vaccine had been developed by Johnny Helix, who used to be Tyrek's golden boy before he disappeared. Tyrek being the big Genetics Factory somewhere in the Dome. Word was that he had been headhunted, probably by Genoa. Bastards, they came up everywhere, like a fungus, or a virus. So it didn't look good, unlikely it could be altered to a symptomless version, something about antibiotics and drug resistant strains of bacteria. It was all way, way too technical for me.

Apparently back in the twentieth century the scientists at the time had discovered something that wiped out all bacteria, the Magic Bullet they called it. But, life adapts, and the bugs got smart. So they had to produce more vicious antibiotics, until the drugs they were prescribing were doing more damage than the illness. Suppressing the immune system. That's why immune deficiency diseases wiped so many people out. Their immune systems were already shot. Then came Ebola. Fucking animal research bastards. Well, I guess the monkeys had the last laugh there. Lot more space for them now. Some of the forests are even growing back, now there aren't any humans in Central Africa or the Philippines. They said it would burn out by 2100. There just wasn't anyone left alive there to see it.

I was still confused but I had a name and I wasn't going to let that go, so what about Genoa?

Genoa Genetics, for more acceptable offspring. They patented CPO, you know that?

Of course I did. I had the rumours but might as well get hold of info from a more reliable source.

How I put it before is how she put it.

I wouldn't work for them if they tortured my grandmother. Some of the stuff I've heard. There was this woman, used to go to a gym I went to, born on the street bur married a corp, security bod for Genoa, Jesus, some of the things Mel told me.

The afternoon drifted on and I got a name, an address and thank God the gym was on the streets, almost Domeside, but not quite. This was the best information I had had in a long time. The money was running really low and well it really hurt to spend it on clothes that I wouldn't think of me wearing. Almost dome type, so I tied my hair back with a cutie little bow, pulled on pretty pink trainers, yes you are reading this straight, pink, and a pretty pink track suit. Crisis, you owe me big time for this. Thank God nobody I know saw me. Dress up, put on a plastic mac and scamper through the rain to "The Wonder Gym". Yea right. Still it wouldn't hurt for me to work out a little either, its tough on the streets. So there I am pumping iron with the best of them, watching, listening and sweating for my art. Showers are good though, sheer bliss. White tiled cleanliness, chemical but the sensation of hot, clean water washing the soap off. The gunfire still echoes outside but just to be able to stand there, in the water jet and relax, priceless. Worth wearing that pink suit for, probably not, fair trade off though.

It took a month of questioning, getting to know people but finally I found out who Mel was. Pretty looking woman, small, blonde shoulder length hair. In every way she looked like a little doll. Immaculate hands, synthetic personality, cliché phrases, the perfect dome wife. It took a lot of control not to shake her. But not Dome, she lived on the periphery, not in the Dome, aspirational. The thought that someone could live on the streets and still be that dim. How had she survived? Still, I was grateful that she wasn't the brightest spark in the fire as after a month in hell I was able to get sat down with her over a cup of coffee within an hour. It was almost too easy. So I suddenly develop this husband who sounds pretty much like any of the others I had heard moaned about, armed with this I offer it like a token of peace and she takes my hand off. She just wants someone to listen to her high pitched excited explanation that she cannot take it anymore. All the hardships of being a corporate's wife, how he disappears for weeks on end, saying he's working. Of course I agreed with everything she said, sympathized mine was just as bad, except for the weeks away. I wouldn't tolerate that, not without knowing where he was. So she couldn't wait to tell me.

"It's dreadful. I don't know where he is for that time or who he's with. He comes home covered in all kinds of dirt."

I tried not to bite although the anticipation was killing me.

"…and you have to get the uniform spotless, or it's his job. PLEX property and all that."

I got real interested in laundry.

"Well, in the end, I just got so suspicious you know. I mean, it looks like mud. Now why's a security guard for a major corporation coming home like he's spent his day mudwrestling? I mean it is not like they have Corporation HQ in the wastelands of anything is it?"

Too right, this was good stuff.

"And I swear he smelt of perfume the other day. Oh God, it's another woman. I just know it."

Too right, but not in the way she thought. Result! So I rabbit on about this and that, like the bastards think we are really stupid and all that. She's really biting, swallowing it all, hook, line and sinker. Time to push it further so I get real helpful, real interested in the truth. Real interested in helping her, just to put her mind at rest. I'm suddenly the best pal she's ever had and she's loving it. I knew she was going for it, I just carried her along on a wave of her own suspicion and there I was, agreeing to get an old college buddy to have a look at the overalls. Its like I felt like I already had the results in my hand. At worst I'd possibly get the location of a secret Genoa installation banged to rights, pay dirt, literally, a little bit of info for Crisis and Doc and I could ditch the leotard before anyone I knew saw it.

She went for it. The silly bitch fell right into my hands, giving me the overall and off I went, into the sickly red sunset, clutching my prize, never to be seen again by her.

It was at least looking better, my funds were almost out so I used the last of them to get a corporate breakdown of Genoa and to take a cheap shot at them. I used one of my contacts and put the word on the streets that they were grabbing test subjects. Oh yes, and fed some fake reports to PLEX Media but I wasn't going to hold my breath over that one. They had a pretty bad rep on Ho Street, the rumours spread like a tenement fire. I laughed.

There I was with one set of well-worn bar clothes, a berretta, but no bullets and a burning need to find out what was going on with Crisis. Then I get a call, Monday 18th September 2058, ingrained on my memory. Its Crisis.

"Been incommunicado for purposes of security and cos we have had no leads and nothing to go on which has left me in the shit, you can appreciate. Make sure this is a secure line before I keep speaking."

Like I'd use anything that wasn't.

"Right, ain't got time for pleasantries, here's the info I've got.
One, Domino is missing, presumed dead or captured. Two, due to point one. Surveillance operation concerning Genoa has been a washout. We have no date from that avenue. Three, Netrun took place at 15.30 hours yesterday against Genoa Holdings' data fortress. Upshot is, three aint no way we get past their security and keep our frontal lobes. Wot we did pull down was a list of employees phone numbers and area codes and I'm going to go round and fuck them up. This is our best chance of retrieving data without doing a suicidal netrun. Four, the Yakusa are now involved in our problem. We tried to negotiate some assistance, they've agreed to lend unspecified help, the cost has been Lightning, sorry Chrystal aint got time to be sentimental. Five, we will be moving against Genoa carjack style tonight. If I don't get to you with information in the next five days I'll meet you at Jared's bar with anything

I've got, either that or there'll be an empty seat marked Crisis and the show's over. Have a better one, Crisis."

Click and the dull hum of the empty line. I stood there, frozen and I felt cold, very cold, and very, very angry. "The cost has been Lightning." Bastard. I screamed so loud no doubt the whole of the tenement heard it. I walked to the window and looked out over the expanse of decaying urban sprawl, black and grey, lights on in windows, different specks of colour from sign boards down below. The sky hung immobile, heavy and pendulous, bearing down on me as my mind screamed. I needed something, I wanted something to help, to take away the pain that I felt inside. Then I really realized it, I had begun to care and it hurt so very much. All I could see was Lightning's face with a backdrop of the thunderclouds. I could hear his voice but I couldn't, I could feel him there but he wasn't. It was like a huge fucking hole had opened up in my world. Let's face it, I loved him and I'd never had a chance to tell him. You've got to understand that was before I got together with your father. Crazed, I didn't know what to do next. I reached ragged curtains and shut out the world, sat on the moth-eaten sofa and tried to shut out the voices and screamed in my head. Why! Why did all this matter so very, very much.

Then I remembered, then I drank to forget but the memories were there, tearing at me. The reason why, why it was so important that I did something for a woman I had never met. Why the thought of her chained in the dark burnt on my mind. In one word, Jade.

It had been years ago, and miles away, down the other side of Ho Street. I'd been running some work for one of the nameless corporates down there, and doing good work too. Do I tell you this, hell its probably more information than anyone needs but if you are going to see the Ho in all its splendour then you have to face what people are really like. Also, we are the sum total of that which has happened. Some things are best forgotten but they just don't go away, they don't die.

When you are born on the streets it is a way of life, who you know and how well your face fits. It is easy to move about if you've always been there. It is like you are everywhere and nowhere. Good work if you can get it and I got it alright, in abundance. Then this "suit" comes to Jake's Rest, asking for me. I have words and turns out he is working the area, wants a local and has cash. Real hard currency you can hold and feel and a bit of security. I wasn't doing bad at the time but that bed-sit was really bad, like Prior Heights was bad but the other one, the walls moved I'm sure of it, crawled like living entities with the amount of mould growing there. You look at the Fixers, you know, the guys with the power and position and you get to thinking yea, why not, get a bit of that action and who knows. I threw my lot in with him and ran a few deals. Not much different to before. Then he comes to what he wants after building up to it after months. Some really serious stuff, like he's talking domes here. Cards, ID, the works, he said that I looked like the sort of girl they won't question, with the right ID and gear of course. So, I give it a go.

True to his word, the card and package arrives. I get tarted up and you know, there's no telling me from those Domer Girls. You know, did the nails, the works, put the hair up and dropped the street talk. All I had to do was catch a combat cab to one of the entrances, pay the driver off in NewYen, less traceable if things went tits up, and watch him go.

The wide expanse between the end of the zones and the dome, open concrete plaza proclaiming the rules of the PLEX and policed by well-armed and overfunded guards. My cab slipped to a halt in the bay marked out for cabs. A PLEXCop walked past, I took just a little bit longer handing over my card. I didn't speak to the driver, I didn't have to, just slip the card into the slot and punch in the number and the door unlocks.

You know the domes look so much larger close up, they sort of sweep away from you, away and up, like it touches the sky from where I was standing.

I swung the door open, stepped out onto heels that were far too thin and concrete that looked far too smooth, trying to keep an air of corporate disinterest. The cab sped away, not much call to take Domers into the streets, some must though, they keep turning up. A large armoured carrier trundled past me. An armoured impersonal slug.

My heels cracked ominously, it was as though I was the noisiest thing on the Plaza, I had to be drawing attention. A group of PAYCops were coming towards me. I held my breath, one of them looked me up and down. It felt like he was undressing me with his eyes. Instinct made me want to give him a kick her would remember. I breathed out, relaxed, smiled a cold and hopefully enigmatic smile and carried on walking. Talk about into the fire. I focused on the entrance, it was getting closer, all I had to do was keep my cool for a bit longer. Why look nervous, I had every reason to be there. Well Melissa Masterson did. I had a card, I had the suit and hopefully I had the attitude.

I swiped my card through the card reader, the red light flashed to green and the electric doors swished open. I was faced with a long blue carpeted corridor. The PLEX logo woven into it at regular intervals. Notices on the walls, proclaiming the rules of the Dome, had to be, I couldn't read them but by the pictures I could work out that much. There were so many, so what I had heard was true. Sneeze in the wrong place and you are history. The cyclops eyes of all the security cameras followed me along the corridor. At the end of the corridor there was a large white desk, with the PLEX logo emblazoned along it in red. Behind the desk a besuited, bespectacled official armed with two huge bodyguards, one on each side, with railguns. No way I was going to argue with those two. I just hoped my ID checked out. I could feel the softness under my shoes, making it more difficult to balance. I couldn't falter, looking nervous was alright. Domers always had an air of nervousness about them by what I've seen. Too nervous and he might ask questions. Then it occurred to me that I ha no idea what I was supposed to do next. I was going to have to wing it this time.

I was getting closer to the desk, fifteen feet, ten feet, I stopped. The man looked remotely interested, raising an eyebrow behind his bottle bottom thick glasses. No cyber replacements, had to be scanners, no way the corporate would have that much of an uncorrected defect. Now I was worried, fortunately I was unarmed, I'd thought to leave my little friend at home. I almost fumbled as I reached into my pocket to pull out the card again. Mentally cursing that I hadn't kept it in my hand. It cut into my finger a little as I pulled it out of my pocket. The corner was slightly chipped, something I'd carefully done earlier. I used a handkerchief which was also in my pocket and carefully wiped it . I was glad now I'd thought of bringing that. Leave no trace, that was important. I held the card between long fake fingernails and handed it to the official.

The official smiled. His voice was weak and creepy. "Careful darling, don't want you suing the PLEX for damages now do we." He seemed so ordinary, just Jack Nobody doing his nobody job. I relaxed a little, I had an angle on this now. You could see the little flashes of silver around the iris, cyberware, definitely not Chiba, that was quality stuff, this was better then streetwear but noticeable, PLEX issue. Just another way to get their employees for life, they end up owning most of their bodies by the time they have finished with the regulation enhancements.

He swiped the card through the card reader. "Well Miss Masterson, enjoy your break. May I recommend that you try Armoured Air Transport next time though. Crossing the zones can be dangerous." As if to reinforce what he said the doors opened behind me, a PAYcop staggered in, blood spattered, obviously bleeding from a wound in his shoulder. The desk jockey looked up casually. "Requesting medical assistance, port 457, PAYcop 2589 kindly step back outside, we don't want blood on the carpet now do we? Medical assistance will be with you shortly." Voice enhancement, the man didn't shout but his voice boomed down the corridor. The cop looked sheepish, stepping back and the door slid closed in front of him.

The official held my card out as I turned back to face him. I took it from him, his fingers brushing against my hand. I don't know how he did it but it was unpleasant. His skin was cold and the look on his face, that look was the same as the hopeless drunks that hung around the women on Ho Street. Kind of leery. A door opened to my right. Taking my bolt hole I turned to go, casting a quick eye over one of the bodyguards, a shiver ran down my spine, no reaction, no movement, either synthetic or conditioned. I passed through the open door as the official issued his off pat comment of

"Have a Nice Day." I felt like whispering "and PLEX loves you" but good sense and knowing that I was being monitored every step of the way curbed this desire to answer back.

I was trying to not look at any of the cameras as I stepped into the crowded area beyond. Standing booths were there to order whatever you wanted pretty much, a room, transport, a personal guide, all PLEX approved of course. One archway led to the Dome, a moving blue walkway, safe and secure "Suregrip" with the PLEX logo emblazoned on it. PLEX looks after its employees, yes, while they are useful.

How can I describe Domeside, a seething mass of people going somewhere. Suits everywhere. The walkway took me over a shopping mall area, in the distance the buildings rose up high into the dome roof. Tenements much like streetside but no windows. Solid concrete blocks. Airborne vehicles circling the building tops, hover vehicles disposed with any need for roads, more room for shops and walkways. Cleaner, definitely. Then this was the face of the PLEX, the Entry Zone as the signs so clearly announced. Smartly dressed PLEX Hostesses handing out guide chips to visitors, checking your SIN number and offering deals on transport, pushing the corporate image to visitors from other domes. Apparently I was visiting from the Manchester Dome.

Everything moved so fast, the walkway whisked me from the entrance to a lift, a glass encased bullet that flung me carefully down to the wide expanse of white marble consumer friendly shopping mall down below. Designed to be aesthetically pleasing. The central mall was the home to long tubs of huge plants. Genetically engineered to cope with he atmosphere no doubt, some were real, some not. I sat a while on one of the marble carved benches, little nymphs bolding briefcases in mock Greek design at its base. The music was beginning to annoy me as well. Classical but interspersed with promotions for PLEX goods and services. The leaf closest to me definitely wasn't real. The tiny PLEX logo imprinted on the stem was a give away.

The air was so clear it was choking. The scents had to be synthetic, there was a bit of a metallic twang to them. The tiny holes the aromas were coming out of were between the plants. There was no litter and nobody was hanging about so I decided I had better move on before I attracted unwanted attention.

I was still having trouble with the thin heels and the polished marble so I didn't have much chance to relax and take in what was around me for a while.

Shops, fountains of clear sparkling water, plants and crowds milling about carrying bags instead of guns. It was the casual way in which everyone walked around that I noticed first. They were more interested in showing themselves off and their latest fashions, they walked and chatted to each other, taking no notice of other people. Not hard to work out why they don't last long when they go on their little "holidays" to the Street.

I took a deep breath, clearing out the stale air of the street. I nearly choked but stopped myself. I was beginning to look like a tourist. Much as you could tell the Domer on the Ho the same had to be the other way around. I had to look up though, the buildings stretched to the sky, there was a sky up there. Blue with little fluffy clouds and the sun. Its golden glow synthetic but just to see what a clear sky might be like. The skies had a sickly red tinge these days, since Mexico. The deep radiant blue, the pure white, quite a contrast. I had to be cautious, I looked down, it didn't rain of course, wouldn't want to get any of the precious domers wet. It was all a sham. Up above the holographic image there had to be moisture evaporators and the cooling systems. We had enough of the greenhouse effect outside the domes, this was a greenhouse in a greenhouse if you want to look at it that way. Word was that some of the less well funded domes look nothing like this. Condensation clung to the smoke clogged apex of the dome, rain ran through the cracking panels of the dome. All a matter of funding of course.

A small child ran out of a shop. A woman was chasing her, she caught her by the arm and spun her round. The child looked up and whined. "Why can't I have it mother? I want it."

The woman glared, lifting her hand she slapped the child. Then she froze. A security guard came from nowhere, swept the child away from the mother as the woman cowered away from him. The guard's voice was monotone. "Public Order Offence, Section 229.7. Your identification?"

He held out a black metal plated gloved hand as the woman fumbled in her handbag. She was obviously terrified. "I, I was just.. I don't seem to be able to find…" It seemed as though her body just wouldn't do what she wanted it to and her bag fell from her hands and skated along the polished floor, her flowing it, almost crawling in her desperation. A small notebook tumbled out with the rest of her bits and pieces. At this she froze. The guard stood back, pulling the now screaming child behind him. "If you would pass that to me." He pulled out a large handgun from his leg holster, the red laser dot creeping up the woman's chest as she crouched looking up at him.

I saw her close her eyes and breath in, trying to calm down. She turned away from him, her fingers curling around the book, she stood up just as somewhere to my right someone shouted distracting the guard. The woman ran, the guard looked back, took aim and fired. The shot was silenced, just a dull whistle, a thud as the bullet hit the back of her head, then her face exploded in a fountain of blood and gore. Momentum kept her moving forwards as the shoppers screamed and got out of the way. The lifeless body fell onto its knees, then forwards onto the stark white blood splattered marble, a pool of dark red flowing over an ever increasing area.

The security guard looked down calmly. "Requesting clean up unit,

Sector 7". He tipped out the rest of the contents of her bag and picked up the elusive PLEX card, ran it through a reader on his sleeve and slipped it into a top pocket. He entered a few numbers onto the key pad and the green light turned red then flashed off. Then he took the notebook from the woman's hand and slipped it into a plastic zip lock packet, pocketing it as a small hovering wagon arrived. Two men in green overalls sprang from the doorless cabin onto the concourse, lifted the woman onto a stretcher and slid it into the back of the van. A chrome door closed. The guard handed over the small girl and she was lifted into another compartment in the back. Her screams silenced as the door slammed shut. They got back n the cabin, drover over the red mess so the cleaning equipment beneath the main body of the wagon could do its stuff ad the red mess that was once a woman's lifeblood was gone. It was as if nothing had happened.

    I walked to a nearby shop window. Staring past my reflection my eyes were drawn to the Chiban Cyberware, expensive decks and all manner of chips and wiring, all gleaming chrome, clean and state of the art. Nothing like the old and damaged equipment we got on the street, so far from it. Then our stuff had once started out this way. This was a world away but it fed our world with its cast offs.

    I wandered on, past the moving holograms of Aztech inviting you to bask in the sun with her in some SIM-Stim or the other. Shame about Mexico, still what does the PLEX need with the real thing when it can sell the image. It was worth a look. It didn't take long to find one of the many SIM-Stim vendors. I stepped inside, I had half an hour before I had to find the others. Might as well make the most of it.

    Thickly carpeted floor, blue carpet tiles. I was getting used to the PLEX Logo on everything now. The shop was bright, metallic smelling with a strong hint of lemon, neon and UV lights and VID-Screens showing what the SIM-Stims were playing. Kids hung around, ones out of each group lost in the headset, his mates watching on screen. Terminals on the back wall to place your order hung in immobile subservience. Just run your PLEX Card through the reader, punch in your number and enter the user friendly interactive program and order what you want. It's either delivered to your home or the metal doors slide open and there it is, your goods, in your PLEX carrier bag. Didn't take too long to work all that lot out. No need for anything as personal as a shopkeeper and no chance of theft either. Key in what you want, get it. Brain death, sorry, that's my personal opinion. I've heard the word on subliminal messages. If they think I'm going to plug my brain straight into some PLEX-Created software, get a life! Not that you can trust everything you hear of course and I have to admit watching those screens, the images to clear, to be there, to be part of it, but on reflection, no thanks.

    Availability, that was what really struck me. Everything was on sale openly. So many shops selling so many things, just swipe your SIN Card and your PLEX Card and it was yours. No long search, no complicated deals, no human contact.

The exception had to be the clothes shops. It must have been a pretty up market area, the prices were phenomenally high, even by what I had heard. The people were different as well from those where I'd come in. They dressed in an even more conventional way and didn't have that casual air about them I'd seen down the other mall. It was as if they looked down on everyone, and each other. Their conversation, yes I was listening, was different as well. It centred on what was new and what they were going to buy or have next. Have, have, have, buy, buy, buy. I'd had enough, I walked into a dress shop. The androids walking about in the clothes, explaining in monotone voices whose label it was and from which collection it came from if you stood too close for too long. An assistant gracefully glided across the shop floor. Bet she was synthetic. She began to tell me which colours were "in" and which would suit my skin colour and body shape. She explained at the end of her little speech that the product she was running was the most up to date PLEX Sponsored research into the social acceptability and aesthetic something or other. I'd lost interest. I snapped back into concentration when she began along the lines of everything being coordinated to my own personal specifications so that my look would not be spoilt by any personal misjudgements. Yes, no doubt, simple mishaps like personal choice.

I thanked her and left, fast, to her singsong perfect PLEX generated accent telling me to "Have A Nice Day."

I had to get to an apartment in one of those impersonal blocks. I was moving in a dream as I keyed in the location on a synthmap I'd purchased. I don't remember how I got there and to be quite honest the faces of the team that would be going in with me are a bit of a blur. I remember that there were five of them and they were hardly more than children. I should have seen there was a problem, I didn't. I take the blame for that one entirely. I just thought it was the employer cutting corners on a simple job. You live and learn.

It is like the darkness closed in. You can always make sense of something when you look back on it. Then, I was just working my way towards something and I'm not even sure I knew what that something was. Just business I suppose. Well the temptations are always there and it is always easier to earn a fast buck if you don't think too much about what you are doing. I can still see their faces if I think hard enough. They were so young and I had to take them into offices out of hours. I sat with them for at least three hours, just watching them, trying to get some idea why these corporate children had been employed. The answer seemed simple when I'd listened to them enough. They were typical bored rebellious teenagers looking for kicks. I wasn't sure but it was quite possible they were even paying for the experience, they didn't seem short of money. That worried me more than anything else. Not the situation to be asking questions and I knew it was something pretty dodgy. Most of the jobs I had been doing were but with the amount of corporate takeovers that were going on. Don't ask me, I only worked there. Me and hundreds like me at the time when it didn't add up, before we realized just how big some of these Corporations were getting. I can put my hands up to that one. I helped, albeit unknowingly perhaps but if all of us hadn't done that little thing that we did to help them. Well it all could have been simpler. Still there is nothing I can do about it now.

They were hardly more than children as I've already written and terrified. Just doing it for kicks? Well I don't think they thought it was so funny then. Strange really that none of them would admit it. The whole crazy situation. We on the Ho spent our lives trying to keep out of trouble and there they were doing it for fun. I overheard one conversation and it sort of made sense. I don't know how "the boss" had managed it but somehow he had managed to get hold of the kids of some major corporation owners. He was actually getting them to do his dirty work for him. Rebellious youth, playing right into the hands of the corporation while trying to rebel against their parents.

We left the tenement and they followed me, like really close. I got past the security and into the offices. Well the shit really hit the fan and so did they. Sushi, the lot of them, sprayed over the walls of some oriental headquarters. I couldn't get one of them out, not one, the deal had gone sour. All we had to do was take the hard drive out of one of the computers. The disc we wanted would be in it so it wouldn't be obvious what was being stolen. We had to make a bit of a mess, make it look like a burglary and get out. Then the PLEX turned up. I know we hadn't tripped anything, clear as glass it was a set up. I knew the call, I'd seen the MO before, well heard about it in stories. So the box goes in the air conditioning while my little street babes take on the wrath of the PLEX. Then boom, the box blows sky high, takes out the team and blows the side off of the building. So there I am learning to skydive without a parachute, into a large pond, cardiac arrest for several very large and very expensive carp before I disappear into a side street and off into the night. Except this isn't the street and the evening is just dusk. It did involve knocking out some poor sweet girl just out for the evening. She gets soaking wet clothes, I get her dry ones and I get out of an exit on the south side of the dome.

Standard procedure, I go to ground, the streets are empty of one Chrystal for weeks. Then I try to call. Disconnected line, I'm not surprised. So, I cut my losses and go back to working the streets, just small stuff, the odd package here, the odd escorting job there, showing people around , nothing too noticeable. Just long enough for me to think its all blown over and then some wise guy kicks in my door and tries to deliver a lead calling card. I'd not been back long so I was still awake. He hit the bed first in a blaze of muzzle flash. I was already standing by the time he sprayed my blood around the walls. I found the window, couldn't think of anything else and well it seemed to be getting to be a habit. I caught more lead as I rolled out into the canal. I lived on the south end then, where the water ducts throw out their black oily water that washes off the streets. I could takes blood and I knew I was losing consciousness so I just swam for it. I was fairly sure that whoever was in my room wouldn't be following me. I went under water, it was the most frightening experience I think I have had to date. It is pitch black there and the water is "sticky" and holds onto you. It clings to your clothes and drags you down. As I kicked my way along I could feel my feet touching things, some solid, some unnervingly soft. I just didn't want to think about it. Somehow I found my way into a drain and came up into a warehouse and passed out.

    I woke up to darkness, cold chilled darkness, well I think I was awake. I was laying on the floor, the floor was uneven, cold, damp, I could hear water dripping and someone breathing. Heavy guttural breathing. I tensed up, feeling the cold stone under my back. I moved my right arm and felt something on my wrist, heard the metal sound that chilled my soul, chains. I sat up and tried to stand but the chains on my wrists pulled me back down onto the stone floor. Then I realized how much I hurt, all over. I could feel the dampness where I had been bleeding. The wounds had been bound but I'd bled through the bindings so the job obviously hadn't been done very well. A white flash cut across my eyes as my head hit the wall I didn't know was behind me and something heavy landed on top of me. Something large, hairy and warm. I could feel its hands pulling at my clothing and it was too late when I realized what was happening. I was too weak to fight him off, too frightened to call out. All I could do was struggle against what was an impossible strength with all the strength I had left. To fight what was inevitable, I could feel it happening but there was just nothing I could do about it. His hands pawed me, I felt his teeth on my face, his tongue and I bit him just as everything faded to chilled nothingness.

    In the darkness I could hear water dripping from the walls. Somewhere behind the wall I leant up against I could hear water gushing, perhaps pipes behind the wall, I had no way of knowing. It was black, not just dark, no light at all. Then I remembered, then it all came back, the pain, the fear and I screamed but no sound came out of my mouth, it was the silent scream as I shook uncontrollably. I was too afraid to move, too weak to fight and too confused to make sense of it all. I could hear him breathing somewhere out there in the darkness. Day after day, in the darkness, once a day food was put in my hands. I couldn't see who did it, I could smell something different, soap, washing powder, aftershave, then the dank dampness overpowered the new scent. I could smell him as well, a sickly sweet clinging odour which hung around after he had gone. I could hear him grunting and cracking bones as he fed, I didn't want to think what manner of man he was.

I don't know how much later it was when I was dragged in the dark. I felt stone under my feet as I stumbled for a foothold. Then I was dragged into a lit room which really hurt my eyes and was thrown on the floor. The room was red, the walls were hung with red velvet curtains and red lacy nets hung at intervals, draped around Greek style statues of nude women. The lights were so bright, blurring my vision. Was I dreaming of hell? The flames burnt so brightly, no not flames, red neon floor lights, glowing holograms of fires around the edges of the curtains. I lay at the bottom of some steps which were richly carpeted and you've guessed it, blood red. At the top of the stairs there was a couch and laying on the couch was a man. The light was too bright behind him, it formed a red glowing halo around his head but I recognized the voice and I knew I was really in trouble.

Jade, the dealer who pushed all the cheap rubbish onto the streets. Shady deals, badly cut drugs, all manner of really lethal stuff, real poison. He sold cheap to those who would never know because when their brains died they didn't care, then the price went up when the addiction had taken hold. He didn't have to say anything, it all became clear in a flash.

A year ago, a man in a bar. A big "suit" with contacts. He was new to the area but word had got round that he was poison. He offered work, I turned it down, I don't run poison. I didn't then and I don't now. Especially for scum like him. He took it personal like, like up close and personal. The pleasantries then became heavier. I don't know what he was on a the time but he was high and looking for some action. Simple rule with me, I run stuff on the streets but I don't turn tricks, plain truth. He got his action alright, a boot right where it hurt, a fist to the jaw and kicked back onto a table in a bar where he had walked in to set up his turf. Kicked over by a well-known local. If he hadn't been a cold calculating bastard up for every cheap trick in the book he would have been finished on the Ho.

So now he had me. I took a deep breath, expecting the flash of a gun and the sharp pain in my head I had expected on so many other occasions. Anticipation, I could feel my arms shaking as I tried to stand. If he was going to blow me away then I was at least going to face it standing up. What was left of my clothing hung torn on my shoulders as I stood to face him, my sight clearing as I got used to the light. Then I saw the image projected on the wall behind his head, images of what had happened in the basement room. All the time he had been using infrared, computer filtered imaging. There had been some light in the room, I could see that now, he' been putting sight suppressant in my food. He turned to me and laughed. "I knew you would be of use to me one day." His voice was deep, slow and calculated.

He held up his hand and two men stepped from somewhere behind me, dragged me back downstairs and threw me back into the dark with the man-thing but for some reason they didn't chain me up.

I could see now but that really didn't help. I did throw something at the camera and broke the lens, just as the hairy ape like man thing leapt at me. I don't know how I did it but I dodged and he hit the wall. I don't remember much other than hearing a sickening snap and thud as he hit the floor screaming. His neck was broken but he wasn't dead.

I collapsed beside him, I remember two men coming in, they were stunned by what they saw and somehow I managed to grab the Colt out of the nearest one's hand. I shot them both, it was close range, I couldn't miss, then I turned and emptied the rest of the bullets into the man thing until It stopped moving. Then silence, I was shaking and I felt myself sliding down the wall. It took all my strength and I still have no idea how I got out of heat hellhole.

That is why it all made sense, that is why I had to help. I hadn't met Blue but if she was. Well it didn't bare thinking about, I still can't think about it without shaking. This is the really real world, no picture books, no pretty stories, this is the sort of inhumanity that lives on the streets. I had never met Blue and to be quite honest I didn't really care who she was. I was really beginning to hate Crisis. Somehow he got people to do what he wanted, lat it on the line for him and then wham, a quick call. I guess I hadn't realized how much Lightning meant either. So was Crisis the devil incarnate or misunderstood man? In my eyes at that point there was no doubt.

"Daniel. I sort of knew but never."

Daniel thought for a moment. "Jared knew, he tried to find Jade but it's a good job he didn't. Cut it out of your mind. It's her pain. Something she had to relate. If you come across him in the future its your call what you do."

Lightning read on.

I met Bill down at the bar. He was sitting at a table on his own, bowed over his pint. He looked up and beckoned me over. I joined him. It was flaming, I wanted Crisis' head on a plate for this. Bill was sympathetic, everyone was. One word was running through my mind, betrayal. I had the answers, somehow I felt that there was something in what I knew but he had no right to do what he had done. I hope he can find some peace of mind over this. The bar echoed with it but where was Crisis, where was the big man, holed up with Diane no doubt. The fire burned though, the fire burnt out and I gathered the anger and pain. Jared was being really great at that point, he started putting beers on the slate. Muttering something about the Yakuza owning the bar now anyway. He was a man so weighted down by trouble, he didn't even chat with the clientele anymore. He just wandered around giving them what they wanted and taking the money. Him and many others, the faceless and the known.

Bill had been doing some research, he came up with Genoa as well and the word was that they were big. Everyone seemed to be coming up with the same stuff. Still, the next day would bear it out. I hung around the bar until closing then dragged myself home. I couldn't face staying over at the bar that night. I only had one set of clothes left. I had to get myself together for the next day. Not that I had anything left. I wasn't going to sell the jacket, even if I didn't eat, food now I vaguely remembered what a good meal was like.

It was a long and lonely night. Lightning cut into my broken dreams, waking me to stare into the darkness. It was like a madness had taken over my world. This sort of thing wouldn't have touched me before, now well that was a whole different story.

The morning came so very slowly, I dressed and got off down to the bar. I hung about outside, trying to get myself together enough to decide what to do when I met Crisis. Just let him ignore me. I went in through the front door and he saw me. He and Diane crossed the bar. Everyone was watching, waiting. I looked at Crisis then I looked at Diane. Something inside me flipped a double somersault. He might be the devil incarnate but a that point it was so blindingly obvious. That was what real friendship is, you might hate them for what they have done but somehow you will let it go. I just said something to him like "we have a job to do." It was the hardest sentence I have ever spoken but the deepest meant. I don't think anyone could understand. It was one of those emotional mountains that the romantic fools speak about I suppose. He was arrogant and an asshole but he was still him.

I took a seat at a table on my own and Crisis began a long spiel telling what we were there for but it was all going over my head. All I could think about was the past. The words missed me. It wasn't until Diane sat beside me, I felt her there and realized she was talking to me. She gave me a letter, a letter from Lightning explaining that it had been his choice to join the Yakuza. I hugged Diane, I was just so glad in a way. I wanted Lightning there so badly but at least he would be safe, they would teach him so much and well, this was something we just had to do. It was really strange, you don't realise what it is like to be hugged when you aren't used to it. It's sort of warm and reassuring. Diane couldn't have known how non-contact I was. Something had changed though, something was gone forever but something else had taken its place. That new something was going to hurt and cause trouble. Its called giving a shit.

A long and twisted journey, we shared what we had. I tried to give Crisis the information I'd found but he was being arrogant so I thought stuff him, see if they can cope up with something. Then Diane came over to see why I was being quiet. Lovely Diane, she really did care about people. I was just sulking but I told her about the soil sample and the analysis I had got off of the chemist. She took it and shoved it in Crisis' face pretty much. So that was the way to deal with him. Anyway, it all hit the fan, net runners leapt into the net lists compared with addresses and we had a location. Impressed me, but then they usually did.

Then this SINBitch walks into the bar. Good looking woman, long brown hair, immaculate and with a mission. Well you don't know things about people until something happens. She headed straight for our friendly neighbourhood barman and gave him real hell about her alimony payments. So Jared had once been a henpecked husband, no surprise now that he had taken on the bar on Ho Street. After that little tirade the gunfire was probably easier to deal with. Then the whisper goes round that she works for Maas Biotech. Problem. Considering who was in the bar and she saw everyone. I wasn't quite sure of the connection but by the way everyone was in a panic this was probably not good. Apparently she couldn't be removed because of her link to Jared. I didn't feel anything about it, I just felt sorry for him. If that was what marriage meant then I think I'd stick to the single life. Go where I wanted when I wanted and leave all that grief to others. Marriage was pretty rare anyway. She stormed in, erupted and stormed out, leaving Jared looking battered.

So what was this help that the Yakuza offered. He turned up, the Ojabund's son. Tall, dark and oriental, more stocky than Lightning but wiry all the same. Not the same style and definitely no replacement. Still it was something I suppose and he would have skills we may not have. Then again I took it sort of personal so I didn't have much to do with him. They had given us the software to do VR simulated runs on the Genoa Site as well. Not that I was going to have anything to do with that either. For one thing somebody had to keep an eye on the "bodies" while they went off on their little joyride. For another, I hate technology.

So we had the layout and everyone jacked in, even the non-netrunners. We had a plan, it involved Bill and his rocket launcher. After the VR main house exploded in shards of wood and metal we decided that we would have to be a lot more careful if we actually wanted Blue alive. Most of the afternoon was taken up by more complicated and different ways of getting through their defences. None of which seemed to be working very well. Then again what did they expect.

Crisis jacked out. He sat there just looking at the wall. I walked over but didn't say anything. He just looked at me. "Chrys, I'm a DJ, none of us are cut out for all this." He shook his head and jacked back in.

Again and again until it got dark and we knew we had to make our run or we weren't going to get in at all. So we tried something completely different.

We had a van, provided by the Yak, and we bundled into the back of it and drove out to the map location we had. It was only just off the Ho so we didn't have to infringe any seriously dangerous areas to get there. We travelled in silence, checking and rechecking our equipment before scrambling out into the night and the sickly woodland. Well it had once been woodland, now it was a mass of broken and blackened trees, rubbish, pieces of metal and abandoned cars. It was off my turf and I was out of my depth with the undergrowth. No light, pieces of wire and other stringy objects winding around my boots, I was not happy. My clothing squeaked in the silence of the "country". I had got too used to the constant hum of the street, traffic, conversation, gunfire, I wasn't used to the silence, it was unnerving. I wondered if there were birds in the day but then with the atmosphere the way it was, probably not.

This was not the sort of forest that you dream about. It was twisted, the wood was charred, blackened and covered with a sticky residue, lifeless. Even the grass as we crawled away from the treeline was sticky, oily and ragged. The residue clung to clothing and it smelt really strange, as did the sticky orange soil. Distinctive soil though and weren't we grateful for that. Nearing the rise we found a dip and a report came in from Bill who had taken up a vantage point with a long distance sniper rifle. It was quiet and there were patrols. It all got very chaotic at that point, we all crawled into a huge crater and dug in there. Jared, Asrael, a "fixer" who hung around the bar too and myself made a break for the main building under covering fire, others were meant to follow.

It was like it all happened in slow motion. Jared took a round and went down as we kept running. Asrael and myself made it to a small outbuilding. Slater, a medic was not far behind us so I stepped round the corner. I had seen gun flashes and a body had gone down but it was like I was in a world of my own as I walked around the balcony around the main building to the front door. It was running through my head, why don't I just knock on the front door. Then it all made sense. Crisis was nowhere to be seen, nobody was, I was on my own and I had a really bad feeling that I had been left out in the cold. I turned to go back, even if I had knocked on the door, what would have happened other than they would have got themselves another hostage. To go in the building a that point I needed backup, there was none.

I walked back around the balcony and found Asrael still behind the outbuilding. Jared was still on the floor. Where the hell was Slater? I turned and at that point I remember bright flashes and pain in my chest. One word flashed through my mind and the word running through my head was "Betrayal", as I hit the concrete.

Grey dust, charred black landscape, red rain fell, endless red rain. It glimmered with a light of its own, exploding in starlight as it hit the tired red earth. Buildings around me were burnt out shells, wood skeletons craving sanctuary from the angry sky. Children were crisped to paper images, crumbling in the wind but untouched by the rain. A rippling blue wall of smoke tumbled down the street, blasting the grey shadows to a cloud of dust. Then bright white light, blinding, drowning everything as I ran, through the light, through the white dust storm, burning particles of dust fell on my hands, my face, burning through the skin, to the bone. I looked down, the skin had all but burnt away, blood poured from open vessels, the flesh burnt away, I saw bone turned from white to black to dust. Then there was nothing, no rain, no buildings, no life, just emptiness.

A dragon raised its head out of the ashes, sinuous it climbed into the dead sky, its wings flapping silently, breathing across the whole land, a gout of cleansing fire, her tears falling as rain, pure clear water that ran in gullies, formed rivers of pure crystal water which ran to the ocean. The ocean was clean and blue. Where she landed grass sprang up around her, where she walked acres of grass spread like spilt liquid. The land was carpeted with flowers and trees sprang up, from shoots to saplings to thousands of years of growth in a moment.

A dark shadow fell over the land, its chill curling the grass, snapping off trees. A face in the darkness, silhouetted by black thunder clouds. Lightning, where was Lightning? I had to get to him but something held me back. White light, pain, I called but strange voices answered, dragons wee all around me, black scaly images. Then a dragon that sounded like Lightning, it smelt like Lightning, it was as if I felt his hand on my cheek, on my arm. I wanted to call out but I could not. The drums pounding in my ears, the rhythm of life, growing and growing, then red, everything was red, then nothing.

Floating in a sea of white water, silver streaks of fish that bit, I could see them biting but I felt no pain. It was dark, I could smell antiseptic as I struggled to keep a hold on consciousness and not to slip back into the dreams. Bright white light, everything was white, a woman in white, black hair tied back, oriental eyes. I tried to call to her, a needle in my arm then it went dark again. Pain in my neck, a burning.

Lightning looked up. "I was there. I remember when they told me, took me to her. She was with the Yakuza and they'd patched her up, really well. I can see where the dragons came from. They all had dragon tattoos on their necks. I didn't want to wake her, she was well sedated."

Nothing made sense anymore, nothing was real. Walls moved and shifted, white plain walls, no cracks, no mold, no dirt. They shifted and moved. I stood in a sea of white, no buildings for miles. I looked down, the floor was liquid, I looked up and the sky was pure white. I began to walk but I got nowhere, I tried to shout but I made no sound.

A shout, the room was real, it shifted a little but at least it was recognizable as a room. Pristinely white, clinically scrubbed, a hospital, it had to be. Not a street clinic though, this room dripped of credits. Chaos outside. I sat up and everything really started shifting around. I was wearing paper, it was smooth and clean. The door was only ten feet away. I had to get out. I swung my legs down to the floor, cold tiles on bare feet, legs that didn't hold me. I had to grab hold of the trolley to stop myself falling. They could be my only chance to escape. Never to be chained, ever. I could see there were restraints on the trolley. Nothing made much sense other than I had to get as much distance between me and that trolley.

Staggering I launched myself across the room, ripping the drip out of my arm, sending the blood bag skidding across the polished floor, leaving a trail of red until it hit the wall with a dull wet noise. Its contents pooled out onto the white floor. I didn't care as I'd made it to the door. I clung to the chrome handle and hung onto it as my legs gave out. I threw myself against the wall to steady myself. I felt pain as bone and skin collided with the solid stone but I didn't care. Using the wall as a lever I pulled at the door. It couldn't have been heavy but It might as well have been. I had no strength to pull it open. I took a deep breath and put everything I had into getting it to move just a crack. I felt something pull in my chest, like something cold sliding across it and I saw the red staining coming through the paper. I jammed my foot into the gap. I was beginning to breathe faster and faster, the walls were closing in, I had to get out. I felt the shooting pain from my foot as the wood door trapped it against the door jam but I didn't care. I pushed toes, ankle and then leg through the gap, sliding myself through. I left a streak of red blood on the white wood as I levered myself into the opening and launched myself across the corridor to the handrail opposite.

The black and white tiles swirled in a moving pattern of their own. There were red blood handprints on the walls and voices, someone somewhere was shouting. Clinging to the rail I began to slide down the wall. Turning I dragged myself up by the rail. It was then that I saw a trolley, not ten feet away, I saw a woman on the trolley, I saw Diane. I know it was Diane, her beautiful long hair matted with blood, her face pale, her eyes closed. I focused on her face as everything started to go a bit blurry. I tried to pull myself upright. Then I saw the blood, the chest cavity pulled back and pinned with vicious metal pins, pink froth, nothing but a mass of pink froth and no internal organs. What had they done to her?

I couldn't make sense of it all as I slid down the wall. A sound behind me, a woman, oriental, smart. I slid onto the cold floor as I heard her say. "Pity, and he thought she was going to live."

My world went dark as I thought. "Why didn't they give her suppressant?"

That was too close, a rumble and the van tilted about 40 degrees, must have been a mortar. Shook us up and now everyone's awake. Time to pass around the PLEXMax.

It's still dark in here though it must be well past mid-morning.

It feels like its slow going out there. Most of the road is a lunar landscape of craters and cracks and by the way the van is weaving we're having to pick our way carefully. There was a minefield about a mile back. That set us back about an hour but that is something you can't rush. Well not rush and live and as we're not doing too badly for time we can afford to be a bit careful. We decided to go across country, hitting a small "B" road to the north and then cutting back to the main highway. The old 1984 map we have is of no use at all. Most of the minor roads have been barricaded by local farmers. Apparently it has been like that for years. When the soil wouldn't support crops because of the pollution and PLEXGlobal put so many embargoes on British produce, well the farmers were left with no choice really. They just dug in for the duration and lived on what they could produce. They barricaded their land and stuck it out. Some say they've gone mad out here in what is known as the Wasteland. I don't doubt it by the state of the road and the amount of ammunition they are wasting on us. Still, it's their home and they are going to defend it. For the past hour we've been hearing the tiny ping, ping of bullets rattling against the armour plating letting us know that they want us to move on. At least the rain seems to have stopped for a bit.

So, we carry on, on and on. We always carry on, what else can we do? This is probably as bad as it has ever got I suppose. There has never been no way back before.

Life after the Yakuza Hospital as that was where I was became different. I didn't get away that day, they sedated me and it was a while later that I was finally strong enough to leave. I didn't talk to any of them in that time. I got talked at a lot. They made it very clear that I owed them but they were fair about it. So that was when I ended up with a tattoo as well, part of the payment. I'd seen Diane dead and when they left me on the street I just sort of wandered for a while. It wasn't that I didn't want to go home, it was that I needed a break and to get my head straight about a lot of things. Crisis and the UHC for one thing, Diane, the BFA, it had all been a bit too much, a bit too quickly and it was all tumbling together. I had another problem as well. Can't say I've exactly been a pacifist, who on the streets can be but I've never been violent. Since the hospital well that all changed. I got such dark moods. I was walking the streets and I'd see something and a real rage would come over me. So I just walked in the rain for hours, taking on anyone who challenged me until I realized I was really, really hungry.

I saw a light over a doorway, and a sign. It said everyone welcome. Well I was nobody but I thought I'd give it a try. I was about as low as I could get. I walked in, soaking wet in totally unsuitable black shiny pvc bar clothes. The bullet holes were patched with some sort of tape. I just walked in.

The hallway was clean. There was a notice board with pieces of paper pinned on to it and a hatchway. An elderly woman pulled back the hatch, she had kind eyes. She said her name was Sally and that I looked like I needed a bed for the night. Old, that woman was nearly forty if a day. She slid the bolt on the door and let me in. She had a well-built "practicality" about her. She came to my side of the wall through a side door and put an arm around me and I let her lead me inside. I hadn't realized before but tears were running down my face. She took me down a long corridor and pushed open a door to a small room. Action after action but the actions were not mine. I was walking in a dream and at that point she could have been anyone but to me she was the Archangel Gabriel! The room was just a bed and a box but it shut out the street. It took away the pain, just for a little while. A towel was folded up on the end of the bed, she picked it up and led me down the corridor to a green door. "Get yourself in there and have a good shower. Get that rain off of you. I'll get you some dry clothes."

Half an hour later I sat on the bed in the small room in warm practical clothes and Sally sat beside me, holding my hand. There is something so calming about that. Her hands were rough, work worn, her nails bitten down so far they looked painful but the peace I got from just that little bit of human contact. That contact I so badly needed. I hadn't spoken for about ten minutes when she looked me in the face and stroked a stray piece of wet hair behind my ear with the rest. "You've had a rough night haven't you sweetheart? Don't worry, no questions asked here. Can I have a name or shell we give you a name? It makes no odds to us here."

I looked at her, she was so genuine, so real. Who says angels are supposed to be beautiful? There was such a practical warm beauty in that face and I don't mean looks. I choked back the tears. "Chrystal."

"Yes and you're as breakable as glass aren't you? Don't worry, you are safe here. Three good meals a day and all we ask is that you help out a bit around the place. You're so thin, wouldn't hurt to get a little meat on those bones. You've missed dinner but I'll bring you something. What shall I do with your clothes, there're not really…"

"Not suitable anywhere…" I managed a smile.

"That's better. Look, I'm not prying but you don't seem like that sort of a girl. How about I find you some more comfortable bits and pieces. Is there anyone we should call?"

Images flashed through my mind. Crisis, no; Lightning, no; Jared, I thought about it but no, nobody to call. "No, I mean yes, I mean thanks for the clothes but no, there's nobody to call."

"Poor mite." She hugged me. I wasn't so sure about all this hugging but I was in no mood to fight it. I needed someone to be there. "If there is anything you want to talk about."

I looked at her.

"Better you rest. I'll be back in a while."

She was true to her word. She came back with a bowl of steaming stew. Real chunks of something that looked vaguely like meat. She left me with my meal saying she would collect the empty bowl in the morning.

There was a single light bulb, no shade, no window. I looked in the small mirror on the wall and I saw my dragon tattoo for the first time. It nestled under my jaw line and curled off down my neck. I was alone, I took off the baggy jumper to take a look at the damage. The dragon curled down my neck onto my collar bone. Three distinct bullet marks mostly healed up were all that was left of my visit to the Genoa installation. I guess I'd managed to shower without looking down. Not vanity, I'd been caught in the crossfire before but nothing had left a scar like that. No more low necks for me, not that that sort of thing was practical on Ho Street anyway if you didn't want to be mistaken for a hooker. I sat on the bed and cried for a while. A luxury not often allowed. I didn't even know why. It was like the universe was so very big and I didn't belong anywhere in it anymore. I had flown too high with Crisis and Lightning. I was a street kid after all and expendable. I'd always been so used to being alone. It becomes a part of your make up and you don't allow for anyone to be there so when they are its good, when they are not well you just get on with your life. Then something happens and you get used to people being around you. When they go away, well it really leaves a gaping hole. What the morning would bring I don't know. I would probably walk off into the morning smog and send them a donation sometime. For now I climbed into the clean sheets and drifted off into broken dreams of dragon tattoos and the faces of those I had known.

The morning did come. I woke up a bit disorientated, then remembered where I was, climbed into my clothes and stepped out into the corridor. A girl, about twelve, pushed past me. She spun round. "Hey, you're Chrystal." I didn't really want to be recognized but it was sort of like finding a friendly face. She was very keen to show me around, explaining that she had been at the Kitchen for about two months. I got to meet quite a few of the Kitchenfolk that day. Silkin the lovable rogue, even the street couldn't wipe the smile off of his face. If I hadn't been feeling so dark I would have really enjoyed his company. He was always laughing, always ready with a tale of an anecdote and they were always funny. Then there was old Batch, he was always full of a good tale, mostly tall ones but he meant well. Elsa, not I really got to like her. I spent quite a lot of time helping her around. She had been a netrunner up until the Brownout. She was very quiet, totally blind now but you could see how good looking she had been before she had had half her face ripped off. It was healing slowly but the maze of cuts and stitches were going to leave horrendous scars.

I hung around the kitchen. Sally seemed to have plenty of time to teach, even though she was always busy. How she managed it I will never know. I'll never forget the first batch of soup I made. I don't know how I got talked into it either. Then again, neither did anyone else but I got better. It was Kirch I really got to now. She reminded me of me of me. Then the silly bitch went and got herself killed. One of the Wombats got blamed but somehow I doubted it at the time. Turned out later I was right. I've still got no idea who did but lets face it the streets are a dangerous place. You might think I'm being a bit light over this. I wasn't at the time and it still hurts. You get used to losing people, it's the children, that is so unfair.

I got to know Elsa a bit better after that. We spent long late nights talking about things. You know, like a world without technology. She ahd been a talented artist before PLEX had got hold of her and wanted her to do slogans and artwork for their artwork. She began to angle messages into her artwork, the right sort. Anyway, in the Brownout she was attacked by a gang. They tore the cyberware out of her head when taking her deck, leaving her badly scarred. The damage was bad, it left her blind. The neural damage is too fresh to tell if she will ever get back into the net again. She could still dream and we began to come up with so many stories and ideals. She spoke to Sally. I know she did because Sally had a long talk with me and after that I started to learn to read and write. Not a necessary skill on the street but somehow Sally believed I would have a use for it. I guess she was right, without her I wouldn't be writing this now.

I learnt to write over the months and that was only the start. I put together SINless, a magazine of thoughts and ideals. Not in my own name of course. I got some hard copies done and started getting them out on the street. It was all so very slow but it gave me what I needed, a meaning in life. Not from what I had been told but from something in me. I wasn't following anyone else's ideals anymore, I was following my own. I could read the Eden Dream for myself now and it meant so very much more. It was a dream I had to fight for. I explained that to Sally and she didn't seem too surprised when I told her I was going back to the street. All she said was that "Doc and Birdie will have missed you" with a very knowing smile. Realisation dawned.

It was hard leaving but it was time to go, I could do no more there and there was something I had to do, even though I had no idea at that point what that something was. I promised to visit. I'd seen people come and go myself and I knew now how hard it as to let them go. It was like the kitchen was safe, somehow untouched by the outside. A place of peace where broken people could recover. I never regret walking in that night. Places such as that were what Ho Street was all about. No doubt it is rubble now and they are just memories but they will be with me forever together with the ideals they helped me develop. It's just such a bitch that the gentlest of people have the most to say but don't have the voices loud enough to get their message across. Still, the quiet whispers will go on forever and a single blade of grass can break concrete given time.

I walked out onto the Ho, its streetlights as mournful as ever. My boots splashed on the rain-soaked pavement as faces passed me by. Tired, lost people, most of them had abandoned their respirators, they didn't work, the pollution was too fine. The plague too virulent. The slogans, daubed in paint, I could read them now. One in particular stuck in my mind.

"First they came for the Jews
And I did not speak out
Because I was not a Jew.

Then they came for the communists
And I did not speak out
Because I was not a communist

Next they came for the trade unionists
And I did not speak out
Because I as not a trade unionist

Now they come for the androids
And we do not speak out
What's your reason?

'Cause when they come for you
There will be no one left
To speak out for you
Your brothers, sisters, friends and family
All will have gone before you.

Pastor Niemoeller, Victim of the Nazis

I could read it all, the slogans, torn down signboards, the sheer hopelessness of some of the messages and it all made sense in a moment. It was like all that had happened didn't really matter, not the personal hurt, nothing. All that mattered was that we had a chance while there was still time left to fight for that Eden Dream. I wanted to speak to Doc Harley so badly, I went back to the bar.

I couldn't expect too much. I'd been away for so long. I rounded the corner but it wasn't Jared's Bar anymore. The blue neon sign flashed out "Eryn's Blue". I stopped in my tracks and went out onto the street to look in through the window. It was like the world was folding up around me. But, Jared was there, behind the bar, it was early and there were hardly any customers but I ran to the door and ran my hands over the spent bullets, realising how much I had grown to love that place. I opened the door and stepped inside. By the door were photographs taped to the wall with silver music tape. Photographs I recognised of a woman who had been with us that night we had raided Genoa. Her face smiled from the photos, wearing anything from a smart uniform to overalls tinkering with a plane. In all of them planes, in some she had oil on her face, in others make-up. In all she looked so happy. A rose taped to the wall had wilted, it was a real rose. I wanted to touch it but I was scared to in case I broke it. Something had happened since I had been away.

I suddenly felt very awkward and slipped back out of the side door and into the alleyway. I just felt that Jared wouldn't want me there for a while, nobody would. I realised I'd been away quite a while and I'd changed so very much. I thought of going back to my flat when for some reason I felt like hanging around for a while and just watching. I had to sort this out in my mind. Why didn't I want to go into the bar? I leant on the wall at the back of the building and watched for a while. My boot touched something and I looked down. Now this is going to sound really, really odd. The number of people who used the alleyway and the likelihood of me finding it. Diane had left a package. By some luck I had found it. I'm not going to speculate but I'm just glad I did. In the package there as a letter the rest was for Crisis.

"Dear Chrystal,

Please excuse cloak and dagger stuff, but I'm scared. And I thought maybe you'd understand. It's Crisis getting the Yak in and us losing Lightning. I can't begin to tell you. But I promised Lightning I'd guard Crisis' back so I will, but I can't see me coming back; I'm a secretary for crying out loud. Am I making any sense? Anyway I keep having this really bad dream about me being dead and everything going to shit and, well, your in it so I thought, tell Crystal and if I'm right then OK and if I'm wrong we can have a good laugh about it.

I wish I'd never gone shopping with the silly little bitch that day. I'm sorry: I know she's dead, but really, I know she was trying to get rid of me. I'm sorry we never got a chance to talk about Lightning. You have fine taste sister.

I guess what I'm trying to say is. I'm sorry for all the missed opportunities Crystal. It would have been good to have had time to know you better. And I wanted to say: keep at 'em girl. You have a future, I can smell it on you. So choose it, and soon. I took down Cooper Peaks and had six months sharing with someone I loved. Not bad for Street Slime. What you gonna choose, girl?

'Cos nobody lives forever anymore.

Diane

Oh, enclosed is for Crisis. It's tacky but if you could get it to him for the Rave: Forever and Ever, Amen – I'll be glad. To sum up (he's very stupid and may need help. "Get the fuck out- or find a good bodysculpter")".

I wish I'd had time to talk to you as well sister. Life's a bitch and there's never enough time. Yea, I'll go on, I'm Chrystal, if it's not a choice it's a duty.

Dead, so Blue was dead too. Couldn't get upset, never knew the girl. Still could feel sorry for Crisis and Lightning. No mention of how but then a lot would have happened after I got blown away.

"Darn, corrupted text again." Lightning read on.

We talked most of yesterday afternoon. Chuckles and Runt are in her too, they were so tired they hadn't woken up until now. We're still holding on to some form of hope though. I'm just glad for the music system. Its just really easy to think that we might a swell go and find somewhere relatively safe and live out what little time we have left. I'm not looking for forgiveness, there's just one thing I ask now, that is that if when we make our final stand, if we can't win that I go out in a blaze of glory. Let me do something that is worth leaving you. It is pulling me apart. Out of this decay, out of this pain, let something grow from the ashes that is beautiful.

I've discussed it all with Jared and we have decided that we are going to run with this plan to its completion. We have each other, we have enough money with the Professor to start up another bar. Wherever we are for this final stand we will make it as much like home as we can. I'm still a little confused about talking about the domes. I know we all have access to SINCards. I think he is just a bit tired. We don't have any option, we are in one of the Yakuza vans and we go where Daniel takes us. I'm not going to use it, I'm in this for the long or short haul.

I had a dream last night, we were all together, in the bar. That hurt, waking up and realising it was a dream. They say that dreams are supposed to mean something and I suppose what the dream meant was that as long as we have each other, and I mean all of us from the Eryn, well the bar is where we are. We can question about the sense in all this, if we try to find reasons then we would surely go mad.

So I had to find Crisis and deliver the package. Nothing changes and somehow having something so practical, so "normal" to do held me together. Trouble was that I didn't know where to start. He wasn't at the bar and by what I remembered he had a flat somewhere but as to where, that would take some finding. Then I catch something fluttering in the wind. A rave leaflet. Yo, good on you Crisis, he's organising a rave, at a place called the Coop and the next day. Great, so I knew where he would be, all I had to do was get myself to that building in Bordertown. Avoiding the street wasn't a problem, I went roof-side most of the way. It was the way I felt. Running in the shadows on top of the world. Somehow at the kitchen I just had found time to dream, I had dared to dream, and time to write and hope. Now I saw the world in such a different way, not just the slogans. I saw it how it was, dark and full of death. You can smell it, along with the petrol fumes. The buildings, standing on a wing and a prayer because in places they were so patched and propped that the existing structure has nothing to do with the finished creation. What have we done to this world? We've destroyed it and then tried to hold it together with metal and glue. Would it be better to let it fall apart and trust in mother nature to rebuild? I thought that the Ho Street area was bad. Moving into the border areas, it just got one hell of a lot worse.

The slow decay between the outer Ho and Border Town is obvious. The buildings are more patched, some of them have whole walls that are made of patched and broken pieces of cars, lorries, whatever the wild inhabitants could find. Plastic bag windows, anything and everything used and reused. The further out the wilder it gets. This was gang territory and they wandered the shadows in packs. It was a long trip, a very long trip. Made longer by having to run and hide a lot of the way. It was not a territory to be wandered on the street. I had no choice but it took every scrap of experience to get me through. The roofs were too fragile and those which would hold me up were inhabited by locals and the locals were definitely not friendly. Every shadow seemed to have someone unpleasant in it. It was like one of those very surreal dreams where you run from shadow to shadow and there is someone there trying to kill you. Not kidding here, these are real nutcases, crackheads, gangers, worst of all Spirals. They openly showed their colours out here. Spiral tattoos on their faces. I spent half an hour under some rubbish to avoid a group of two of them. They are so high on something so unpleasant that I didn't even count on being able to outrun them. Something was not quite right. I couldn't work out what it was at the time so I just kept quiet and kept my head down.

I reached the area of Border Town where I had heard this building was. The Coop, a huge mammoth of a building, an old warehouse or something. Now it was a safe haven for those in Border Town who had something to sell or needed a place to trade in peace. Huge, black and forbidding. But I had to go in there, no choice. I was soaking wet, exhausted and beginning to wonder what this was all about.

I circled the building, there was a gravel area and two entrances at least. That was good. I made my way round to the front door. This was new territory, I couldn't count on just being able to walk in. I knocked on the door and it swung open. That was good, there was someone there, that was also good, he looked offensive, I don't mean unpleasant, just enough to make me change my mind about going in. It was the chainsaw I think, that and the helmet. He asked me why I wanted to come in. I couldn't think of a good reason, my mind was just concentrating on that chainsaw, I've heard of them but I hadn't actually seen one before. I muttered something about getting out of the rain and he stepped aside. There was something familiar about him. Then I put a name to the man, Gridlock. Then there was something familiar about a lot of people.

It was strange, walking into a place I didn't know and seeing a lot of faces I did. Chuckles, Asrael, Jared, Yali, they were all there.

Asrael came over. "Chrystal, good to see you. Food?" I nodded, I was so grateful, I had no money. I was feeling a bit lost. I had sort of got used to being with someone when I was with this group. Az put up the money for food, coffee and booked me a bed. I couldn't remember doing him any favours, so why was he doing all this? I guess I was just naturally suspicious. He wasn't the only one either, people I had known from the street we rebuying food for people they knew who were out of money. Loaves and fishes, the dark cloud lifted, it said so very much about how far we had come and what we had achieved.

"Asrael, why are you doing this?" I had to ask.

"You're with the UHC. Who knows when I might need a favour." Something in his eyes, so he was after something.

Then I remembered how much we had all done for nothing over the past few months. I had been away a while. "Thanks."

"No problem. So what's been going on?"

"You probably know more than I do. What happened to Blue."

"You were... Sorry, Chrystal, I forgot. It all went horribly wrong. When you got shot we heard it but we didn't see. Crisis was next onto the balcony. He found you, well steppe don you actually, that's the trouble with wearing black. There was a gunfight on the balcony and quite a few people got hit. We didn't count the number of patrols that had gone out from the building and come back. A concussion grenade and most of us were down. Crisis, Slater and the rest of us that were still standing by the time we got to the hut well we blew away the bad guys and had Blue there, in the middle of the room with a wedlock collar on."

"Which is?" It sounded familiar but I couldn't place what it was exactly.

"Exploding device put round the neck to keep someone in line."

"Shit."

"There was a trigger. Slater put it in his pocket to keep it safe as most of them were set off by pressing a button. Then he went over to Blue, to check her out before they started tampering with the device. Problem, it was proximity activated. Took her head right off."

I didn't know what to say.

"Yea, then Crisis took Slater's off with his rippers. He was well pissed off. Any news on Diane and Crisis?"

"Isn't Crisis here?"

"Not yet but he better be soon."

"When he gets here I want to talk to him."

"A lot of people do."

"I've got some bad news for him. Diane's dead. I thought everyone would know. She died in the Yakuza Hospital."

"I'm sorry. Did you know Eryn?"

I remembered the woman in the tent with Jared. "Not really. We spoke."

"She flew in the AV to get us out and the bastards blew it out of the air. She was Jared's daughter."

"I didn't know, I'm surprised to see him here. He was in the bar earlier tonight. Still I expect he had transport. It's a long walk. A lot of death on the streets." The food was good. The conversation didn't help though. "Any news of Lightning?"

"I don't know how to tell you this."

Now I was worried. A cold feeling, like water falling inside me. I somehow felt I didn't really want to be hearing this.

"The Ojabund's son died on the way back to the bar."

"He what? How?"

"We came back through the sewers. Ratty was down there."

"Ratty?"

"Some mutant bundle of teeth and claws that fancied eating Japanese. That's an understatement. By what we know about Ratty, it's a genetic mutation that can take on the form of whoever it kills. It's a vicious predator that has bee seen a few times around the bar."

I vaguely remember Doc mentioning something the night of the Brownout. I hadn't seen anything like that in all my time on the streets, something I was glad about. "I'd like to offload some of this equipment if you'd excuse me."

"Sure Chrystal, catch you later."

I wanted to clear my head, so Blue was dead, Eryn was dead, the Japanese man was sushi, this was bad, very bad. Crisis was going to be "having one" soon if he hadn't already. There were friendly faces but I really wanted Lightning to be here. If the son was dead the chances of getting him back, didn't want to think about it. I dumped my bags in my coffin bed. I hate those things, the walls close in on a normal room, with them, didn't bear thinking about. Somewhere to store things though and I didn't want to walk around with the package for Crisis. I didn't even want to see him. It was a "love-hate" moment.

I checked out the building, at least two more ways out of the main part of the room, that was looking better. I walked around and went back downstairs to have a look around the booths and stalls. I don't know, somehow the crowd was closing in. I was wandering saying "hi" to people I recognised but I had so much on my mind that it became a bit of a blur. Chuckles stopped me. He looked agitated. That was not good. His reputation had grown, guarding clinics, I had no idea he was such a touch EuroSolo. To me he would always be my friend Chuckles though he looked upset. Memories flooded back, in the bar that night when he'd had some sort of an episode. Muttering something, flashback, but something more sinister than that, something I couldn't hear, couldn't understand. I gained a respect for him then, if he was worried, I was going to listen.

"Good to see you Chrystal. Have you seen Runt?"

"Sorry Chuckles, I've been helping out at a soup kitchen since the raid. Tonight is my first night back."

"You did what!" The look on his face was priceless.

"Yea, yea, so the girl can cook now, there's no end to my talents. What's this about my mate Runt then?"

"She went missing in the Brownout."

"I don't know, it all got so confusing, I don't even remember her being there." Then it flooded back, yes she had been there and she hadn't but I guess I was so used to her disappearing. We both worked the same territory on occasion and slipping away was something we did best.

"How are you feeling?"

"Chuckles, that sounds like a loaded question?" there was something in his tone of voice.

"It is. I mean really."

"Sort of odd."

"Sort of angry?"

"What do you know about it? I could feel my hands shaking. The anger had been my worst nightmare."

"When you went down on the raid on Genoa, Slater got you patched up. When everyone went down he had to get everyone into the hut. You were almost conscious. Doc Josh had to do something, he was in a panic. Diane was down, most of us were down and he had to act fast, he gave you the clinical form of."

"Chuckles!" I didn't want to hear it, I really didn't want to be hearing this. I hate drugs, I don't take drugs, I hadn't, I… "Please.."

"Sorry Chrys, it's the clinical form of Grievous Angel."

"Holy Shit. Why am I still alive?" It all made sense, the cold shakes, the depression. No wonder Sally had warned me she would get someone in to help. Trouble was that when I went like that I couldn't tell the difference. It all made sense. When I had been at the kitchen there had been nights when I had been so off my head that they had had to hold me down. I had no idea why then, they had no idea, or perhaps Sally did. She never let on. She just sad and held me when I cried.

"Clinical form. Not so many unpleasant side effects. Look, I'm sure we can get some to stop the shaking."

It was that noticeable then. I looked down, it was. "No, I'm going to kick the habit, I only took one hit."

"Chrystal, its addictive on the first hit."

"Then I'm in for a very bad year."

He smiled and gave me a hug. Then he froze. "Chrystal, turn rond very slowly, where's Diane?"

"Sorry Chuckles, she died in the Yak… Bastard!"

There was Crisis, large as life, big grin on his face and a Yakuza bitch on his arm. The hospital, Diane on the bed, the woman in the corridor. I could feel my temper rising. "Chuckles, talk to me… keep me talking… I."

"Why?"

"Because I'm going to rip his head off if you don't." I didn't like the look of the bodyguard, tall, well-built hard guy. The tattoos of the Yakuza but European looks. Steely expression, Daniel. The anger was rising, I could feel the red haze coming down, clouding everything, drowning out the sights and sounds. All I could hear was Chuckles' voice, calming, he haze lifted, rational though returned, rational hatred of someone I had called friend. Explanations, I needed to know.

When faced with situations like that you realise how cruel the world can be and how easily we are forgotten. Love for some is fragile, it is words and convenience. Music drifted, the UV light, cigarette smoke, the unnatural glow. It was all too much. I stormed over.

Crisis brightened a little as he saw me. "Chrystal, good to see you."

I was feeling like being cruel. "Crisis, can we have a word?"

"Of course. What…" He must have seen my face. We moved out of earshot of the woman.

"Crisis, who is that?"

"Marakiko San, the Ojabund's daughter. She wanted to see this place."

"What about Diane?"

"I haven't heard anything."

"Crisis, Diane's dead."

"What… how?"

"In the Yakuza hospital. I found her on a trolley."

"Are you sure?"

I cast a nervous look towards Marakiko. "Yes, most of her major organs were missing as well. They killed her." It sort of came out but it was what I felt so…

"You heard about Blue?"

"Earlier."

"Look, the UHC's still together, Silicon's going to get here later. Sorry about the party Chrys, there's one tomorrow night though, here."

I shook m head and sighed. I wasn't going to give him the package with Marakiko around. He could wait, as long as he had it before the rave. Marakiko was watching him with the eyes of a predatory animal and there was no doubt what was on her mind. Great, that was all we needed. We lost the Ojabund's son and then Crisis gets involved with the daughter. I took a quick look and wasn't too surprised to see the end of his little finger was missing. Lucky that was all he lost.

"Look I had better get back, catch you later." He looked upset which was reassuring. I had to keep my temper, perhaps this was a plan on his part to get Lightning out of his little arrangement. I couldn't tell.

I went for a wander. There was a lot for sale, even a news stand with reports coming in on the screen. I could read them now which helped a lot.

6

Crazy and broken, the drams of people and the buildings they lived in. Offbeat, the place and the people. Mismatched but somehow it had a beauty, a broken, dark, sinister gothic feel of imagery that was self created. I don't know why but even the coffee seller had something about him. His youth, that he had been raised by the sisters, I don't know. His name escapes me now but he was memorable enough. For a while. What that it? Were we so used to seeing people come and go that we didn't even bother to remember their names?

Would names make them personal to us and then it would hurt more? That's not a question I can answer. Scavengers, scarecrow people, life's gypsies, that was us, that was what we had become. Crisis and the others, they stood out, because of their clothes and because of their attitude. I guess we'd had it lucky on the Ho. That was something I thought I'd never see or think. We'd kept our identity, not that these people hadn't but it was like… Unexplainable, mismatched with no street identity, things to trade but so very precariously perched on the edges of gang territory. How had they survived? Something was bothering me, several things actually but…

I ducked under some plastic and bumped into Yaki and Shade. They had a "thing" at that point and were screaming at each other. That was what I thought all relationships were like. Reasons to hurt another person. She was screaming at him about something so I backed off. Had to be love, if that was what love was.

I backed away and bumped into Chuckles. Someone so strong physically and mentally, probably because of his military training. But he looked worried. I was glad in a way. Someone like him cared about my little pal Runt, that sort of gave me a warm feeling. Better if she was here though. I'd be happier to know where she was. I smiled, he managed something like a smile and then we sort of wandered off, nothing to say, nothing we could say. She was still missing.

Vortex, I haven't mentioned him before much. Well, he is quite a character. I still can't work out if he has his head screwed on the right way or if the wires had burnt what was left of good sense, leaving what we can understand. He had his own distinctive style, torn jeans, plain mac and a blue peaked cap scribbled with anti-PLEX slogans. Guess he was making his feelings felt and as much of a statement as any of us. He is a man who is giving life a go for what it brings or too plain crazy to really care. To the outside world he is just your friendly neighbourhood netgod with a sense of humour that could put everything really into perspective. He lived in his world, the net, nowhere I could ever go and nothing I have ever understood as it is like a world of its own. You can walk about there as an "icon" by what I've been told. You step into that person and you walk around talking and doing what you want to do. Say you want information about your bank account, well your icon walks into your virtual branch and asks. There are no counters or tills as you are attended by your personal cashier. Same with everything, on line shopping is walking into a virtual store with your icon and your virtual credit card, you check out like you'd check out physically, all goods being added to your card and delivered to your real self later. It is amusing that you can walk around and see yourself in the "real world" dressed in all the items you see. Better than a mirror.

The netrunners had to understand it completely as there is so much that can be achieved there, so much in that unreality. We'd spoken often, it was not unusual to talk that night but for some reason I told him about SINless. Dangerous but what the hell. Somehow I felt tit was the right thing to do. Can't write something for a reason and then keep it to yourself. It was a good idea, do you know what that nutcase did? He took the text and put it in the net as a self-spreading virus so that anyone who logged in got a copy. They log on and there is this well-endowed nymph holding a copy which she holds up at the screen and the watcher can scroll down. She could be deleted easily enough but she made sure she left a copy on the hard drive before she went. That had to be deleted as well or it would pop up again later. Good on him, at least he got it read and I got more airtime than I cold ever have dreamed of. Vortex, he was a strange one. I didn't know how to handle him to start with. He's bright, you can tell that, sharp but no edges. You know he's storing up credit but you can really talk to him. Like he knows things, understands and more importantly he will give it a go. He has that angelic look of innocence as well. Pah! Not likely, not surviving in this world. Raphael on acid more like. Deadly nightshade, he keeps a brain under those golden locks.

The place unnerved me. Why then I don't know. I'd walked into thousands of strange places but somehow I really wanted Lightning with me at that point. No it wasn't the place, it was the person. A dull ache that nothing could calm. So, I'd go up an see who was up there. Attitude, walk with attitude, passing people on the stairs I rounded the corner and looked up. Jared, at the top of the stairs, back-lit by a shade-less lightbulb. He looked worried and that worried me, he hadn't seen me at that point. He was turning people back down the stairs and I wondered if he'd hassle me. Still, something made me want to go up there. He just stood there, solid as a rock. There was something in his eyes, something had happened, something bad. Solid stairs, sawn up doors, smooth, they creaked with age, straining against their bolts. It was like I could hear the sound. Jared had his gun out. I froze. The hollow sharp feeling shifting. I was missing Lightning, ti was like a piece of the puzzle was gone and because of that the whole coherence of the group was gone. I didn't really hang with them anymore, preferring to spend time with Jared. That was the beginning of it all I suppose. I missed Lightning though. There was something that linked us and I didn't want to lose that. I'd not had friends before, he was a really close friend and the burning thing was there was nothing I could do about it. It was like that moment on the balcony all over again. I couldn't just knock at the door and ask for him back.

There were too many people about for my liking. No room to move really, but at least there was a crowd to disappear into. Everyone was wearing body-armour and dull colours, black and grey, concealed weapons not so concealed when they stick into you in a crowd but there was little effort at concealing weapons here. Everyone knew they were there so there was a general acceptance. My head was beginning to spin, I focused on the red hair, the grey duster coat, the gun that could stop pretty much anything. Fighting back the red mist. He looked shadowy, his brow furrowed, something real bad had happened. I knew that look.

I didn't know him all that well. We'd talked, yea, I suppose I knew him better than I thought. I melted back into a corner while he got rid of the crowd thinking I'd follow them down. Though he showed no inclination toward getting rid of me. That was good, that made me feel good. Guess I belonged. The way he looked at me unnerved me, like he watched my every step. That was dangerous, it felt dangerous, he was in that sawn off shotgun mood I'd seen before. Had I pushed it too far? Wat it fear I felt? As I stepped onto the landing he stepped close, so very close that I could feel the heat from his body. Warmth, the smell of gun oil that same old excitement. Fight or flight, I stepped past him and kept walking. His hand on my arm, electricity ran through me, he looked worried. He pulled me closer, too close, far too close I didn't like anyone that close, he knew that. Now I was worried, this had to be really serious.

He whispered in my ear, I could feel the warmth of his breath on my neck. "Chrystal, we're in big trouble. The Yak bitch got herself trashed in the ladies."

Ming back to reality. "She what?"

"She's history, slashed, decorating the walls as Crisis is in there with her, covered in her blood and hysterical."

"Great, it gets better and better." Lightning, that was all I could think of. Crisis could go to hell. He'd made his bed and more than likely slept in it. Lightning was what mattered. If Crisis had lost our chance of getting him back. The red mist started rising.

"She came up here on her own, he came up later and found her on the floor, blood everywhere. I found him kneeling in a pool of her blood."

I looked at him. "I guess they wanted a bit of .. privacy." The anger was rising. Diane's face was all I could think of. Poor sweet Diane. That man needed putting down. "Where's Daniel?"

"No idea." Expressionless, he was cold about this, in shock perhaps, thinking over what this meant quite likely.

I heard a footstep on the stairs, I guess we must have been standing there in silence. I turned. Daniel was dragging himself up the stairs and he looked like he'd been asleep all his life. Eyes heavy, limbs looked like they weighed like lead. He could hardly get up the stairs and it didn't take a genius to work out what had happened. You had to feel sorry for the guy. Crisis on the other hand, I didn't know whether to shoot him or sympathise with him for his bad luck with women. What was he? Some sort of reverse praying mantis? Having sex with him was pretty terminal by what I'd seen.

I pushed the door open. Daniel staggered in and I followed him. It was beginning to make sense, she'd drugged him to get some time with Crisis. Didn't make much sense though, even Lightning had toxin binders, surely as a bodyguard that would have been high on his priority of wants. Still, not for me to question. The light-bulb was swinging gently where someone had knocked it. It was casting strange shadows about the coffin somber faces. Crisis was crouched on the floor, howling like some primeval beast. Hands were trying to comfort him. Comfort him! I felt like kicking him down the stairs and handing him over to the Yakuza at that point myself. Still, I knew what it came to it I'd feel different. He looked up, dammit, I did feel different. How did he do that? I guess because whatever he may have done he was always so damn unlucky. So he wanted to get his "end away" with the Ojabund's daughter. Not such a bad move with her power and their contacts would have been ours if he'd played his cards right. Shame he always pulled the Joker.

It looked bad, again. The Ojabund would be there in the morning and his daughter wouldn't exactly be in a state to cheer him up even if we scraped together all the bits. So then we would have the head of the Yakuza on our tail wanting blood. We were either going to have to fight our way out of this or come up with a killer. I wanted to throw the package at Crisis at that point to make him remember. That was the problem. I wanted to be angry with him but I couldn't. I guess I must have stuck around with Jared because somehow we ended up downstairs talking like we had so often before.

The smells, sights and sounds. His voice so calming but there was something that made me uneasy. It wasn't the conversation, I loved talking to him, too much. I always had but there was something in the conversation, an intensity and it was nothing to do with the words. The subject was pretty basic but it was the undercurrent. The smell of instant coffee and the sounds of quiet conversation drifting around the huge expanse of the Coop. It was easy to forget how big the building actually was when you're sitting in one of the booths. The ceiling and walls brought down to a comfortable height, the walls towered and the wide expanse of the ceiling swept up into darkness and rafters.

It had got a lot quieter in the main trading area. The traders had drifted off. The netrunners were somewhere upstairs, I'd check on what was going on up there later. They were hardly exciting, they'd be sitting around a table, their decks carefully laid out with only the odd twitch showing anything of what they were doing or seeing in there. At that point I just wanted to sit, just for a while and let everything sort of catch up with me.

The lights were dim, the blues and whites stark contrast to the huge strip lights that lit the main bulk of the hall. Jared sat in silence. It's easy to forget how much that man has been through. I had always been glad to have him around but that night, more than ever. There was a sort of comfortable ease I always felt when I was around him. I don't know why. We'd talked a lot at the bar but somehow this was different. He was glad to talk to someone about Eryn I suppose. I found it a little strange at first. I guess I was guilty of the same prejudices as the rest of the population about synthetic people. Lets face it, what really is the difference. They are given a personality which develops. The inventors themselves know that they have to do this to stop psychological problems. Excuse me, if they can have these sort of problems then they are real people. Our bodies are a bit like machines which function on a day to day basic level, it is our personalities and beliefs that make us something else. If they have that too, what really is the difference. What makes a person, certainly not the physical shell, that can be cloned, I don't know. Would I have been and felt the same if I'd been born in the dome?

Thankfully I'd never know and I didn't really want to have to think about it much more. It was a distraction from thoughts of being turned into Sushi by angry Japanese but I needed to think of something at least.

Jared's love for his daughter was natural, and his pride. He didn't care if she was synthetic or not. She had been as much a daughter to him than any other could have been. That seemed important to me too that he did care. I guess it was a bit of a test, if he could care for her then when it came to making a decision that I wanted to be with him later, that decision was easy.

I knew he'd care so it was safe to care back.

I had met Eryn at the bar, just before the raid on Genoa Genetics. She seemed alright, a bit harsh perhaps but then these were harsh times and I wasn't exactly being my usual friendly self. He love of anything that got her off the ground was so evident. It had surprised me at the time, she flew us into the area herself, no remotes, she had piloted it herself. I remember that now, strange that I had remembered it earlier as getting there by van but we couldn't have done. That is how the memory plays tricks I suppose. It has unnerved me that I may have remembered some situations differently.

Still pretty risky to fly yourself into a war zone but then again I didn't know at the time that Jared was her father and I suppose that changes a lot. It was the personal moments that he talked about that mattered, like her getting a job and her love for Drake, another pilot. Drake didn't know yet, Jared had been trying to contact him since the raid but nothing came back, a brick wall. That surprised me, that androids can love. It shouldn't really, if they develop personalities, why not? Again it makes us who we are.

Crisis broke into the conversation about this point. He seemed agitated, which was pretty standard for the situation. He was muttering to himself and I couldn't help wondering which of is many and varied pills he had taken to get that effect. Ok, so he was in one hell of a position but he had got himself there with very little help from the rest of us. Any standing he had gained with the Yakuza was history. Marakiko's death had seen to that, Diane was gone too. I know he'd instigated it but Lighting his Home Boy was gone too. Also too many people had lost a lot of respect for him since the raid and the dwindling finances had pretty much gone now so he couldn't keep the respect he had once had by being King of the Hill. He had unceremoniously rolled to the bottom of it and was finding his circle of friends getting less by the day and for a DJ who traded on being "the man", it didn't look good. He was going out for a walk. Foolhardy but it was fairly quiet around the Coop by then. Jared was worried, I was just angry and snapped something like "don't follow him, he won't kill himself if he doesn't have an audience". It was cruel but then I wasn't feeling particularly charitable at that point. I just took a long drink of coffee and stared at the graffiti on the wall. I don't know what Jared much have thought of me at that point but quiet frankly I don't care. I'd had my loyalty pushed to the limit and to be quite honest I felt it was being used a bit like a weapon. Everyone seemed to need or want something and it all took a little bit ore of the woman who was once Chrystal. I was tired, I was angry. Not just at Crisis, at Diane for going on that stupid raid, at Lightning for leaving us, at the world for not leaving us alone. It was one huge, horrible mess and it just wasn't going to go away. Not then and by the way I felt that night not ever.

It was like Jared was breaking through whatever shields I had put up, and it unnerved me. There was nothing disloyal about talking to Jared, after all there was nothing between me and Lightning, there never had been. I still felt awkward so somehow I made an excuse and wandered off somewhere.

I thought about going back to my coffin room and trying to get some sleep. If I was going to have to take on the wrath of the Yakuza the next day I had better be ready for it. There had to be more. We had a killer to find at the least.

I stood in the open doorway staring out into the rain-soaked night. It was perhaps a bit fresher than on Ho street. So, as the sun went down behind the dark thunderclouds we didn't give it a thought enough to watch it. Perhaps one or two hanging about by the door smoking homemade cigarettes might have, I don't know.

Those who were still awake b the time the clock crawled into the small hours clung to their coffee cups and looked at each other. So, what was new, it was late, we were tired and we were in trouble. We had a dead body, an important one but nothing much by way of clues that were going to get us out of this mess. We'd gone over the room what felt like a thousand times looking for clues but there was nothing available to give us any clue to the identity of the murderer. By now there had been too many people going over it. I for one had been in there twice just hoping and I know others had as well. If we hadn't bagged up any "evidence" by now it would be damaged and useless. We had a glove and with all the technology in this room we should have been able to do something. That was what was bugging me, we weren't we were talking, we were discussing other things, we were getting more and more tired and we were getting nowhere. Then again, nothing new there.

I couldn't just sit there, there was so much I needed to know. I'd heard rumours of trouble on the streets all night but outside seemed so quiet. There was the odd burst of gunfire in the distance but nothing too major. Nothing for it, the only thing I could do was surrender to the feelings that were digging far too deep to be ignored.

I called Sally a the Soup Kitchen.

I could see the place now, in my mind's eye, the scrubbed threadbare room, the phone jumping into life, spitting out its dull ringing tone, click and Sally answered. She always hated the telephone, she still did, I could hear it in her voice. That and the way she always sounded out of breath. "Hi Sally, its Chrystal."

"Thank heavens you are alright." Only she could sound that genuine and actually mean it.

"How's it there?" I was just hoping.

"Pretty bad. Spirals hit the place about three hours ago. Chrys, they have guns now. Really heavy stuff, the sort it's kinda hard to get hold of. We lost the front door to a rocket launcher, we've patched it but they'll be back. Don't try to get back tonight. We've dug in for the night, whoever is out there stays out there. The children, you've got to understand."

"Not a problem Sally, I'm out in Bordertown. Just worried, know what I mean?"

"Sure kid, appreciate it. Keep on at 'em kiddo, you know you've got it in you and well, if we don't speak again, thanks."

I should be saying thanks to her! "Don't be daft. I'll catch you on the flip side."

"Sure Chrystal, you'll be there on the flip side, no doubt 'bout that. Just remember the Dream, hold it with you every day of your life. One day..." A loud explosion "Gotta go, keep your head down." Click...

The line hummed its disconnected tone and I felt cold and empty inside. A true feeling, that was the last time I spoke to her. The next rocket launcher shell took out half the building and the place burnt to the ground. Most of the people were caught inside and those that didn't die in the rubble were caught by the Spirals. I wanted to be there more than anything else, to be there to help. The walls closed in then and everything looked so unreal. I was walking in a dream, not it was a nightmare. The trashiness of the place no longer seemed the same and it made me angry. What right did anyone have to make people live like this while they lived in their ivory towers? What about the children? Hiding under beds in shelters, just hoping they could make it through just one more night. But what for? To live another day of pain with no hope of a better tomorrow? NO... No way, there had to be more, we had to be fighting for something. Hey, listen to me, so who died and jacked me into Doc Harley? The image returned of that balcony that evening at Jared's Bar, the freedom fighter who had so much belief, who fought for a cause. That was what it was for, him and the rest like him. What had been bugging me, it still did, then realisation dawned. Spirals with guns. Psychotic maniacs with guns on their side. They didn't have the ability to barter for them, they could have stolen them but they wouldn't have known how to use them. Not unless someone had taught them and had found something to control their crazy attitude long enough for them to be able to reload.

Crisis sat by the stereo, head in hands. Silicon Avatar, the UHC Zen, stoned, netrunner was with him. They say he's got to be good as he runs while tripping. Then he's a strange beast alright. Long white blonde hair, radiating energy, a life in perpetual motion, tapping out the tune of his life on anything he could touch. Crisis flipped a Portishead CD into the machine and hit play, all we needed, music to top yourself to but good all the same. Daniel, like some skin statue stood motionless, the lines of worry so evident, arms folded across his chest. We were a group of people bearing silent witness, heads bowed, clustered around a small neon lamp and a table of disposable coffee cups in a huge darkened room as the main lights went off and we were left with the lights from the booths and the security lighting.

The plastic sheeting was swaying gently, like disembodied spirits, hung out to dry. We drank more coffee, we always do, gets you through the night when sleep won't claim you. Black and two, known as BFA. None of hose foul tasting synthetic whiteners. I can only hope that real milk used to taste better or I would wonder the sanity of anyone coming up with such an idea as white coffee. Then again, I think cows were extinct then, its hard to graze cattle in a war zone and where in PLEXUK wasn't. That and a campaign to eat less or no meat, I guess there were reasons.

Rain on the patchwork roof, somewhere up there in the darkness. Raindrops on metal, rattling. Music drifted its disembodied rhythm and words that at one moment meant a lot, at another meant nothing. I listened for a while. I could literally feel my mood change as the music changed. Perhaps that was why some of our music was so angry. We were angry, or if we weren't we really should be. Strangers by the door looking out into the black emptiness, but we all knew it wasn't empty out there and there weren't really any strangers, I just didn't know who they were yet. If we were attacked by Spirals our lives would all be in each other's hands.

Jared was being real quiet. Something was on his mind, but as we'd been talking about all night he did have a lot to have on his mind. I caught him looking at me a couple of times, not moody quiet, just a haze that comes from exhaustion when you can't give up and go to sleep. It wasn't as if any real ideas came in those hours before dawn. It's the surreal time when the head floats and the spirit cries out. It is the time for sitting and taking in the atmosphere, for being with people or alone depending on the mood but everything smells and sounds so different. A time for reflection, for thinking and for being. It's the time when you realise that you are still alive, that the world is falling apart and, depending on the mood that it's all going to fall apart around you whether you care or not. It's the time for philosophy, personal ideals and those conversations that wouldn't make sense at any other hour of the day. The theoretical truths of the universe seem open to you as the sleep deprivation takes over the conscious mind and everyone becomes a scholar. I sat back down with Jared and the others and pulled out a water bottle I'd brought with me, the last of the Peach Schnapps seemed appropriate for that night. Not enough to render ourselves incapable of defending ourselves but enough to take the edge off.

Crisis broke my concentration. I'd been half listening to him, having sat back down with the sorrowful group that was us in the corner. The music drifted, Portishead interspersed with something a lot heavier. The mood flashing from memories to sheer blind panic. Crisis had been talking to Silicon, off in a world of their own of street talk and chatter. I guess I must have been talking to Jared, I as drifting into that calm of needing sleep so badly but not wanting to be alone. Then again was it a total unconsciousness of what was going on around me? I don't now but I certainly didn't notice

Crisis stand up and walk into one of the booths. No reason to I suppose. The owner had gone to bed long ago, leaving his deck on standby. It was probably monitoring something or processing something. I'd spoken to the guy earlier. An ordinary sort of man. What I mean is that he dressed streetside but not eccentric, he was quietly spoken and didn't carry heavy weaponry. How do you classify people? I would remember his face, round and friendly, dark shades, the man was blind and of course that distinguished him from the start. He was a trusting soul to leave all the equipment up and running but then he probably had programs out there doing things. He hadn't protected access because Crisis and Silicon sat down and attached the wires and plugs into the sockets just behind their hairline. Well I thought they had until I realised that Crisis had a deck of his own. Can't say I'd seen him use it before but now his fingers ran over the half keyboard.

If you grow up seeing people with the connections near the hair line I suppose you don't really notice them. To someone who hasn't I suppose it must look a bit strange. The whole idea of having wire interfaces and other circuitry embedded in the brain just under the skull doesn't appeal to me. It's a simple operation apparently these days, depending on cash of course. If you are going for the up market stuff, the stuff from Chiba, then you are not talking street prices, nobody has that kind of cash here. If they did then they wouldn't be hanging around without an army to protect it. Everything has a price and to be honest, the price for second hand cyberware wasn't that low that it wouldn't interest even the most timid street punk. I wouldn't say that surgeons didn't have the skill but it was experience as well and supply. Surgeons, more like mechanics these days. No Streetware was not Chiba quality by a long way. Anyone who could afford it wouldn't' be seen near the streets as I've said. If it was it was old, third or fourth hand and I don't even want to think about that. Most of what we had was, like most of the equipment we can get hold of, second hand. Domeside construction definitely but not high quality. Not too bad as long as you don't think about it too much or where it came from. Seeing the mess they had made of Elsa when they took her hardware I wouldn't want to risk it, even if I did have any interest in jacking in, which I don't. Her hardware would be back on the streets by now, walking around in someone else's head.

I hadn't really seen Crisis as a Runner. He had the jack socket but then quite a few street kids have sockets they stick on for a bit of street cred. I'd not really thought about it. I suppose I'd seen him with small plastic bags of chips and I had seen the socket but well, how much do you really look at anyone? Just enough to know what they look like, not enough to give any other messages. So he could use the net, but for what? The netrunners had already been in the net most of the night looking for answers. "What you up to Crisis?" I had to ask, just before he went in.

"It's getting dull here, We're going looking for Soulkiller."

My feet went cold. I'm no netrunner but I've heard that word banded about. Again, I had to ask. "Silicon, what's Soulkiller?"

"Yo babe, nasty bastard ice that does your head. It's out there, hey it's the devil in the net. So, let's dance with the devil." He jacked in.

"And your going out looking for it?" He didn't hear me.

"Hunting the hunter." Crisis had an odd look on his face, then he jacked in.

"What will you do if you find it?"

No answer from either of them. Now I was worried. It's hard to quantify something you don't really understand. We had enough problems and the thought of those two with their brains fried as well was not appealing. Then again, this was Crisis, no, the temptation to just leave him to fry his brain was appealing but somehow I just couldn't do it. There was no way of knowing what was going on though. They would communicate between themselves in the net. As far as they were concerned we were literally in another world.

This was bad, this was very bad, particularly when Crisis started shaking. Jared was on his feet and half way across the room. We couldn't pull them out, we didn't know how. I had no idea about how much mental damage I'd do by unplugging them. Jared stopped and looked back, he looked pale. "I'm going to wake Vortex."

Poor Vortex, I remember a short while ago when the little guy had gone off to bed. He needed to sleep, all he needed was two hours to take his contact lenses out, that was all he got, well nearly.

It was a good idea, I wasn't coming up with any, somehow I was frozen to the chair. This was one thing that I have no interest or wish to get involved in. All I could do was watch the little pageant unfold. The two in the net, flicking and flitching, Daniel standing beside them and watching, as helpless as the rest of us. Vortex scampered across the room, half asleep in his crumpled T-Shirt and torn jeans, skidding to a halt, jacked in and then they all jerked violently and were back with us in the real world.

Vortex was mighty pissed off. I was too but I wasn't going to let it show. All that was running through my head was that the stupid idiots had probably alerted PLEX that we were here. Not that I had such great confidence in the intelligence network of the PLEX, just a firm confidence in our bad luck.

I know how I felt, we were in enough trouble, although it wasn't exactly Crisis' fault he had played a big part in it. Simple rule, if you are going to do something really stupid, don't involve someone else, especially someone as easily led as Silicon Avatar. There was a childlike innocence there. He played with life, well if he'd run into Soulkiller I don't care how good he was in the net. I'd heard about it, there was only one deck that could deal wit it and that deck wasn't here. Neither was the woman who could use it. I know enough about the net to know that every time you go in there, there is an imprint that you have been there. He was someone they were after. I would have thought that with the amount of interest there was from certain circles in getting hold of him he would have wanted to keep his head down, not go public. Still, that was Crisis for you.

Jared's face was like thunder. He stalked off across the room. "I'm off to bed."

I didn't blame him.

More coffee. Crisis took a long drag on his cigarette. "Yea, like the bitch just wanted it, now this Gaijeen is history. My arse is toast tomorrow morning."

"Tomorrow?" The comment startled me. Then we hadn't really questioned him on what was going on. He had to know more than he was telling.

"Honourable little daughter gave her proud new father a call when she got here. Wilful bitch couldn't just come here quietly and then go back to him tomorrow. No, she had to go and tell him and he, and his little Yakuza mates with their very sharp swords will be here in the morning to escort little daughter home. Want to know what is worse. I didn't tell you about what happened on the way back to the bar the night we hit Genoa Genetics. You know the Yak boss' son was with us. We were nearly back at the bar when we went underground. The roads were crawling with PAYCops. Then this "thing" jumps out of the darkness and rips him to shreds. So Yak boss gets my little finger an I get a whole world of pain. Then in the bar is Marakiko, waiting for her betrothed. She didn't show much interest in what was left. So I guess she figures that I sort of owe her and she came here to collect. Yak boss decides he's run short of heirs and adopts her. As I said, tomorrow morning I am history."

I'd heard rumours earlier, this just confirmed how much trouble we were in. No clues, no ideas, no Lightning and as I saw it not much hope of escaping being made into Sushi in the morning.

The grey wisps of smoke spiralled up to join the hazy darkness above. The neon light illuminated Crisis' heavy set dark features, he looked slightly demonic. What that it, was he sent to wind us all up in things that were going to be the end of us? Was the devil bored of waiting to get his claws on us.

I remembered the package. No, not then, it could wait, it would be better in the morning, after what happened with Marakiko's father. Let him deal with one problem at a time. Was that why? I doubt it, no I wanted to have a little power over him for a while. He wanted everything his way, wanted the whole world rotating around him. Well he'd pretty much succeeded in that. I'd keep my little card one more day. It made me feel better.

I thought that perhaps I should try sleeping, nothing was being said now. It was sit in silence and drink coffee moment. I said my goodnights and went upstairs, stopping for a moment by the half open front door. The music from the stereo echoed strangely where I was standing, the darkness had mellowed to the dull grey of morning and the scent of the air had changed. The distinctive smell of morning, despite the fumes and the pollution, nature's little reminder that she was still out there, still in control somehow, time to sleep.

It was dark upstairs, a feint glow from the shuttered window at the end of the corridor, the read security light had broken , leaving only the bare bulb. The walkway was clear, who would be stupid enough to leave their equipment outside their lockable "coffin". I moved as quietly as I could but the whole room resounded with the rumblings of snoring and heavy breathing, echoing in the tin box. It was like being in the belly of some huge metal beast with bronchitis, still with all the pollution who hasn't got a few problems. I keyed in the combination and the latch clicked. The internal light didn't work either so I crawled into the darkness, shut the door, locked it and just stretched out on the flimsy, lumpy, musty smelling sleeping pad. I struggled out of my coat, rolled it up and wedged it under my head. I pulled out my berretta, checked the safety was on and curled up with it.

That gun had been with me for a long time. It's black sleek shiny exterior battered but every dent was done with loving care. Like hell. It was the only thing I had left of a friend I had once known, Max. Somehow he felt close that night. Memories of hearing him snoring on my sofa night after night. Waking in the morning and sharing coffee with him, coming home at night and finding him there. Not that he was big on conversation, especially at first. He kept his head down and kept out of my way. He was just glad to have a place to crash. Guess he stopped drinking in the time he was with me. He actually started teaching me a few things as well, like how to use his berretta. I learnt fast and he seemed really pleased with me. It was like his payback for me having let him crash I suppose. Never know when it would come in handy. I don't know, perhaps I'll find him again one day. He's probably dead, but those weren't thoughts for a few hours sleep. I held the gun close, as I had on so many other nights. It was like a reminder, that all he had taught me would always be with me and the gun he had left for me when he split would be there to protect me, even if he couldn't.

The wheels keep turning, rolling us on. The van nearly went over back there. We got sideswiped by a rocket. We've had to stop for repairs. Daniel is out there now, looking at the damage. Got to go, its taken out the outer shell and we've got to repair it and it is faster if we all lend a hand of course.

That metal was hot, still smoking from the explosion. We've managed to patch it up and thankfully it didn't get through the second layer. It must have impacted on the ground and we got caught in the blast. It made quite a mess of the outer shell. It was strange being outside, it made me feel sort of light headed after the oppressive semi-darkness in here. It's the colours you miss in here. It's black, chrome, flashing red and blue lights, the odd flash of colour on clothing but mostly black. Out there it was actually green. I mean grass green, there is grass, real growing grass and well it would be a rural scene if you ignore the craters and the barbed wire. There are fields on both sides. Skeletal hulls of vehicles litter the road, burnt out and picked clean, but the fields are green. Not that sickly black-green you get near the Ho, no, green-green. Bright, dazzling colours, the brown wood fence posts, bleached by the sun, the heavy grey sky, the bone white skulls of men and animals nailed to those posts, dark grey-black tarmac of the road, the light grey where holes have been blown in it. The broken white lines, leading from crater to crater like some insane join the dots.

It's hard to imagine that once there were streams of cars driving along here. Families, mummy and daddy and two kiddies, bored by long journeys and following the car in front. There was a saloon car, on it's side, burnt out, no idea that colour the paint was once. You can almost hear the echoes of the children, the incessant questions and the noise, the engine, the radio, all gone now. At night I could imagine the stream of insect like metal carapaces one behind the next, lighting the night with white and red, the constant stream of red lights stretching out into the distance. Must have been quite a sight. That there were that many people left to drive like that, that we could be free to do that. The question is, will you long for what we have now, will it get worse?

We had to move on and fast. There was movement in the field. A shot bounced off the bodywork. Hardly any paint left out there now, just a pitted surface of dents. Somehow she's holding together and they missed with that last shot. Good job, by the way it rocked us as it hit the ground, it had to be high calibre. I did catch a glimpse of the road bridge, well what was left of it. Locals, had to be, their scavenged clothing and what looked like a rocket launcher. Must have been where that shot came from. Definitely time to move on or become special delivery "materials" that these guys were shopping for. Another rocket missed, made the back of the van jump a bit but not enough to do serious damage. Everything is pretty much tied down here, except for a stray coffee cup but thankfully it was empty.

Back at the Coop I must have drifted off to sleep as I woke in a panic. Sleeping in those boxes is like being buried alive. I heard voices, checking my watch, 11am. There was still snoring echoing round the chamber. I holstered my gun and clicked the latch. Knocking the door open with my boot the light streamed in, yellow lightbulb light, illuminating the dust and dirt. I jumped down onto the floor, shut the door and reset the combination.

Downstairs the cooks were busy with breakfasts for the hungry and I was very hungry but very poor as always these days. The smell of instant coffee and cigarette smoke. This made some nearly human, don't try talking to them before though.

The traders were setting up for another day, just another day. The NewsNet stand had the screen on, psychedelic spirals and lines. I didn't watch too long. It's been a thing with me for a long time that I worry about subliminal messages. All to do with my fear of being controlled I suppose. The colours were bright, then there were the other surreal pictures. Printouts, I'd have bought one if I had the cash. I checked my pocket, nothing is not enough. The NewsNet guys weren't up yet. They'd been around the day before but I'd kept away, they had their camera but I don't think anyone was much up for being interviewed. Old news, an old sheet, a piece on the serial killer. Well they had a story now, there were enough people here, so who would be next? Apparently somewhere in the milling crowd yesterday I had missed that fact that there were a couple of PAYCops as well. Great, that was all we needed. Paid by who? That was the question. One tall, male, dark haired and silent, the other a woman, smartish, long light brown hair and glasses. Streetside, fit in anywhere types, just the sort that make good PAYCops. Not really in uniform. Boiler suits are common. Not like the flashy, in your face, "here I am", PLEXCop uniform if you want to look at it that way. They are around in the morning though. Those guys get up early I guess. Didn't bother me much, I wouldn't be speaking to them. Others were though, particularly to the man. Word was his name was Carter and he was being really helpful in looking for the murderer. Now that made a change, a helpful PAYCop. Then if he was here when the Yak turned up he'd probably get caught in the crossfire, so, wise man, looking after his own tail.

No sign of Silicon or Crisis. Then again I could hear Crisis, who could miss him. Then I suppose Silicon had gone to sleep off his enthusiasm or to try something chemical somewhere. I then worked out when I had actually gone to bed. I'd had about two hours sleep, oh well, there you go, should be used to it by now.

Gridlock was back on the door. I did know him, I knew I did. Didn't know anything about him though. Just big and dangerous with a chainsaw. People were coming and going all the time. Those who had just come in to spend the night were now back on the streets. I couldn't remember what day it was but then days seem to run into each other. No such thing as weekends on the street.

There was a face I recognised, Runt. Street runners were my people, I remembered them easy enough. She looked a bit bemused and was just wandering into the Coop. So where was Chuckles? I was just about to go looking for him when he stepped out from behind a stall and hugged her like he'd missed her as much as we know he had. I had questions. I left it, let them talk it out. I went back upstairs, couldn't put it off any longer, I got the package for Crisis, the small plastic envelope that held a CD-Rom and a note. I wasn't sure how to do this. I thought about it all the way down the stairs, crossed the trading area and just walked up to him. "Crisis, can I have a word?"

"Sure."

"In private."

He looked bemused. "Sure."

We stepped outside, it was quiet, here wasn't much cover but the fire escape steps seems like a good place. He was looking worried, he must have caught something from my expression.

"Crisis, Diane left me a note. She has asked me to give you this." I held it out, my hand shaking in the chill air but then my hands always shook these days.

He looked at me and took it. I looked at him and was about to leave when he caught my arm and pulled me back. It sort of put something together, bringing me back to the UHC. It was a warm, oh my God we are in real trouble, hug, the kind I really, really needed. I was going through hell trying to get over the dependency on the clinical grievous angel and trying not to let it show.

Don't you ever think of taking anything. I certainly wouldn't have done.

I walked away a short distance, leaving him to read the note. That was between him and Diane. As to whether I would show him my note from her, I didn't know. The bit about Blue, they were both dead, what good wold it do now.

I wandered back inside. Somehow I had lost my peripheral vision. No, I'd just worked out that life, and death, seemed to have a habit of happening anyway. The morning was drifting on, it was time we needed answers. There was a gunshot, the woman PAYCop was slumped into a chair.

I can't say I exactly know what happened there. I can't even remember who explained it but she was the serial killer. The tests on the glove had proven it. She'd tried to escape and I think it was the other cop who had put her down but I can't remember. It all seems so long ago now. They'd been doing tests on all of us and she had resisted. When forced to take the test, well, the results were obvious. Problem solved I though and wandered upstairs. I stopped on the stairs, leaning against the wall. What was happening? What had we all become that someone's death could be seen as a solution? Was everything decaying? I went up the stairs, I was looking for Jared I suppose,. I'd been doing that a lot lately, and I didn't really know why.

The netrunners were sitting round a table when I got upstairs. Suddenly Vortex stood up and started shaking, blood trickling from his nose. He was muttering words that didn't make sense. Something was obviously very, very wrong. Doc Josh was there. Josh, about my height perhaps a bit taller, heavy set, long thick blonde hair and quick reactions. He was checking out Vortex as Vortex tried to explain that this just "happened". Josh sat him down and got his box of technology out. This was going to take time, Vortex seemed alright and the room was getting far too crowded for me. I couldn't do anything so I left.

Jared was by the back door, just watching. He looked like one of those western sheriffs, standing there, rifle in hand, silhouetted by the morning light. There was something so steady about him, so real. I felt it even then. I walked up beside him. He turned and smiled. "Thought I saw movement, by the building line. Could be spirals."

"Don't they ever sleep?" I was trying to think of something clever to say but I couldn't.

"Hmm, not when we want to. How's it going?"

"Just ruined Crisis' day. Diane left me a note, and something for him. I left him to read it."

Shade stuck his head around the door. "Hey, he Yak have turned up."

I looked at Jared, he looked at me and I was past him and down the fire escape. I was oblivious to where he was, everything was grey and white, grey building, white gravel and this rising feeling of excitement and I had no real idea why. I turned the corner, saw the black cars, Crisis talking to a man in a black suit, but I didn't see them, I just saw Lightning. He was standing with them, in a black suit, his long black curly hair spiralling down his back, the sunlight reflected in his mirror-shades, a dragon tattoo curling elegantly down his neck. He stood unmoving, radiating a steely confidence. I was caught, like a victim in the gunsight, it was that laser pointer on the chest moment. The midday sun just about braking through the thunderclouds, no rain, it was as if the moment was caught in time. He must have seen us but he wasn't going to react. I was too far away to hear what was going on but the Ojabund shook Crisis' hand and turned to leave. Was that all? Not a word. I thought that Lightning was going to leave without even a word.

The Yakuza left, leaving Lightning standing there. He went to Crisis, I couldn't move, I was cemented to the spot. I saw them hug. I heard him say "I'm back." Then he saw me and I was caught again, I couldn't run. It was like all my thoughts had been open to him. I heard his boots on the gravel, it was like everyone was holding their breath. Yali was there, I heard her say "Good on you Chrystal." He got closer. Stood in front of me and then took me in his arms and held me so close. I could feel that strength, that incredible strength but with such gentleness. I was breathing so fast and it was as if the world didn't matter. Everything I wanted at that point was right there. He pulled back, still holding onto me as he told me how he had missed me. I didn't know what to say as he ruffled my hair like he always did. I could see Jared to my right, he was watching but there was something in his eyes, a sadness. I was so pleased to see Lightning that I didn't really take much notice.

"I couldn't be there Chrys. I couldn't help, we weren't getting anywhere, it was all I could do. I had to get us some help. We're not cut out for that sort of thing."

"That's OK, you got us the breaks we needed. Just sorry it ended the way it did."

"What do you mean?"

"They haven't told you?"

"I have no idea what has happened."

Crisis came over. "Lighting, she's dead, they both are."

"Oh man, look I had no idea, they kept me away from everything."

"Look, I know…"

Lightning looked devastated. "Anyone else?"

"Chrys took some serious injuries, put her out for a while. Yak fixed it."

"You OK now Chrys? I knew you'd pull through."

"Yea, but I'm not showing you the scars. You were there, weren't you?" I felt him tense. He looked a bit strange and then got sucked into he crowd of questioning people. There was something I was missing here. I wasn't sure what it was.

Crisis looked uneasy. "Let's get inside."

Once inside it seemed like everything got very surreal. Crisis had to sort out a lot of deals he had put on hold so Jared, Lightning and me, well we found some comfy chairs.

Then this Tribesman sat down.

"Hi, I'm Tictac." He sounded friendly enough. Strangely dressed, a bit like the gangs but more rustic.

He was tall and lanky, good looking in a sort of Domeside way which was odd because his clothes said otherwise. "Here, try this."

That was not an invitation I usually took up. "What is it?"

"Water."

"What?" Now I was confused.

"Water from home." He offered the bottle.

I sniffed it, smelt strange. I tasted it. It was clear, pure, tasted like nothing I had ever tasted before.

"It's from my home. You guys haven't seen trees I hear."

I'd read about them, seen an old vid-film but the thought that they still existed somewhere. "You have trees?"

"Lots of them. Look, why don't you come and see. I'm trying to get together a group of people to come and see what we are up to. You know, there's not enough people to fight or be unsociable."

Right enough. "Where are you from?"

"Wales. Far from any Dome. I can't see how you all live like this."

His eyes were honest. You can tell when someone is up to something. They don't look you in the eye unless they are very good at lying. He seemed really genuine.

Crisis was making a lot of noise. He sounded alright though, not in danger or anything, just arguing over something. The afternoon dragged on. It was an odd sensation, I know its caused by the body's reaction to the drug it is trying to kick out of its system but it was like the Coop phased out. It had been happening a lot, it was something to do with the complete depression that took over. I couldn't tell anyone, it was a real weakness but with Lightning and Jared both watching. I just phased out and drifted off. Tictac pulled me over onto his shoulder and that was it. Strange that in an open hall like that I actually felt safe for the first time in my life. Looking back on it, I was. Far safer than in any coffin room on my own. I had Lightning who was wired to hell and like a hawk for noticing trouble and Jared, ex-android hunger, ex-cop and keen to blow anything to bits and as I learnt later Tictac, warrior of his tribe and something really rare, an honest and genuine man. So the afternoon slipped away.

I think we all knew something was going on outside. It was the reports coming in that woke me up. It was a moment I didn't want to ruin though so I just sat there for a while with m eyes shut, listening to the conversation. It's not often you get a chance like that, you know, to be that little bit secure. Something that calmed the wild spirit in me. If we had a chance it was because of moments like that.

Barcode, that was the catchword. So it was real, not just a rumour. Runt had got one when she got caught on the street on her way in here. She now had an interesting tattoo. I smiled, not a problem, could get it skin grafted surely. That was before I saw one. The bastards went down to the bone, black and sinister. Hell, we were no more than groceries in the store, check us out when we die.

So Carter had been sent to Barcode us perhaps? Credit to him that he hadn't tried. Wise, more like he would have been dog meat, if we'd had any dogs of course, except for Cerebrus of course.

I haven't told you about him yet have I? Some sort of genetic dog mutation. I'd heard of dog gangs, he was different, tougher. I'd seen the red boiler suit first, then saw him from the front. Another dog creature half dog, half man, I have no idea. I saw him from a distance and that was enough. Then I thought, food and went to get food and he was there. Then I saw his problem. He wanted food but he couldn't get his money out as his fingers although more human than dog paws were a bit too clumsy. Doc Josh seemed to have befriended him and was helping him. They had formed some kind of understanding, man meets dog. I don't know but it was good to see. I had a bacon sandwich of something and he was in front of me, looking hungry. So I gave him some and that was it. Friends for life I think. I knew, and he knew and there was no dog intelligence there. If you can imagine a nearly six foot mass of muscle and danger. So, I was glad he was on my side, well I think he was.

Crisis' voice cut into my thoughts. We were supposed to be having a rave tonight, first in a long time. Trouble was with all he barcoding people had a lot on their minds. The sun was dying in the sky, its sickly red reflecting off the grey cloud, too much dust and pollution these days for a proper sunset.

Voices at the door, not quite believable, too high pitched, squealy voices. No doubt, had to be them. The Sisters of the Perpetual Railgun. Sisters was a bit of a misnaming or nor so much. They were men in nun's habits. Loud and very strange. It's like seeing a transvestite who doesn't bother to shave his beard off. They strode in, and everyone wanted to talk to them.

"Time for confession boys and girls, form an orderly queue."

What the hell. Why not? To get out of the queue I had to move. Let's see what they were all about. So I stayed put. Jared seemed really pleased. He hadn't bothered to tell me at that point of course that he grew up with them did he? I wondered why he didn't make any comment.

Confession with the sisters was interesting. I saw on a cushion on the floor. "Well child, what do you have to confess?"

"I killed somebody."

"With what?"

"I don't know, a Glock I think."

"Did the corpse deserve it?"

"Yes, he was keeping me prisoner, well his boss was."

"Did you kill his boss as well?"

"No."

"What were you doing child, whistling Dixie, come on kid, why didn't you blow him to hell?"

"I was having a few problems at the time, anyway I don't kill."

"Get real. Give him death, it will set you free. We'll loan you a railgun, even help you out. What did he do?"

"Had the man I killed rape me."

"Kill the bastard, vengeance will make you free. He took away your dignity. He will be your boogie man, death to him, it will make you free. Ride the pale horse, to him you will be death. He is guilty, judge him so. He is like the devil in the first degree. You have to get over this unable to kill thing. Death to him, it will make you free."

The sisters moved around the one who was talking to me. It was very strange, I had expected something so different. They smiled and waved guns around their laughter manic and I began to wonder. The streets can make you mad but then, who isn't a little bit in this crazy world. A chance to have a go at Jade, it did have a good ring to it. I wanted to have power over that man, to see him crawl out there, just like I had crawled. I just wanted to see him on his face in the dirt. They aroused such an anger in me. I was stirred, if I had known where he was I would have gone for it, I'm sure.

"Go child, in peace, let your forgiveness come from wasting the bastard."

Great, so now I'm not forgiven until I waste him. Still the thought of him kneeling at my feet, putting a gun to his head and then walking away. It wasn't the thought of someone else doing it, it was the fact that someone would love me to get rid of my pain. I'd never felt like that before. It was like something that was ancient, you know, the white knight that comes in and sort it all out. Still if it came to it, I don't really know what I would do. I've asked questions, I've looked for him but most of me wants to forget it all.

We sat down at the coffee booth, the hot black liquid holding my attention for a moment, the kick of the caffeine mingling with the kick I always had from the drug that always ran in my system. Chuckles was right and even I knew enough that it was now part of my cellular make up. I could fly like a kite on nothing and then rip a door off just because I could. Stable, not a chance. Psychotic head case I'm afraid, but the lucid moments were more than the crazy. It had a chance of getting better, unfortunately only in my mind. Still, hope springs eternal and I needed to know what Lightning was thinking about.

"Chrys."

"What's up?"

"I's all of this. Look I haven't told anyone before, except Crisis, but I was in love with Blue."

I nearly went through the floor. It was like everything had fallen apart. "But, I thought you... She was. That explains the perfume you gave her. I got the wrong idea, I thought you and I." I couldn't help it, I blurted it out.

"Chrys what are you saying?"

Now I was embarrassing. "I've got to go." I didn't know where I was planning to go.

"Don't you dare. Look this has come as a bit of a shock. Look we're still here, still together, still UHC. This was all so much more than I expected." He looked really worried as he pulled me back into the chair and I let him, like I was some rag doll.

Moonshine broke in. He was tall, thin, with a small goatee beard and brown curly hair. "We need people upstairs. Crisis is calling a meeting."

There was a woman I didn't recognise, white blonde hair, said her name was Angel but everyone kept whispering that her name was Freak. Even I had heard about the high tech silver cyberhand and there it was, beautifully made as her hands seemed to glide over the silver deck. I could see the netrunners stare, Vortex whispered, "That's a Crystal Deck, it's worth more than I can imagine and I can imagine a lot. You know what she's got in there, Archangel. The Soulkiller hunter. It's a chance. It gives us a chance to get in the net and get what we want and get back out again without getting fried."

Then, she chokes, then she spasms, the deck falls onto the cushion beside her as she falls onto the floor. I'd seen it before, so often, bleed out. Poor bitch, all her internal organs and blood vessels were exploding. But why? There was enough suppressant. He had to have taken it, she had to, everybody did. We were all wasting away, we knew it. I walked away, I couldn't watch. Doc Josh was there. I couldn't watch anymore, I just wanted to scream. This was the wrong way to go and too many people were just ceasing to exist this way if they didn't get the suppressant. No fault of their own and nothing they can do if they can't get the dose. The voices of friends vanished and gone. Black and whispery as the rain. Weren't those the words from a song. I didn't feel like music. Too right though there aint no angel going to greet me, it's just you and me my friend. The disease was in all of us. We had committed no crime, done nothing but it was there, in our blood. Our only sin was having a developed immune system. That was why it didn't hit the Domers so badly. Bastard, Jared Matthews, just one chance, let the only person I willingly kill be him. Put me in a room with him and he would know what pain felt like. I'd feel no sorrow seeing that bastard die. For once in my life I might give up the fight against this internal desire to rip hell out of those who really do push their luck. Just one chance.

Perhaps I ought to explain this. Not killing people doesn't mean that I don't want to. Or that I don't think that they deserve it. I just happen to value life, it's the most beautiful gift anyone ever has. It is all they will ever have that is truly their own. It is why giving birth to you was the most wonderful thing I could ever do. It is the sign that we will always carry on. I have seen people who deserve to get what is coming to them but somehow I know that life will deal with them. It is in their lack of peace. I know that I have all I will ever need. I didn't have to kill anyone to get it. I didn't have to steal or lie or cheat. It makes what I have so very special. I'm no saint, far from it. But by god I'm real and what I have is real and what I believe is real.

How something like the plague could be set free on us. It was something I firmly believed, that it was engineered by the PLEX to wipe out the people on the streets. It's just a thought, it kept creeping into my mind.

It is seeing her face again, in memory. One minute glorious, hands flying over the exquisite deck, the next gone, just because she didn't take suppressant. Like a broken doll she was carried away to be disposed of.

This was just a thought, we have the AI. How would a full confession from Jared Matthews sort out the situation? How about if he told the populous what he had done and why he had done it? The AI is his brain, it can mimic his look, his manner, his voice. How would that change things? The truth has to be free but what would riots in the domes cause other than to make them suffer as much as us and that wold make us as bad as him. No, that is no answer.

The choices we have, its poetic justice. We know how to fight, we know how to survive but do we know how to live? When I first met Doc Harley I saw him as a man of vision, a man who cared. That is something I admired. Now I've seen him go to pieces too often. He's no leader, even I can see that. We need someone who is going to be strong, who is going to listen to reason and to the voices of people and consider what is right. Perhaps he can be that man again? Where are the heroes? We have a voice now, but who will be that voice? Will nobody take a stand? Trouble is that we don't really have any answers. Everything has been polarised into saving Ho Street for so long. What would we do about say the tenant farmers, the petrol station communities, the ecology and economy? The last thing we can do is to bring down the PLEX. It's a truth that is screamingly obvious, they have a rational power base, they have the basic needs of the countries sorted out. It's a problem that seems to reoccur. Just because someone is very wrong on some fundamental points doesn't mean they are totally wrong on everything.

Those were the thoughts when we first got access to Danforth. How different to the final decision? Have we become what we detested? We are sealing the fate of billions and by what right?

Oh God, let us make the right choices now in these last hours. We are just ordinary people, all we needed and wanted was to be left alone. Why did he have to destroy the street? If he had been able to accept it he could have made life so much better for the street people for very little cost. I wouldn't have taken much to have started trading with the fixers, subsidising the bars to make repairs and clinics and getting people on side. He could have rebuilt but he chose to destroy. I think there was an offer for everyone to move into the dome. I don't remember it. I wouldn't have gone anyway. I don't think anyone would, well a few perhaps. Well even if he did offer we obviously didn't take him up on it. My mind is in chaos, I can't sot this out at all.

Back at the Coop I left Lighting with Crisis and went downstairs with Jared. The smell of instant coffee and the sounds of quiet conversation drifting around the huge expanse of the Coop. It was easy to forget just how big that building was when you sit in a booth as I was, with Jared. It seemed almost intimate, that was it I think, it brought it all to a personal level, we were talking but the walls were plastic, it was not seeing the rest of the building and focusing on what we could see. It was a bit like our conversations. We could talk for hours and it was like nothing else existed.

It had got a lot quieter in the main trading area as well. Most of the stalls had actually packed away and the traders had drifted off. It was a chance to just sit, just for a while and let everything catch up.

The lights were dim, the blues and whites stark contrast to the huge strip lights that lit the main bulk of the hall. Jared sat with me, in silence. He was just sipping his coffee and relaxing back in his chair. It had been a long day and somehow we knew it was going to be a long night as well. It's so easy to forget how much that man has been through, he just deals with everything. He always seems to know what to say and even in his grief is handled with a dignity. He's a strange one. I just wanted him to be the first to speak.

He did, finally. "It's not going well is it?" He looked so sincere and I knew he wasn't talking about the day.

"Not on average, no." I didn't know what to say.

"We've got a long way to go. I've got some ideas though."

I tried to smile. "That's a start. What about the bar?"

"Belongs to the Yak now. I just get a salary."

"If you need a hand."

He stared, one of those world stopping stares that you know needs an answer. "You could help me run it."

"I've not had much experience as a barmaid."

He laughed. "I didn't mean that."

Somehow this made me awkward. "Got to get back alive first."

"Sure. Look we're pretty much committed to this eco stuff but what are we really doing? So I let them stay at the bar, it's a little bit I can do and I now you've done stuff."

"A little, not enough though. What is enough? I can't see the answer. You know I felt so, oh you know, when I found out about that Genoa place but lets face it, it was a wipe out. We lost Diane and pretty much 100% on the other side. What about the husband of the woman who gave me the overalls? She killed her husband and she's never going to know it. I hope she doesn't anyway. So, he was a bastard to her and perhaps some would say he deserved it but it was a job and lets face it that gym was pretty pricey. She didn't mind taking and spending his money. Careless talk and all that. Cost his life. Consequences. Lets face it getting married these days is rare, so she didn't have kids but that doesn't mean much. There was no chance for reconciliation, no chance for anything. He could have been saving to get out, who knows? They were just ordinary people. That's the problem, even the PLEX, they don't have two heads or horns or a tail. What makes us right in what we do just because we are right in what we believe? They wanted to trade, we never did truly find out what they wanted did we?"

"Crisis I think."

"Why the hell is he so important, perhaps we are doing the right thing? Any idea why corporations want to get their hands on a DJ? His taste in music is pretty iffy sometimes."

"No idea. It's just the decay that gets to me. You know, you can see it on the faces. I get them coming into the bar, I have for so long. Why I wanted the Eryn in the first place, it's a place to go. Where do you go when your home has disintegrated and you don't belong anywhere. Sit in a musty crumbling flat and wait for the walls to cave in or get out and talk. But the talk, down and down that spiral,. How they're fed up with their lot. Not just money worries, would that it were, it sort of gets you down after a while. Some worries are so trivial, some so serious you just want to let them slip into that oblivion. Takes some doing on the watered down PLEX brand barrel stuff I get these days. It's like everything is so watery. I don't water down anything. Honest truth. But it arrives that way. PLEXBeer."

"So."

"So. Chrys, I've seen that look, what do you mean?"

"I mean I can get hold of better stuff."

"And…"

"Well, just run the other barrel from under the counter into the pump on one of the PLEXBeer pumps."

"No chance, can't risk getting shut down. Too many people need that place."

"Fair call."

"You can get me some more Saki though."

"Fair, I have a new contact for you. He could supply whatever you want. Haven't met him as he's a big name. I'll get him to call you."

"and what will that cost?" He looked concerned.

"You'll find out." I smiled but it soon faded.

"What's the matter? Something has been pulling you down all evening. I know you well enough for that."

"Lightning."

"But he's back, doesn't that solve it all."

"No."

"Why?"

"Because he's in love with someone else."

"Sorry Chrys, don't know what to say."

"That manure occurreth. I think we both know that."

"Hey kid, don't let it get you down. This hellhole is bad enough. A least you're not married to him."

"Yea, fair point, forgot about that one. What about the Rave? Are you much up for that?"

"No. Not really, not really in he mood. Look, I don't know what you think about synthetics but she was my daughter. I don't care who created her. I was proud of her, you know, when she got her job, when she met Drake. She had a life and was building herself a future. When she came to the Eryn that afternoon I couldn't be prouder."

"Yea, I remember her, nice looking girl."

"Damn straight, and devoted to flying. Why she didn't just use a remote I don't know."

"Because her dad was on board. She cared." I was trying to help but I didn't know what to say.

"They aren't supposed to you know."

"I know a bit about all that, about the incept date being to stop them getting a personality."

"What about humans who live so long that they stop caring. A bit of a role reversal don't you think? She was all the daughter I ever wanted, synthetic or not, what the hell was the difference?"

"I guess I've been guilty of being caught up in the old prejudices from time to time. Then I had never met one... I mean I didn't know she was."

"She was a very advanced model, escaped from Chiba and lived for about a year before I caught up with her. Well, I sort of ran into her I suppose. I saw someone in trouble in the alley, jumped in to help her then found out I was supposed to retire her and she was next on my list. Trouble was that I'd spoken to her, got to know her and hell she was so real. I couldn't do it. I lost my job over it. I think it brought about the end of my marriage as well. Jezlyn is a corporate dream, you know, housewife, worker, wouldn't buck the system. Then her husband goes and adopts a synthetic and when it all goes to shit at home he moves out of he Dome to Ho Street. You know what she wanted that afternoon?"

I shrugged, feeling a little uncomfortable with the conversation but glad he could share. "No, she seemed pretty angry."

"I was late with her cheque. She earns nearly twice what I do and the bitch comes down to the Ho to have a bitch about her blood money. It's worth it to be rid of her."

I was about to say that he didn't mean that but, I don't know, I sort of accepted that he did. I don't know about what it would be like to live with him, well I didn't know then. Jezlyn and I were so different. She needed and wanted him home, we just have to live day to day.

I was conscious of movement. Moonshine, packing away the booth next to us. He looked up. "Sorry, go to get some of this stuff moved away for the rave."

I was conscious of Crisis. He was with someone I didn't recognise. Shorter than him, wearing a waistcoat. They seemed very pally, I went over. "Hey Chrystal, met Domino."

So that was the florist. He seemed nice enough in the few moments I had before he went symptomatic. Great, I meet him, he falls over and then I find myself outside the Coop, in a ruin of a building with Domino's body and a quickly built funeral pyre. It was what Crisis wanted. So, Crisis, Lightning and myself stood in silent witness as another member of the UHC was no more. It's hard to get upset about someone you don't know. I think I was getting a bit numb to it all anyway.

Crisis had a scrap of paper he was looking at intently. There was something that we were looking for a the time and I can't remember what it was. I now that it was important to Vortex and Azrael as well because all of them wanted to go and check out the name and address. I did what I had to, knowing that I had no SIN number, and that they were barcoding. I went out with them. I would keep my promise to Diane, yes Crisis was pretty stupid but we had to do these things. I guess now I do need that good bodysculpt.

So, we called a Combat Cab and drove off into the night, to get caught by the first roadblock. I thought about making a break for it but it was too closed off a road. If I had got out of the cab they would have been able to get me with long range weaponry. So, I had to stay put and get out at the roadblock. Anonymity went by the board, I got barcoded and it stung like hell, physically and emotionally. Just one more tattoo to join my little collection. Still, wouldn't be to difficult to get rid of it. If it was to the bone then they would have to take some of the bone too. There had to be a surgeon out there who could do it. I bet that Slater could have done it. But he was gone too.

So we go to a tenement block and make like the old fashioned SAS. Up the stairs, covering each other, kick in the door and there is a woman with a small child. The woman tries to get away, we catch her and scare the living daylights out of her. Then we find out that she is Domino's woman and that the child is theirs. Guess Crisis' information about him being gay was a bit off then. We had just half scared the poor woman to death. Just another Crisis cock up. Not the best way for her to hear that Domino was dead either. I caught the child as it tried to run. It was the first time I held a small child, albeit that it tired to get away and scratched me. It felt so strange holding someone so small. So fragile. It must be a woman thing, I felt so strange about it, it was like a warmth inside, as the kid calmed down. Of course it ran back to its mother when I put it down but at least it went back to the flat. Crisis gave her money. That wouldn't help on the lonely nights but it would give the child a better chance.

We went back to the Coop, tails between our legs, feeling pretty fed up with ourselves but glad to get inside those patched up walls.

I hadn't been back long when there was gunfire outside. Heavy calibre. Guns emerged from everywhere, carefully hidden or just holstered under clothing and the mood changed from sitting around chatting to running around loading up as we went. The distinctive slide and click of clips slipping into automatics and the whurr click of revolvers to the heavy thump of rifles. Well-practised, these were Ho Street people, most of the locals had gone by now.

I got to the stairs, crouching with Jared and a couple of others. There were Spirals in the main room downstairs. I got to the door at the bottom of the stairs, opened it a crack. Daniel and Gridlock stood in front of the main door, the last of the spirals cut down by a beautiful clean blow from Daniel's sword. The body hit the floor as Daniel finished the elegant arc. He brought the blade forwards, changed his stance from combat blow to resting and ran a cloth over his blade before sheathing it. The hum of Gridlock's chainsaw became a splutter and they looked at each other. At their feet four dead Spirals.

Tables had been turned over, people were tentatively unwinding out of crouching positions and staring into the dark room, all the lights had been put out.

Jared was behind me. "Chrys, why don't you keep on the stairs. If we need to retreat we'll need you for covering fire."

I was glad to take this option, it meant that I might just manage to avoid killing anyone. I really had no idea why I was staying there, the likelihood was that when or if it came to it I'd have a real problem what I was there to do. All part of it I suppose, I wanted to be there with them but I wasn't prepared to compromise my values.

The air seemed to be getting thin, I could feel that rush of adrenaline, it was like a buzz that ran through me, emotions running from one mood to the next. There were holes in the banisters so the stairs were a good place to take up covering fire, if that door opened and we didn't recognise someone then whoever it was would meet a hail of gunfire. The back door was covered, I heard a shout, can't remember from who, it was a good position to cover anyway. The stairway was open metal, it would be almost impossible to get to the top without getting shot. That was the plan.

All hell broke loose. Gunfire, screaming, something heavy hit the door and the door opened and Jared backed through, carrying Crisis. I had no idea he was down there. We'd been too busy to notice. I was so sorry, I had promised Diane and I'd lost him somewhere in that confusion. I had just assumed he was upstairs. Now he was being carried upstairs, the blood pouring from his chest. Jared looked ashen white. "He just couldn't get out of the way, we took most of them down but it was point blank. Help me someone, get a medic."

There was a double coffin bed just beside the door upstairs. They laid him there. Crisis was out of it. Doc Josh crawled in him and began patching him up.

"Chrystal."

"Doc?" I crawled in beside him having a very big problem with the space and people. I started to feel sick and the walls were closing in. There was a small side door, I clicked it open. Runt's head poked through the hole.

"How is he?"

Both of us looked at Doc who was covered in blood and wildly spraying Crisis' chest with a white liquid. "Chrys, did you know he was on CPO? This little baby is a CPO pump and he's taken a direct hit. I'm getting the damage to the chest cavity sorted out, there's a lot of internal bleeding but it's the pump, its cracked and most of the CPO liquid has leaked out."

My head was spinning, from the space problem, from the adrenaline and the GA problem and now I was trying to cope with this as well. CPO, that means that Crisis isn't Crisis or he is but the body wasn't. What the hell, the body that was there was my friend Crisis, the CPO made him who he was but if the liquid was leaking away, the words "may not reboot" came to mind. "Doc, I didn't know. Can you do anything?"

I'm doing all I can, believe me. That should hold it. Just, but I need you to keep the pressure on this for me and time me 15 minutes. Then call me, get someone to come and get me. Just keep the pressure on."

It was dark in the coffin bed. I could hear Crisis breathing, it echoed in the musty air, rattling around in that damaged chest. Then the NewsNet reporter tried to crawl in with his camera and I really lost it. "Get the hell out of here. He needs space, can't you give him some privacy."

The reporter looked struck, his insistent expression fading to confusion. He backed off and stalked away.

I hadn't realised but there were tears running down my face. I didn't want Crisis to die. I was willing him to live with every part of me. He couldn't die. So many street kids had wanted to be like him, he had made a success out of nothing. So the real thing wasn't always as good as the image but, hell he didn't deserve all the problems that seemed to track him down. I watched the time and 15 minutes passed like the hands of the clock were running in treacle. Gunfire downstairs, the building rocked, bits of plaster and paper falling off of the walls. The structure wasn't sound enough to take this. We were in trouble.

Doc crawled back into the space and had a look. He shot more drugs into Crisis' chest cavity. "He's doing fine, well for someone in his condition. It's a mess. Hold on there Chrys."

More gunfire.

"He'll be coming out of it soon. Keep him quiet. Tell him what's happened and call me, I need information. Hang in there kid."

I had relaxed back against the wall of the coffin bed, my hands sticky with Crisis' blood, making a handprint on the clean dressing the Doc had put on the wound. I kept up the pressure.

Crisis moaned and opened his eyes. "Chrystal, what's going on?"

"You got shot. In the chest, it's cracked the CPO pump. I didn't know."

"Sorry Chrys, I thought you knew." He choked.

"Hey, take it easy, I'll call the Doc." He caught my hand.

"Thanks."

I wasn't sure what he was thanking me for but I'd take it for everything. "Doc!"

Doc crawled in just as there was another burst of gunfire downstairs. It was followed by a scramble of people being carried upstairs. Lightning was being carried too. Christ, I didn't know what to do. Crisis clung to my hand, Lightning lay on the floor opposite, blood pouring from his shoulder. The air was thick with the smell of cordite and blood. The lights flickered and it got darker. It was as if everything was closing in. Gunfire, almost constant. Someone bundled through the end door. I didn't recognise the voice, it was all getting so very crowded in the room. Legs obscured the entrance to the coffin room and the walls closed in. It was so very dark and all I could do was hold onto Crisis and hope. He was more lucid now and reaching for his drugs. Doc had done a really great job. The blood had stopped and the wound had been temporarily closed with medical sealant. Crisis saw Lightning and half sat up.

"Chrystal, go to him, he'll need you."

"No way I'm going to leave you." I wanted to get to Lightning, Crisis was out of danger now.

"Go… It matters, doesn't it?" He gripped my hand.

I turned to Runt who had been sitting there getting the reports and relaying them on. "Runt, could you take over here for a while?"

"Sure". She scrambled through the impossibly small hole as I edged my way down the side wall trying not to disturb Crisis who was far too busy selecting from his collection of pills and powers.

I crouched beside Lightning and he put his good arm around me. "Ouch!" He smiled and leant back against the wall.

"Baby!" I hissed at him. I don't know but I'd got myself so wound up that saying something like that seemed appropriate.

He turned his head towards me and brushed my hair back behind my shoulder with his uninjured arm.

Jared was to my right. He looked away before muttering. "I'd better get downstairs. We've lost the main room, it has been overrun. I put in a call to the Yak to ask fan to ask for an evac. Don't know if they are going to come up with anything. We aren't exactly their favourite people at the moment." He put a hand on my shoulder and went. I looked up and smiled at him as he turned away. Just don't let him get shot as well I thought.

Doc began work on Lightning's shoulder. "Nice piece of dermal armour, bit dented now though, better get it straightened out when we get out of this or the pressure will make your shoulder ache. Lot of blood there but nothing serious. Hard little bunny aren't you."

Lightning smiled and pulled on his jacket. Doc responded to a call down the corridor then stopped, grabbing a bed as he fell, choking, convulsing. We'd seen it so many times, he was going symptomatic. Panic and movement, screaming and gunfire downstairs. Gildae, the dog woman medic I haven't told you about yet who had been supplying us with suppressant leapt out from the corner where she had been treating a gunshot and opened her little box. It didn't take long to administer the white liquid but it seemed like an age. It was like every was moving very, very slowly.

It went quiet downstairs. It went quiet upstairs and the Ojabund's right hand man walked into the room. Silence, we knew we were going to be in trouble for this. An evac wasn't going to come for free. He turned to talk to Jared who had come up with him and then everything moved like a blur.

Crisis leapt out from his bed, off his head on something and shot the suit in the back of his legs then blew him away. Lightning and I just grabbed him. We had to get him out. I was conscious of Jared there as well. Crisis was just going crazy, he had his gun out an looked like he was going to use it on anyone. Somehow we bundled him to the back fire escape, climbing over people. Doc Josh was laying on the stairs, still gasping for breath as Crisis went down the stairs. I pushed in front of him, screaming at him that if he wanted to shoot them he would have to shoot me first. They hadn't done anything wrong apart from coming to get us out. If we could just get Crisis to a car the rest would get their evac. We would have to take our chances.

Staggering we got round to the back of the building. Lightning and Jared keeping us covered, Crisis looking for someone to kill. It had to be the drugs. Then this woman came from nowhere. I didn't recognise her, she was wearing a black Yak suit. I tried to stop her. I saw the suppressant vial in her hand, Crisis must have only seen her coming towards him. He turned and before we could stop him her head exploded in a shower of red. It was point blank, he couldn't miss. Another shot and Crisis staggered, a bullet blasting into his forehead, he staggered backwards as someone else fired. I realised it was Lightning and the Yakuza member who had shot Crisis hit the floor. Another gunshot and Lightning hit the floor. Crisis fell into my arms and I was conscious of Jared behind me. I lowered Crisis onto the floor, he was too heavy to carry. Lightning wasn't moving. I looked at Jared, he looked at me and I turned and faced the Yakuza. This had to stop. I realised my gun was in my hand, I had a clear shot, but to continue this was pointless. Nobody could win. I think they saw it too. For some reason they didn't shoot me although they had a clear shot.

Nothing made much sense at that point. I was bundled into the van with Crisis and Lightning. The doctors were working frantically on Crisis and I knew it was bad, very bad. There was blood everywhere and they had him wired up to the wall with so many different coloured wires. They had cut his jacket off and it lay beside me. I reached down and palmed the note from Diane and the CD-Rom and anything else that looked important. I couldn't look down, I just did it by touch. They would probably search me but if they didn't think it was his perhaps they would leave it with me.

The drive to the hospital seemed to take forever. I just sat there and watched as the medics did all they could. If I had been religious I would have prayed but I had nothing to help me. Just the blind faith that they would be alright. As the sleek black van sped through the night nothing stopped it. The convoy was well armoured and well-armed.

At the hospital Crisis and Lightning were taken away on trolleys and I was shown to a small room. A doctor came in. Oriental and polite, he bowed. Approaching with some caution he lifted my chin and looked into my eyes, lifting the lids. He pulled out a scanner and ran it over me. I didn't want to ask, I didn't want to speak to him.

"Chrystal, you are unharmed. You rest now." He clicked something on the scanner and it went dark.

I woke up on the street. No headache, the blood had been washed off of my hands and clothing. The Yakuza providing a laundry service yet again. Washed and delivered back onto the street. As to Lightning and Crisis, I had to get back to the bar to find out.

8

How I'd love to hear Lightning say "How about some music?" now. It somehow made the worries fade. His voice, the music, the smell of coffee, some things could be relied on to bring the mood back to what it should be. Old favourites, some new ones we'd written himself and the song they'd written for Original Sin. He'd picked up a tune whenever he heard one. There had been a time I'd hummed a tune to him. He'd then rewritten the music until it sounded really good. He'd adapted the words until it was something that really hit home. That was probably why Eve and the lads had liked it. It was as much a protest now as it was then. Original Sin was the band I had put together in the latter days of Ho Street. I'd been going under the name of Spirit then and had been overtly acting against the PLEX. The band, the gigs, the slogans, a big fight back just before it all went to hell. The music Lightning had written had the rhythm of the street but something else, it was ours.

Poor Eve, I wonder what happened to her. She probably died in the wipe out of the Ho.

Eve had been the lead singer and there had been a venue booked for the night and she'd have been mid gig when it hit. Oh well, at least some guys went out to music. She wouldn't have wanted it any other way if she had to go. Strange how everything got tainted, music, life, everything. Nothing was pure anymore, not even the music. After all, the PLEX did pretty much control the media. Try getting anything without its logo emblazoned on it. The fat cat got fatter, until the bubble burst, until that moment. Music was the colour of the street and PLEX had owned that too.

Then there was Dynas Emrys.

Not quite a night like any other. I have to admit I was really keen to see what Tictac had been talking about. I will remember the taste of that fresh water always. It was just so unlike anything I had ever tasted, not like the synthesized drinks, not like the bottles of PlexMax. No, this was something else and I couldn't describe it. It was a bit like a dream. The grievous angel had been getting at me lately, it dragged me down even lower, the ever downward spiral. My head rocked so much with the drug, with the beatings I kept getting just for causing trouble. I needed something so badly, the whole world was beginning to swim around me. I think everyone was beginning to get the idea, contacts were falling away like rain, who would trust someone like me? I don't seriously know why this lot did. What had happened to the Chrystal they had known? She had been worth knowing, she had the contacts, she had the value. Everything has a price, mine had gone through the floor.

Jared wasn't anywhere around that night, neither was Lightning. Bill had been clinging to me like glue, but then he really wanted to go on this little trip and he was using me as a reference. I don't know, I really wasn't sure about recommending him. The only hope I had was that if he was doubtful this might just swing him to do something worthwhile, to fight for us. No, not us, for himself. This world belongs to all of us, not just those who care about it or own huge chunks of topsoil.

Some hope but I guess that is all we have ever had. I couldn't help feeling that night, through the haze, through the anger that there was something out there and I really, really needed it. I needed some hope back when the world was so black and it was dragging me down. There is only so much you can take, even if you are fighting for a cause, before you sit in that corner and think why? I was thinking why now, very much.

All I could do was to hope that I would get something from that visit, something from what Tictac had offered.

Night was falling, I sat at a table watching the people come and go. It wasn't a busy night but you could see through the crowd and tell who was getting ready to go with Gildae. Gildae and Tictac had found a cosy table for two and were making the most of their time. She seemed really happy with him and in a way it was great to see. Chuckles, Runt, I can't remember, do you know I just can't remember who was there. I can't remember who was going. That time was just so clouded in the darkness of the drug and the way I felt.

I sat on my own, I think everyone had the general idea that I wanted to be on my own. I felt like that a lot and it had been getting more and more difficult for anyone to talk to me. I didn't want it that way. I didn't understand it at all. The whole world was swimming around me like it was unreal and I just needed something solid I could hold onto, some reason for all this.

Gildae came over, she put a hand on my shoulder, carefully and I remember looking up at her. Her eyes kind, dark brown under her huge floppy hat, a sort of extended beret with a peak. She looked so human, the only hint that she was Dogclan being her elongated jaw. I'd just got so used to her I didn't notice that any more. I suppose I had, when she had brought the suppressant to the Coop but I think we were all just focusing on that little silver box she carried. She smiled, she had the sort of manner, I don't know, it was a lightness. She always had had. She whispered. "It's time.".

I picked up my small bag without a word and followed the little group of people out of the front door and onto the piece of waste ground. Except it wasn't waste ground anymore. Over the past couple of days Jared had had a couple of tents erected. Their back walls were solid, just for a little protection but the roofs were canvas. It made the outside area more useful though and some of the bares had already started making use of the tables out there.

Nothing made much sense. Lightning had wandered off into the night somewhere, he had taken what had happened to Crisis badly. If the truth be told I think the bullet he took hurt more than he made out. He never said anything but then he wouldn't. I still liked him around but we had become a lot more distant since the Coop. We had to be, but I think it was probably more from my point of view, looking back on it now. I think he had been closer than ever and that may have had a lot to do with the absence. I had been keeping my distance.

There was an AV waiting on the forecourt. A bit up front I though but then we had a long way to go and we could easily lose any tail.

Lights blurred as the AV drove along the Ho. Life flowed around us, the reds and greens of vehicle lights and the yellow tenement lights stretching to the sky. Black and inky sky draining its black oily stickiness onto the streets. The sound of the water under the tyres and silence. Nothing but the cries of the crowds, gunfire and the sounds of the City, of home.

My home, this was it. Black and grey and cold, so very cold. I couldn't stop shaking, my hands, my body. I clung to the metal wall of the AV, feeling the tears streaming down my face. For what, for who? I had nothing left. My independence, my attitude, that was all I had ever had. What had they done but destroy me by making me care. Care for what though? To cry over them when they get shot. Perhaps to calm someone's lonely night and think I'm their angel of the moment in the future? In my wildest dreams I knew there was more to life than this. The cold of the metal wall chilled my cheek, my wet hair clung to my face. I was going somewhere, I couldn't remember where, I had to remember where. It was like anything important was slipping away from me. I was trying to hold onto it all. I could sit by the keyboard and throw the words at the screen, if they made any sense now I don't know. If anyone had read SINless, how would I know? It was only my views anyway. What did I want? That had never really been an issue before. Survival had been all. That, loud music and the talking. You now, just spending time with people with views, people that had something to say. You leave the night feeling you have gained and given. Something shared, not the polite conversation I had heard in the Domes, not the dead rolling out of designer's names and tired ideals of PLEXgiven religion. No, the voice of those who know who thy are and what they talk about. Not the pretty and the pampered, the survivors.

Would death bring peace from this? This demon that rests inside me. The wildness that made me want to tear at the walls. To run at them, feel the pain when I hit and slide down. The anger that made me hate those that I love and believe that all they did had some sort of plot behind it. I knew they had no great plan to get control over me. It was just the drug, just the street, just life. One huge spiralling plughole and we were all being dragged down it even if we didn't know it.

Lights thinned out, the noise got less until the AV stopped. Time to move, shaken from watery thoughts, all thought, all ideas were sinking into a treacle slowness of unreality. I walked like I was in a dream. I saw the seats tilted up, the belts hanging on the ground, the metal floor, the flashing lights but it meant nothing. I couldn't focus, I couldn't see it for what it was. Familiar scenes, sights and sounds meant nothing. I was sinking lower into the sea of oblivion.

Bill caught my arm, I felt his strong grip and just went with him. I know there were still tears running down my face but what did I care, what pride was left, what hope, what part of the Chrystal that had run the alleys with such arrogance. Nothing. I nearly fell out of the AV. Bill caught me and somehow we got into the Airborne Vehicle and I was strapped in and the world got smaller below me for a while. Like I could leave it behind, spiralling into the air, the feeling of ascending, like a spirit to heaven, then the euphoria of the movement through the clouds and the steady jolt as gunfire bounced off the outer hull. Until we left the Ho behind.

Then I looked down on darkness, like hell was below us or nothing. So far to fall but then we'd fallen so far already. The thoughts flowed like the rain on the Ho, dark, polluted and without the hope of promoting any growth other than the dark mire that was there already.

Another window, another dark scene. The bump as the plane landed and we stepped out. Nothing changed, just another drop, another long walk through tired streets. But there weren't any streets, I looked up, towering on either side of me into the distance, trees. I could smell them, I could smell the grass. My head rocked and I tried to hold it together to feel what I was seeing. That was it, this was what we were fighting for. Not a dream, the chance of a future, what the Eden Dream really meant. I walked, my feet like lead, my body broken from too many fights. It was like I carried a great weight with me. I'd read something lately, like carrying my own cross to Golgotha. Every step drained my soul, be it on grass or not. I'd had enough, I'd had nowhere else to go. Just to fight on now. Was I really fighting though? Was I making any kind of a difference? There weren't any real goals either, any real victories other than those we assumed we gained ourselves, that and places like this still being there.

I felt the warmth of the huge bonfire and sat on a wooden bench. Everything swam together. Were they Wombats? They wore tartan, no, not black and white, all colours. I heard words, words of hope. It was really strange to hear people speak in such a way. It had been hours and the hours had drifted away. Now they walked around the fire and they spoke, the power and passion, of the earth, of saving it and of what we were doing.

Hope, that was what was screaming at us. It was what echoed in my ears, fool bitch, I was building my own cross and crucifying myself on it. The power we needed, it was nothing more than we had been born with and the lessons that the street had taught us. They were a family, they fought, they were arrogant, there was no difference, this is humanity. We were a part of it all, not some alien race. Our reactions were animal in a way, envy, fear, hate and the will to fight. Not destructive in its base form, only when encased in concrete and given nowhere to go. We are by nature tribal. It was so easy to see it from a distance. Look at the street, look at the clans, they are no different to any tribes I had read about. They still battled between themselves for power, for place and for a mate. When they got that mate then they had to defend him or her from all comers, care for him or her and make sure that the family survived. Not just that the power is with the women. It's a primal need for the world to survive. Just a need to make the men fight so that the strong survive to care for the women and keep the line pure.

Gildae spoke, like the others but of the dragon. I remember the dragon, I had seen her fly. I'd seen her cry blood, in my dreams she had called me and I had thought nothing of it, in my dreams I had seen her, now I knew who she was, she had a name, Gaia. Gildae spoke about the dragon of the earth and as she spoke a white light fell from the sky. The sky was so clear. A dark blue natural dome. Was that what Jared Matthews was trying to do, imitate her? Would he build his own heaven and make himself a god. The star fell, from the heavens, blazing its way to the earth. Where it fell I don't know, back towards the Ho I think. It's tail yellow and orange against the black sky.

So the dragon fell to earth. It was all very strange, very new. We were welcome here, it was very different. No buildings, just the sky for a roof and the fire cracking its sparks up to the heavens.

There was a woman, I don't remember her face, it was shrouded in shadow but her voice was deep and slow. The people there, they listened to her. So when she spoke to me I listened. I didn't know what I heard. She spoke of a man, a good man, a man who waited for me to get home. She saw a long coat and a gentle expression. I saw confusion. I knew who she meant. It was like something cut through the cloud, through the voices and the anger and screamed at me, listen. I listened and all I could see was one thing I had been missing for so very long. As she said, go home to him. That was what I wanted to do so badly, just go home to him.

Nothing else seemed to make sense.

My head ran wild with thoughts. Not just what I had seen, what I had heard. It was a cold biting terror that now that I had the truth in my hands I wouldn't be able to do anything about it. That was the way of the world, I had seen it happen so often to others, and in old films though why they should matter I don't know. I didn't want it to happen to me. I just wanted to see if there was something in what the woman had said, or was she just a raving lunatic. Hours, in two hours I would know and somehow it scared me.

Holding onto any kind of hope in the world is hard enough. It is almost as if as soon as you dare to hope that is when it goes really wrong. Daring to believe in something is the greatest invitation to be shot in the back or watch someone you love be shot. All attachments were risky and on average to be avoided. Was I being totally stupid thinking the way I was, was I sealing my death warrant?

The plane's engine hummed away the miles and I couldn't talk to anyone. My mind was all over the place, fear, excitement, curiosity, all there. I kept hearing the words, "someone is waiting for you". The feelings were still there, chemically induced depression, spiralling me down to the thoughts that it was just another way of getting at me. Anyway, why was it bothering me, I'd seen Jared a hundred times. It was just her description. Was I just hoping that it was him? We hit some turbulence, looking out of the window I could see the mountains of Wales so far below, they were moving so slowly. That was the problem, the flight wasn't that long, we just had to work our way round into safe airspace or risk getting blown out of the air. Nearing the Ho was the most dangerous part. The vehicle had a faulty hover function so we had to allow for plenty of space to get down. Then again we had to be armed and ready when we did, the pilot would only drop us for a few minutes, the zoners would dearly love to get hold of his plane and he wasn't about to let that happen.

Gildae and Tictac sat behind me, I could hear them whispering to each other but I couldn't hear what they said, didn't want to pry either. The dark green faded to grey-black as the sun went down and we flew over the urban sprawl. Circling the Ho the gunfire just looked like tiny fireflies, burning brightly for a moment then nothing. Somewhere a building burnt, somewhere else a car turned on its side exploded scattering the crowd that sheltered behind it.

So far below, so far away from the peace and beauty of Wales but we had seen something, something worth fighting for. We couldn't rest there, we had lives elsewhere. We could no more rest there than in heaven. For our sins we were some kind of hope for this world. I caught my reflection in the window. Somehow I didn't look so drained anymore, so tired. There was something in my face I hadn't seen before. I felt warm inside, excited like awaiting a gunfight. The plane wheeled, levelled out, descended, bumped and we were on the ground. Seatbelts off we hit the concrete at a run. In moments the aircraft was in the air again and we were running for cover of the nearest alleyway.

Slapping Bill Haley on the shoulder I cut off into a side alley and headed for the minor zoo I called a flat, just to see if the cockroaches had missed me. I knew that the day I started giving them names was the day I would shoot myself.

There was a firefight going on outside so I slipped around the back and shinned up what was left of the fire escape. Once on the rusting landing I leapt through a broken window and went to my door. It had been jemmied unlocked again, it stood on the jar. I listened, it was quiet, I pulled out my faithful berretta and pushed the door open. A bit incautious but I was fairly sure they had gone, still I flicked the safety off. They had and it didn't look as thought the place had been touched. Then again I didn't keep anything there in any case. All I had was in the bag on my back. I flicked the safety back on and while I wondered about all this I looked at myself in the broken mirror that was nailed to the wall. I pulled out a comb and dragged it through my matted hair. I hadn't been taking much care of myself since the Coop had gone down. I don't know why, there was no reason I suppose, other than my general pissed-off feeling I had against the world. Still, I took a breath, sighed and pulled out the battered bag full of make up and did what I could to cover up the grazes and bruises.

I hadn't done a bad job, even though I say it myself. Even pulled out a clean T-Shirt. I looked at myself and laughed. Then decided not to as crows feet were far more noticeable when I did that. Still, that is what the street does to you, it takes your youth, it takes your energy and spits out what it doesn't need and you get to live with that. Well I could live with it. I swung my bag over my shoulder and kicked the door open, stepped through and pulled it shut behind me. There was still nothing there. I'd been crashing at Jared's Bar or the Kitchen, there was precious little point really keeping it on, especially now that someone was breaking in regularly. The building was noisy, even above the gunfire on the street I could hear a couple two doors away arguing, somewhere someone screamed and a gun went off. I shook my head and strode along the threadbare carpeted hallway and shinned down the fire escape and disappeared off into the street.

Peripheral vision, that is all you need. They should write a song about that. I was humming something as I made my way to the bar, keeping to the safer alleyways. I didn't really feel like a fight. Didn't get one either which surprised me, it was a quiet night. Just two dead zoners, Wardogs I think, and a woman wandering aimlessly muttering something about a brown box. I ignored her and carried on, through the streets, through the back of what had once been a shopping mall, jumping over the concrete wall which got in the way of a really neat short cut I had found a while back. I ran for cover under the concrete walkway, crawled through a wire fence and ran up a bank neatly avoiding all the broken glass, sheets of rusting metal and broken down cars. There was enough cover for someone to be hiding, and enough for me to hide if necessary. Somewhere a dog barked and I stopped in my tracks. It had been years since I had heard a dog, well a real one. There was something about it's bark too, that was no dog. It was likely that one of the Dog Gangs was working the area.

The street glistened with distinctively black oily sheen, rainbows of green and blue swirling in the pools, engine oil. It sticks to your boots, covering them with a film. Reflecting and distorting the signboards advertising SimStim. Aztech's face still so popular, be it a bodysculpt or old footage, it was hard to tell. With simulation there isn't much need for the real thing anymore but try telling that to Doc Harley. We all have our loves but for him his SimStim Queen, real, not some adoration from a lustful fan.

We all have our wants and our needs, every one of the faceless creatures that pass me by. Even the crackhead leaning against the broken post. Sights and sounds, the people walking by and the hum of the traffic and the splash of feet on the soaked pavement. Plastic dressed SINless tarts hanging around doorways, part undressed, showing off their wares.

They were OK I suppose, hadn't actually got to know anyone like that, just on the occasion when I'd needed information. They are in a position to know a lot which gives them power. I knew a few down the East End of Ho but that was before the Mission opened up. They've all but moved on now, plying their trade on new turf. They pretty much know everyone that moves about the Ho and its their business to know where they are coming from, if you know what I mean. Each of their own perversion I suppose. They don't generally make enemies, it's bad for business.

What with the Mission and the Yakuza, they had all but gone. I think most of them moved into warehouses down by what used to be the canals, my old stamping ground when it used to be warehousing for goods and a hub of commerce. There's some pretty nice little hovels around that way, sort of secluded if you don't mind the damp. They move in and the associated trade shifts there as well. Pimps, dealers and others, but it gets them off of the main street. Still, there were at least three or four working from doorways within 100yards of Jared's. I'd seen them in the bar but they weren't encouraged. They were too keen to sell information which was not healthy for them. A few disappeared in the earlier days and I think they got the message. Some information is not for selling. YumYum had made a bit of a difference as well or so I had heard before I went off to Wales. No doubt I would be hearing more.

It was busy when I stepped out onto the Ho. Joining in with the flow I went back to the bar. A couple of women hung about outside, their short leather skirts reflecting the neon signs. They smiled, I didn't recognise them and I thought it strange that they were being so open. They were either from off the Ho or completely off their rockers. I was about to say something but stopped. You just can't tell people. As I stepped into the bar I heard gunfire, I looked back. Its never wise. The bar was almost empty. Yali and Shade sat in a quiet corner together. They looked worried, then they always did. Daniel was by the door, silent as ever he turned and I couldn't believe it, he almost smiled! I gave him a big grin and strode past. Most people were out the front by what I could gather. Then tents had been reinforced to sheds and opened up and there was a fire burning in a large oil can. I stopped in my tracks when I saw Jared.

He looked up. "Chrystal, I've been waiting for you." The words stopped me in my tracks. It was alike a huge expanse had opened up in front of me and suddenly everything was very bright. It was like I was in a spotlight. I'd always thought the bar dark, not that night, it wasn't actually any brighter I don't think, I don't know. It just felt different. I was moving, my legs carried me to the bar.

To this day I can't remember my exact words. Typical Chrystal forwardness no doubt. I just told him that I missed him. He stepped around the bar and I felt like my legs were going to buckle. He'd never been this close before, not when I was actually thinking about him. I could smell the gun oil. I could feel the warmth of his body, so very close to mine as he put his arms around me. I didn't know what to do, I was beginning to panic but it was what I wanted, really what I wanted so I looked up at him, into those blue eyes and something happened. It was like a shift. It was like nothing existed in the bar. No peripheral vision, no caution, I was oblivious. He bent down, I could feel his breath on my mouth, then our lips met and it was like in a moment my life came together. Then we remembered where we were.

I looked up and Birdie was sitting there, her distinctive short dark red hair, brown fringed jacket and big black boots, grinning at me. "You two will get yourselves shot if you go on like that. Does this mean that you two have finally got your act together?"

That I hadn't considered. I hadn't considered any of it really. I just felt so very comfortable with it all. He looked at me, I looked at him and it all seemed very unreal. Bravado took over and I just looked him in the face and said something like. "I guess we're on for tonight then."

He mouth fell open and I couldn't help laughing. He closed his mouth and smiled. "Guess so."

There are things to remember always, the music in the bar, yet again it would never feel that way again, ever. Leaning on the bar, Jared making every possible excuse to come back and talk to me, and to take time off to stand on my side of the bar. Nothing different was said but it was like everything was on a different level. It didn't take long for time to pass and now I was really worried. It was like up to this point nothing had really mattered and now I had something I really didn't want to lose.

Jared leaned closer. "Tonight I really don't care if they close the bar early. I'm going to throw everyone out anyway. Just tonight. Some do live here but the rest…"

The door slammed shut, I know, I slammed it. Shutting out the world. I think Jared took pleasure in that, letting me lock up. I turned around and leaned on the door.

"Pull the bolts across." He said it with conviction.

"I thought the bar side door was always open."

"No, not now you're inside. I sort of got used to you coming and going. You were the only one who used it. I'd rather shut the world out now."

The large bolts slid into place and it felt good. The chill of metal, the resistance as they fitted into metal rings, three of them. The back door was already locked and bolted. I stepped back and he was there, I could feel the warmth of him against my skin, through the black silk of my shirt. I turned, putting the world behind me. The bar lay illuminated with a gentle blue glow, most of the UV lights were turned off, the stereo playing Portishead…

I took a deep breath, smelling the smoke and the bar smells but mostly the subtle smell of his aftershave that I had never noticed before. There was something so comforting about it as Jared held me close and whispered. "Welcome home Chrystal." I hadn't thought about that. No point going into all that now, that wasn't what I meant by all this. Panic set in but he lifted my chin and he bend down just as the door to the back rooms opened and Gildae stuck her head in. Jared froze, Gildae froze too, apologised and backed off.

The bar might have looked empty but we would have been fooling ourselves if we had believed we were on our own, the rest of the building wasn't. To get any privacy we would have to negotiate the stairs, get past the back room and the kitchen and avoid getting into any conversations which inevitably lasted all night. I hadn't realised how many people actually lived at the bar.

Fair enough, it was always like this. Most people did their work at night so the bar could pretty much be open 24 hours. We gave up closing the bar. People were still streaming in, in ones and twos but I didn't take much notice of them. They came to the door at the front and we had to let them in. Where else could they go?

I slipped out back for some peace and refilled the coffee urn. I caught the reflection of Jared behind me in the dented chrome. He wouldn't sneak up behind me, he had more sense. He was just waiting and watching. I put the container down and got grabbed and spun round. He laughed, kissed me and mumbled. "Domesticated."

"Not even house trained, so don't even think about it." I wasn't being serious, how could I be? For the first time in a very long time I felt really comfortable about life. Almost to the point of relaxing a little and believing that we did stand a chance in this crazy world. The air was getting thin, I don't know how. I felt incredibly light headed and my head started to spin. I hadn't felt like that before. Well not unless you were talking about witnessing some serious fight or dangerous situation. Was this dangerous? About the most dangerous situation I have ever been in. It was me on the line this time.

Crisis was outside the door shouting. He had his gun out and as I crossed the room he pointed it. I found myself looking down the barrel of the gun and that was it. When I slept that night I had dreams of this sort of thing, it was like a spell cast over me. Two worlds coming together, the rational one and the drug induced haze, like a red mist. Part of me just wanted to cling to Jared and get him to hold me until it was all over. Part of me knew that that gun was pointing at me, there was no rational thought as Crisis wouldn't do that. I was close enough to look him in his eyes and he was wild. I remember reaching in front of Jared and my fingers touched his shotgun. He stepped back, a reflex action and my nails scraped ineffectually down the metal as I felt a sharp pain in my neck and I fell backwards.

Darkness then light, metal, the smell of the musty mattress as I came round in the Yakuza tech room, laying on one of the bunk beds. Walls of chrome equipment levers, dials, and screens. Jared was sitting on the bed, he had been stroking my hair, it was the first thing I felt as I came round.

Shade was in the room. I lay there with my eyes shut for while. He seemed very agitated. "Saul and Nazareth are in the bar."

Who were they?

"That's all we need. What are they here for?" Jared sounded really upset.

"Jared, Saul's my brother."

"What?"

"We all have our past. I was an Adroid Hunter's Netrunner. He was the brawn in the family."

"But not now?"

"Not now, they are here to get us back. He's going to want to talk to you." I could feel the tension in Jared's arm.

"That life is over."

"We're going to have to convince them of that. Another thing."

"What? There's always another thing…"

"My sister's turned up at the bar. She's tanked on Crystal Mist." His voice was shaky.

I racked my brains, damn, that was one bitch drug. It was technically a recreational or should I say terminally unpleasant recreational, that end game fun for the psychotic. Guaranteed lethal, addictive first hit if you live for a second. Lethal long term anyway. Another cellular addiction.

"She's in a bad way. She's survived the first hit and has been doing all she can to get it. I mean anything. It's simple isn't it, I go back with them and Saul makes sure that she gets the right treatment."

"There's got to be another way."

"Your going to have to talk to them."

The sensation had come back into my legs and I managed to sit up. "What happened?"

"Good to have you back." He lifted me down off of the bunk. "Crisis was being an asshole and your little problem decided to sort him out. Don't worry, he's fine." There was a little venom in his voice. There was one very worried Jared. "Come on, lets see what's going on."

"Sure." I felt odd. I rubbed my neck. It was a bit sore and I was light headed. I followed Jared out into the bar.

The side door flew open and Tayl staggered in, carrying Doc Harley. He'd been missing for a very long time apparently. He was obviously in a bad way. It was all happening that night. One thing after the next. Just another busy night on the Ho.

Eva, a medic I had met a few days ago followed the BFA crew into the side room, the one just off the bar. It was a bunk room, I'd never actually been in there up until that point. I followed them in and crouched beside Doc who lay there. Eva was checking him out so I let him know I was there. It was really "soft" you know, a really pathetic thing to do, but then I was doing a lot of things that really weren't the old me. Not that Doc was conscious enough to know I was there.

Slipping out into the bar I shut the door and ran into Vortex. He walked with me out into the courtyard at the front. He had that look, the serious I'm going to be up to something look and it was always best to find out exactly what he was up to. "I know how to get rid of Saul and Nazareth. It will take time though, will you give me a hand in a while."

"Sure, whatever." I had seen something I didn't like. Jared was stepping into the back room with the two Android Hunters. It was like the world fell away. The bar looked so strange as I walked inside. The blue white glow engulfed me but it was like I was in a dark tunnel. They were going to take him away. Lightning was standing by the door, he caught my arm and looked down at me. He just seemed to know something and wasn't going to tell me. I wanted to go into the back room and throw the unwanted guests out of my life.

Lightning, a voice of reason that cut through the mist of depression, the complete despair I was feeling at that point. How could I expect to keep Jared, I'd lost everyone else. I was tearing at the walls, not physically and I think only Lightning knew what was really going on. It was like he had got some sort of link into my emotions. He patted his jacket, I knew the berretta was there. He bent down and whispered in my ear. "Stay close, they won't take him and he won't go."

"How can you be sure?" My voice was slightly higher pitched than I remembered it.

"Chrystal, do you need to ask?"

I didn't, I suppose I knew the answer, I just wasn't going to have that much faith in myself, in everything we were doing and what the bar meant to him. After all, I hardly knew the man. There was an attraction but even from conversations you can never really know what is going on in someone's head.

I don't now what was said in that room. I have never asked. I had known for a long time that it had been Jared's choice not to carry on retiring synthetics. Some things are private, he would tell me all he wanted me to know. I cared enough not to find out the rest.

He came out of the room and he was quiet. It was like a cloud hanging over him. He went back to the bar and had a stiff drink. I can't remember what Nazareth looked like now but Saul was tall, short haired, good looking and looked dangerous. He carried himself with an air of authority as he started requesting that certain people were tested. Time to do something about this. I went to find Vortex.

As the two moved to the back buildings Vortex wandered in. He looked worried. "I need to do a run but I don't want to be disturbed. I'm going to sit in that corner, and I want you to pull a chair up real close and look we are having a real intimate conversation. I they come in here I want you to make it look like we are intimate. What I mean is get between them and me so that they don't see me jacked in. Don't worry, I'll be in the net so it won't be like we're doing anything. Will you do this? It's important."

"Just hope that Jared doesn't come in at that point."

"your hoping, its my head that would get blown off. I'm going to break into the local telephone network and put a call in for assistance. As they are the nearest two they should get called out."

I wasn't too sure about this but I sat down and he jacked in. Then of course both Saul and Nazareth came into the bar and there was no option. I draped myself across Vortex, long enough for him to finish what he was doing and jack out which wasn't very long fortunately but everyone in the bar must have noticed.

Saul got the call, spoke to Nazareth and they both left. I just looked at Vortex who was grinning all over his face as he leaned back in his chair, looking smug and clasped his fingers behind his head. "Simple really, just a call for help, a couple of synthetics running riot down North Ho."

Jared was behind the bar and he looked very relieved. Everyone did. Yali was looking particularly shaken, I think they had done a test on her. Can't blame her, I would be too. That's the most unnerving part about all that business, there is nothing that really shows that someone is a synthetic. Even the person doesn't necessarily know. After all, we have so many hang ups and mental problems due to the way we live who could categorically state that they know everything about themselves.

The mood lightened after the two had gone. Locals began to drift off to avoid the PLEX and others drifted out into the back room.

"Alone at last." Jared had to say it. Alone, at the Eryn, unlikely. He put an arm around my shoulder. "After you." He opened the door and we stepped into the cigarette smoke and hum of conversation of the hallway.

Gildae and Birdie were comfortably perched on the steps outside the "back room". The hum of conversation and most of the cigarette smoke drifted from the right hand room. The "Yakuza" room, the left hand door was still securely locked. Nobody would be stupid enough to mess with it anyway, even if they did know it was there.

Coffee cups and full ashtrays up the stairs, someone's assault rifle propped up on the landing and a box of shells on the window sill. I stopped on the landing to check in the spare room. There were a few sleeping bags laying around and a blanket but other than that the room was mercifully empty. There are only so many dirty coffee cups you can deal with in a day. I closed the door and carried on up the stairs.

This was our part of the bar, well as much private as we could get it. We had the large bedroom that looked out through bars, bullet proof glass and UV filters onto the main Ho Street. Daniel had the room next door. The back bedroom was mainly a storeroom, with a couple of mattresses that got used on occasion. Opposite our room there was a small bathroom. Not a palace but we called it home with its designer peeling wallpaper and bullet hole decoration, riotous parties I've been told, not attacks, from before Jared got hold of the place.

When I got back from the bathroom Jared was in our room, sitting on the bed cleaning his gun. The electric light reflected off of the chrome barrel, I knew that gun oh so well. So distinctive, the sort of weapon that retires unruly synthetics. Works just as well on PLEXCops though. Call it evolution.

He heard me but then the floorboards squeaked tunefully. It was possible to know who, what and where anyone was if they moved anywhere upstairs. Getting up the stairs quietly, even if there weren't people sleeping on the stairs every night would be hard. I wouldn't say impossible, particularly in Daniel's hearing as the master of stealth would probably spend the next few nights perfecting the art, keeping us awake until he did.

Jared looked up, his face warming from the concentrating frown to something softer. I closed the door behind me.

"Good call Chrys." He holstered his gun. I frowned, he unstrapped the holster and let it fall onto the floor with a thump I just knew they would hear downstairs. He shrugged.

The noise in the room downstairs was winding down. It was midweek but we didn't exactly keep office hours so it made very little difference. I could hear Birdie and Tayl, Gildae had joined in. They were arguing about the media and I heard Aztech's name mentioned once or twice.

"Forget all that, just for one night." He was close no, very close but there was none of the usual panic, this just felt so right.

"For a while."

He reached over and turned off the table lamp and the room plunged into a comfortable darkness. I'll tell you the rest when you are older.

I can't believe it, we have just gone half an hour in the AV with nothing happening. It all seems such slow going but hey, the van is in one piece and we're all still here. Bill has proposed we make a stop off at a place he knows to restock. Good idea, the food is getting pretty dull and we're pretty much out of even the basics. Getting out of here for a little while would be great too.

Netrunner corner was empty, pieces of wire laying around where they had jacked out. Shade stood near the table and he looked as stunned as Daniel. A piece of paper in his hand. Coloured on one side. He looked too worried, like this was something personal, I'd seen that look before. He held out what I could now see was a postcard, a picture of an oriental garden. I guessed it was something serious before I read it but the words cut me cold. I can't remember the exact words but they were basically saying that his parents had been given a free holiday to Japan. His parents worked for the PLEX of course. Bastards!

This was the night they dropped a rock on Japan.

I could get philosophical at this point, spout about luck and destiny, not much luck in this world except that which you make for yourself. If you have heavy weaponry then you have a destiny to survive, street logic and its all the logic you need. To survive you talk fast, run fast, have a big gun or have a big friend with a big gun. All helpful. Don't be there in the first place, best advice I have for survival. But, who wants to live their life under a stone? Even then you can't do much if someone drops a rock on a whole country!

Make a big noise, get noticed "Boom". They started making a big noise on the Ho, wouldn't have been just there either. Onosendai, largest corporation in Japan. A real threat to the PLEX. So what does our favourite Megacorporation do. They get out their massdrivers and drop a rock on the country. Why bother with an expensive buy out. Neat and tidy, then they use the media to tidy it up. No mention that they sent some of their "favourite" employees there for a holiday just before the rock dropped of course. Guess its cheaper than paying them a pension.

A nation wiped out pretty much in moments. Unlike many other corporations Onosendai had kept their main power base on their home island. Other than those who were setting up the operation on Ho Street and any they had in the domes that was it, gone. How many thousands of years of discipline and tradition. Just another PLEX hostile takeover.

Mass genocide of an ancient culture, its history and people gone in a moment. Its just so hard to believe, even now. I don't know but I think somehow because Daniel looked so "Western" I sort of forgot his oriental ancestry. I know I was keen to point out his attitude but I suppose that was just a dig. After all they had moved onto the Ho, taken over and started to change things. I don't think anyone really thought that the PLEX would or could do anything as harsh as that. Then in the world of big business and considering what is at stake they obviously could.

It didn't help Daniel or Shade. Both had lost family, friends, Daniel a country. He wasn't the sort of person you could console either. I had no idea what to do. He must have known we were all feeling for him. Shade, what could we do for him? I don't know what it is like to have a mother and father but I know how I would feel if anything happened to Jared or Lightning. He must have been really hurting.

Looking at the faces around the table, all so tired, with the new strain of Helix Diane on the street, with the suppressant being needed every six hours now, things just seemed to be getting worse. It was like a decay that you could smell in the air.

The moments rolled into a couple of hours, broken by Crisis calling the long awaited meeting. In the half dark of the meeting room out in the courtyard. Crisis stood up. It was just so good to see him there, not being brash, or loud, trying to do something. Perhaps we were all calling on too little too late but we were trying to do something and everyone was giving what they could. I mean giving, not selling, not dealing, giving. That doesn't happen on the Ho. I'm just glad I was there to see it.

So we had one suppressant machine and people bleeding out every day. There was no way that supply could meet demand and that would lead to riots. One machine, Christ, that was not enough. That would never be enough considering how much can be turned out and how little that is in comparison to the number of people who died every day. But, it was all we had.

The conversation went round and round, promises of what we had, what we could give. Everything we have, that was about the size of it. A time for reflection and a time to try to put it all together. There were so many questions. We still don't know too much about the plague, we don't know if there was a cure. Rumour upon rumour that Genoa had a cure, not a suppressant. Why did the domers not need it? Why did the PLEX keep raiding the clinics?

All questions we needed answers to.

Sometimes, when the floorboards are rough under your feet and your breath makes smoke puffs in the morning air you begin to wonder. Jared, still asleep, clutching the blankets like someone is going to take them away. His other hand under the pillow, no prizes for guessing what he kept there. The curtains were still drawn, beams of light spotlighting the threadbare reds and greens of the carpet, touching the top of my boots making the metal plates shimmer. Clothes from the night before thrown on a chair, I drag them on, watching my reflection in the chipped and browning mirror. The choice of the morning, take one last look at Jared asleep and reach over onto the slightly crooked table beside the bed. I remember thinking that I really must do something about that broken leg. I picked up the alarm clock and flicked the metal bar to stop it ringing. Let him slip, I would open up the bar.

Smiling to myself, I stepped out into the corridor. Just another morning like many others, trying to remember over the dull haze that clouds everything, another night in the bar and too much of some imported wine or the other. I felt sick but then I always felt sick then. A few minutes and a bit of talking to god on the great white telephone and I felt better. Staggering out into Daniel in his embroidered black satin dressing gown really didn't help. He gave me a knowing understanding look, caught me as I stumbled slightly. He's a pretty solid object to hit. Silk over a well developed and worked on muscular frame. His movements so smooth, elegant and the didn't flinch as in one smooth movement he returned me to my feet and carried on into the bathroom.

Unusual, the stairs were empty, then it was early. Nobody usually dragged themselves out of wherever they had found to crash until Midday. I just got up early out of habit. Daniel for training I suppose. Nobody else was daft enough, we were night people, we had no use for the day. Well not all the time anyway.

The door to the back room was half open. There was a pile of equipment on the table and the sounds of snoring. I stuck my head round the door, carefully, didn't want it shot of by some trigger happy occupant.

Doc was asleep under the table, wrapped in his green sleeping bag with a kitbag for a pillow and hugging his rifle. Tayl was sitting on the floor wedged into the corner, a bundle of urban cammo. His black cap pulled down over his face, HK47 across his lap. He opened an eye as I looked in, smiled and closed it again.

Dr Gildae "Doggirl" was curled up in the corner. I know it was her because I recognised the equipment, she was buried under a pile of blankets, rags and other bits and pieces, curled up close to Tictac who sat upright, back against the wall, head forward on his chest, handgun on his lap, an old Glock I think. I couldn't tell from where I was standing. He didn't move when I looked in, his bare painted tribal chest moving gently and regularly. He was asleep. The wonders of the back room.

I stopped for a minute and looked around. People with nowhere else to go. Then there were a lot like that. I rubbed my shoulder. It had been a long time since I got caught on the street and barcoded but it still hurt. Not physically, but every day I want to rip that part of my shoulder off, to go back to being unknown. The thought of being a number. It feels like being goods in the supermarket, so they can make sure they've got us all. Well they haven't, not yet, and they never will.

Back in the van, it worries me that we have split the survivors up. I know we all got to the AVs but its what happened after that. The gunfire has been pretty much constant for the past few hours and we're moving into unknown territory. Anywhere off the Ho area is out of our territory and we have no idea whose turf it is but clearly they don't like guests. We are as likely to come under local fire as the PLEX. That's the problem, no way of communicating, not without letting anyone who is looking for us know where we are. Now we run and hide. Hunted, homeless wanderers, so we become road warriors, eating up the crater strewn highway to who knows what.

Where is truth, what justice can we call for, does it burn in the flames of the Ho or will it rise like the Phoenix to call us and those like us, to fight again, to have hope.

I heard a song a while back. "Sometimes its hard to tell the difference between darkness and light. Until you have faith in what you believe. It can't rain all the time.."

I covered the bar until Jared came down and then I split. Night fell, I pulled my collar up, that sort of helped to keep the rain out but my hair was soaked. I could feel it sticking to my face, the oiliness of the rain sticking it together. That damn polluted rain. Still, could be worse. I turned my face into the wind and pushed my way through the crowd. Faceless strangers wrapped in their waterproofs, breathing through respirators. Clutching my respirator until my knuckles turned white I paused to wipe the smearing raindrops off of my light filtering goggles which now kept the sticky rain off of my face.

Pausing, I ducked into a doorway. The floor was ankle deep in old PLEXCoke cartons and other assorted unidentifiable rubbish. I didn't look down too much. If you don't bother to think about it then it doesn't bother you so much somehow.

Then I realised I wasn't alone. To my right, sheltering in the corner, a black figure, but then that pretty much summed up half the crowd on the street and nearly everyone I knew.

She spoke first. "Quite a night."

I smiled under all the metal and plastic of the respirator. The voice was muffled but I could easily recognise Runt.

"Yo! Trouble down on Seventh Avenue."

"Chrys!"

"Yours truly."

"How's it going?" Her voice even more distinctive, she stepped from the shadows and we hugged. The clash of metal and leather against metal and leather. She was a bit shorter than me, more strongly built, her long brown hair tied up gypsy style in a black and white skull printed scarf.

"Had better ones."

"Straight."

"Lost the vendor on the border of Shadow. Lucky wasn't there either."

"I heard."

"Bitch of a life."

"If you can keep it."

"Back to the bar?"

"Might as well, it's dead on the streets tonight."

As if on cue a gun went off and somewhere somebody died. We ducked out into the rain and moved with the flow for about a half a mile to the side door of Jared's and slipped into the warm dryness of the crowded bar.

Runt went to talk to Jared. I went out back, waving to him. Habit I suppose, to see who was in the back room.

Doc, he sat on an old wooden chair, tipped back, his feet on the large battered table. The room was its usual state, cups, tumblers and erupting ashtrays, the smell of stale cigarette smoke and dirty laundry. A dark, decaying shabbiness, starkly lit by a single strip light hanging at a jaunty angle over the table. Bare walls, table and chairs, it didn't really need any other furniture.

Doc looked up, took a long last drag on his cigarette before burying the stub along with the others. I smiled to myself. There was a time you could tell who had been in the room by the brand they smoked. Now it was only PLEXBrand, the red lettering stark against the white of the filter. Cigarettes had long since stopped being dangerous. The development of a different way of manufacturing them had seen to that. We have enough dangers in this world without the poison they used to contain.

"Chrystal, good to see you kid. How's it going?" He was making the effort but his voice was flat.

"Been better, we lost Jack Shadow. Bullet in the brain and the stock's gone. Same with three other clinics, except on Seventh where the place was napalmed."

After delivering this news he swung his feet from the table, letting the chair fall back onto all four feet. Burying his head in his hands, I knew how he felt. So many people had risked their lives to get hold of that equipment. Then the PLEX or whoever was doing this just wanders in, shoots the doctors and takes it. No doubt it will be blamed on some organisation, probably the BFA which makes no sense if you know the streets, but makes a log of sense if you know the politics of the Domes. A neatly edited news report broadcast while they tuck into their evening meal. No doubt they will relax on their synthesised PLEX brand sofas with a glass of PLEX wine and discuss the state of the world. Hardly likely, it is more likely that they will pass it by while flicking to the next shopping channel.

Doc looked up and suddenly he looked so tired, so drained. His green combat clothing torn and falling into holes, pieces of technology poking intriguingly out of pockets. His cyberhand moving to rest on his black and silver graffiti covered deck. On his lap something that looked suspiciously like a pulse rifle.

"Sorry Chrys."

I pulled off the goggles and respirator. "What, sorry that life's a bitch and she just screwed us again?"

"That's about it darling."

"So."

He looked at me intently. I tried to smile.

"So what do we do next?"

He shrugged. "I don't have a fucking clue."

I just wanted to hug him. I don't know why. That or cry. Not a time for tears, a time for tears when it was all over. He leant back, his shoulder length brown hair hanging down behind him, clean shaven, a little scarred, but then who wasn't. I'd been hit by more ricochets than I was comfortable with. Too tall for the chair, his long legs stretched out under the table. He was an active member, the leader. Active, that translates as you get shot at, passive, that means you think about being shot at and then get caught in the crossfire.

"At what point do we become worse than the monster we are trying to bring to heel?" My voice was a bit broken.

What do you mean?"

"If we didn't fight then would they leave us alone?" I just stated it, I'd been thinking it.

"You can blow that kind of talk, right away. The answer is probably the day we do more harm than good. Would they leave us alone if we did stop causing trouble? Are you prepared to take the risk? We are the solution, the question. Without us they would go unquestioned and they would do what they want to do."

"No, but I'd consider the question."

I left Doc alone with the thoughts. I didn't know what else to say. Then again what can you say? I hope you have better answers than we had. I hope you don't need them. I closed the door quietly, its click inaudible over the hum of conversation.

That evening nobody looked up as I slipped round the side of the bar. I was being watched though, I could feel it. You learn after a while. Jared passed me a drink. He wrapped it into my hand, his hands amazingly soft, warm. He smiled, lifting his open bottle. PLEX Beer that was all we were allowed to sell or buy. The clink of the bottles was lost but the meaning was silently loud. I smiled and he was about to say something when someone called him from down the bar. I watched him go, smiled, shrugged and turned to find Lightning standing there, towering over me.

Lightning smiled, catching my arm like he always did, pulling me closer and whispered in my ear. "Got a lead, its worth following. Are you up for it?"

Somehow it always started that way. This time I finished my drink. To many half drunk bottles had been left on too many bars when I had to leave in a hurry. Not that night. Somehow I wanted to stay in the bar as long as possible. Then it was out the side door, onto the street and it was raining, it was always raining. I pulled the respirator up over my mouth, wound a long black scarf around my neck and head and followed Lightning out into the early morning.

The air smelt cold, it felt cold and it was of course raining. Another night on the Ho. An AV screamed past, sending a wave of dirty water over the pavement. I ducked into the alley, passed silently around a couple of drunks who had passed out. I stopped, went back and kicked them awake. They cursed me as they staggered off home but at least they would be alive in the morning. The alley was silent, somewhere about a mile away there was gunfire, a short burst then nothing.

It was about 4am and I needed to rest. I pulled out my key from around my neck, slipped it into the lock and listened as the bolts slid back. I leaned my shoulder against the door and pushed. The door gave little resistance, I slipped inside an shut it as quietly as I could and pulled the bolts across. The blue glow illuminated everything eerily. The bar was clean, but then Jared always left everything immaculate, especially when I wasn't there. It was a tough night, I had a tough decision to make. I stepped into a side room and turned on the computer. A sealed unit, and began typing something. I felt like hell, I had been feeling sick for a while now. I typed a few words onto the screen and gave up. I was too tired. I logged out and dragged myself upstairs and into the bathroom. The light shone brightly yellow, the shade-less bulb starkly bright against the cracked white tiles. I ran the shower, let my clothes fall onto the stained lino and stepped into the hot spray. It had hardly any power but at least it was fairly clean water and I could wash off the grime of the street and the sticky rain out of my hair.

I heard soft footsteps and I knew who it was. Somehow He hadn't mastered quiet movement and somehow I knew he never would. I had hoped not to wake him, I needed to talk to him really badly but not tonight. Not after dragging myself in at this hour. I heard him going downstairs, coffee machine, it had to be. Coffee and a cigarette before bed, that was his usual. So he had been waiting up. That was worrying. I know I push it, I've always pushed it, you know, its just that I have a lot I have to do. Not earning money, I know the bar can support us both, its like important stuff. Contacts for Doc, getting information put about, getting hold of it in the first place. I know he understands but it is times like this that I wonder. I need him to love me, I cannot handle the fact that he might be suffering for all this.

Slow footsteps coming up the stairs as I towelled myself dry and a gentle knock on the door. I couldn't pretend I wasn't here, I had to answer.

"Chrys?" His voice was insistent.

"Yep just a minute." I wrapped the towel around me and grabbed my clothes and gun off of the floor.

"Chrys, I'll be in the room."

I didn't like the tone of his voice. I snatched up my clothes and followed him. Catching the door as he kicked it shut, cigarette hanging out of his mouth, coffee cup in either hand. He held the filter in is teeth. "Sorry darling."

He put the cups on the table and put his arms around me. My shoulders hurt, my body hurt but somehow that didn't matter.

"Chrys, come, sit a while. Look this is a bit off, I know but I've invited some people tomorrow night. Look I now its not much notice but hell its been so stressed lately. We never took any time to well.. Sorry." He looked so innocent which was really strange considering. I smiled and he lightened up. "I knew you'd understand. Problem is that I can't be there for the start, I've got to pick up a big order from the South Side. OK if yo let them in."

"No problem."

"Great kid. Now have some of that coffee and lets warm you up a bit."

I took a long drink of the PLEXCaf. You just couldn't get the decent stuff anymore. Something to do with here being nobody left alive to grow the beans and the state of the soil I think. He finished his cigarette, threw off his shirt and climbed into bed. I put down the cup, turned out the light and felt the chilled sheets against my skin.

Somehow the chill always lessened the fire in my shoulder. I put my head on his chest and fell asleep.

I didn't wake up until long after Jared must have gone out. It was nearly afternoon when I dressed and wandered down into the bar. Doc Harley and Gildae were sitting deep in conversation over cups of coffee, the ashtray was already half full so it must have been a serious morning. Lightning was behind the bar, reading some news sheets, Daniel was by the door. Daniel was always by the door.

Lightning looked up. "Morning Chrystal, bye Chrystal, why you being so off today?"

"Got a meet, I'll see you tonight."

"See ya, keep ducking."

"Damn straight."

I slipped out into the street and sauntered nervously a couple of streets down to where Eva was helping out at a clinic. I was really worried. I hadn't told Jared but alongside being symptomatic with Helix Diane I was also beginning to feel really tired and ill. I expected a fair bit of illness but with all the permutations of the plague, well you can't be too careful or you'll end up infecting everyone.

She was in the middle of dealing with a bunch of kids when I got there so I gave her a hand. After a while you get used to administering suppressant, anyone can do it, so I sort of lightened her load for a bit. By about 1.15pm she was clear and we sat down for some coffee before the afternoon rush. Over coffee she sort of asked me why I looked so tired. She knew about the Grievous Angel stuff, so there was no need to explain.

"So Chrys, what's up?"

"I feel like shit."

"You look like shit. Get on that couch." The way things were, no medical supplies, just an old couch and a whole bunch of scavenged drugs. "No kidding, I mean it."

I did what I was told and for the next half hour she fussed around and we nearly came to blows over the amount of fuss she was making and the amount of tests she was doing and then she just st on the couch with me in silence. I was scared. Like was this it? Had I gone and got something really nasty? How was I going to tell Jared? We had only been together about two months.

Eva finally looked up and there was an odd look on her face. "Chrystal, I don't know how to tell you? I don't know if I believe it myself. You know the chances are so, so slim."

This was it, this was the big one, slim chance of survival.

"You're pregnant."

I nearly fell off of the couch. Like the chances of getting pregnant with all the pollution were minimal. Jared was older, I'd been totally shot up in the Genoa raid. It was just so totally incredible. I sat there in silence.

"Chrystal, say something."

"About two month." She was right, you were born nine months to the day after the first night I spent with Jared in the bar after coming back from Wales. Now that has to be some kind of odds. Trouble was I had then to tell Jared and I didn't know how he was going to take it.

"Keep it quiet, I want to tell Jared. Look I know the chances of bringing it to term are well, slim."

"Don't worry, we'll do all we can."

"I'm not going to think about that bit, not yet. Lets be glad for what we've got."

"Youch, that's a bit philosophical."

"Won't be tonight, I have no idea how Jared is going to react."
"I'll be at the party, wouldn't miss it for the world."
"Look, I'd better get back, there's a lot of tidying and moving to be done."
"Hey, take it easy, in your condition."
"Do I throw something at you or what?"
She smiled. "Or what. Hey, its great news, could be what we all need."
"Could be." I walked out and I was walking on air. I just wish that Jared could have been there. Still, I had to wait so I went back to the bar and got Lightning to move the tables around in the big room upstairs.

I was so tired I went back to bed and woke up about seven, in time to open the bar. It was a busy night and it was really hard not to tell anyone. There was a general lack of depression around the bar which really unnerved me. It was like they knew but they couldn't know, I don't know. All I know was that I just wanted to see Jared and the hours went so very slowly. The bar closed and the guests he'd invited moved upstairs and sat around chatting.

Jared was very late, arrived about 1am carrying a suitcase. He went straight to the kitchen and I followed. The case was full of guns and at least one new one.

"Chrys, great to see you. What's the matter?"
"Can I have a word?"
"Sure." He looked puzzled.
"You know I haven't been well lately."
He looked very concerned. "Are you alright?"
"Got Eva to check me out."
"Wise move, so how are you?" He put his arms round me, it was perfect, we were alone and I just sort of told him.
"I'm pregnant".
He didn't react. "Are you sure?"
"Yes, I need some more checks but we're pretty certain."

The doorbell rang. It was annoying. I just wanted some time with him. He pushed past me and went to open the door. I heard the voice and I recognised it. Jezlyn, his ex-wife. That was all I needed. Hand on my berretta I decided it was a really great idea to go and see Crisis. I stormed into the main room and Crisis knew that something was up. I sort of blurted it out. That Jared had invited his ex-wife and they were being really pally and that I was pregnant. Crisis opened his mouth and exclaimed "Preg" at the top of his voice in chock, as Doc stifled him with a hand over his mouth.

Doc, his voice always so calming. Telling me not to worry and that Jared loved me. I went upstairs before I did something I would probably regret.

That was the night I met Julius P Madrid, UN Eco-Warrior or something. He seemed to know everyone, which was strange as I had only just heard of him. But then I hadn't been much involved in all the eco stuff before. We took a bottle of wine and found a mattress to sit on. The upper rooms were mainly used for people who crashed over so they weren't all furnished. They were all in use tonight as guests disappeared off in little groups and circulated around the rooms talking to people. We sat down and started discussing the numbers of clinics that were still open and other such stuff when there was a scream from downstairs. Rule one, scream means trouble when it involves a friend. The stairs hardly got in the way and we found Gildae trying to rip Tictac to pieces, screaming something about him being unfaithful.

I ought to take a leaf out of her book, that was how to deal with men obviously because Tictac was very sheepishly trying to explain that he had been drugged.

I looked around and saw a woman in the corner. I recognised her from the Coop. Tessler, a fortune teller or something.

A typical fun party, so she had been drugging men and well I don't have to tell you why. Then she takes me aside and something really strange happens, she goes off into some sort of a trance an says that her god has favoured me. I backed off and Eva pulled me out of the situation. The woman is batshit mad!

Jared stuck pretty close after that. Jezlyn seemed to be making friends alright and keeping well away from him so my little berretta friend stayed in its holster.

We drifted on into the night, talking about the world and what we were doing and trying to get some ideas. Julius was being very vocal, arguing with Doc Harley, I seem to remember but I was too tired. It had been a long day and I was quite glad when the party quietened down and people drifted off to bed.

The choices we have to make have to be based on what we know and what we believe. I was so caught up with what I was doing, I had sort of forgotten about all the basics in life. Those were wild days but it was like someone had upped the stakes. I was still running the streets but it wasn't just me anymore and to be quite honest I don't think that Jared was happy about it either.

So, the paper was peeling off the wall, the room smelt a bit musty. We sat, we talked and we ate our first meal not taken at a run as one or other of us was going out or going to keep an eye on the bar.

After the meal we just sat. I don't know what he was expecting, it must have been obvious I had something to say.

"Jared."

He looked up. "I knew there was something."

"I've been thinking. I've done a lot of thinking and I've made a decision."

I got one of those Jared disapproving looks the "don't make decisions without me" type.

"I've been thinking that its going to be pretty difficult for me to keep up with the sort of things I have been doing. I want to get the band off the ground."

"What band? How does that relate?"

I'd forgotten that I hadn't actually told him. But then I tried to keep most of the BFA things I did away from him.

"I've met this woman and she has a terrific voice. Anyway, I put together some lyrics and well, Lightning is getting some of the music sorted out and…"

Jared looked a little confused.

"I've arranged some underground gigs for the band. OriginalSIN. With some of the new songs we have put together. Purely street side with the tapes being smuggled into the Domes."

Jared looked disapproving. "In your…" He bit his lip.

"Look, this mess isn't going to go away. Anyway, let me finish, you are going to like this I hope. I have this plan. The band isn't going to be that difficult as I've arranged the dates and venues via contacts and I don't have to be there. I've sorted out security and other stuff, its purely a quick hit, play the music and they get out. She's a tough bitch, she's been streetside all her life and she doesn't take any shit from anyone. The rest of the band are about the same. I can still write propaganda and stuff, from the background. She is the front woman. I'm going to arrange a falling out with Doc Harley so that they don't get associated."

"Damn stupid idea. Can't you let them deal with it all? You won't be pregnant forever."

"We don't have time. Its now that it's all happening. We can't put it all back."

"Look, I know how much you care but be reasonable. You aren't going to be are you? I didn't think so. OK I'll back you all the way, do what you want to do."

"Thanks."

"Just make it convincing."

"Sure thing."

"So what are these lyrics then? We're doing the candlelit bit, why not sing me something?"

I glared.

"I've heard you. Go on."

I can't explain the music to you but the lyrics to the first song we had got together I can tell you.

If all were torn, and thrown down.
How would we remember?
If we were gone and but a shadow
How would they remember?

By the words, written in blood
That's how we remember
By the fire that burns in their hearts
That's how they will remember.

PLEX can break us, and burn our bodies
But none shall forget
They can destroy us and bring all to dust
But history shall never forget

So, with fire in our hearts
We carve out a story that none can deny
We leave a legacy for the future
That none will forget

When the wind blows our ashes
Caught for a moment
In the skeletons of burnt trees
How will they know?

For without life and freedom
Without the wind blowing in your hair
And the salt breeze on our faces
That is the true SIN

That would cast us out finally
From all hope of redemption
Bowing at the feet of the great god PLEX
Cast out of the garden forever

So as the foul serpent crawls its way around the Ho
Swallowing up all in its path
Disease to all from its foul breath
Eating its own tail to do it all again

For it cannot stop
The destruction it has begun
Like splitting the atom
The shock waves roll throughout eternity.

    Someone was hammering on the door. Jared grabbed his gun from under the table and put a hand on my arm to stop me following. Thundering down the stairs I heard him put a bullet into the breach. It just all seemed so wrong.

Couldn't they leave us alone for one night, was that too much to ask, obviously it was.

I followed him, two steps at a time honoured fashion, out into the bar.

Maverick the other barman who had been running the bar had mostly tidied the bar and the shutters were down so we couldn't see what was going on in the street. They couldn't see us moving about either which was good. It was necessary now because of the curfew which had been imposed. Whoever it was still pounded on the door.

Jared had one bolt back by the time I got there and the gunfire outside was very distinct, rattling off of the side of the building. He stood to one side, opened the door and Runt and Chuckles stumbled and fell into the bar, out of breath but apparently uninjured.

Chuckles turned to help Jared shut and bar the door. He was out of breath as he gasped. "That was too close." They threw themselves into chairs and Chuckles put his guns onto the table. "There's a riot about a block away. The PLEX have turned over at least five clinics tonight. We couldn't hold them off, they are using pretty heavy stuff."

Something exploded outside, rocking the bar. I steadied myself against a table as some of the glasses fell off the shelves behind the bar, smashing onto the tiled floor.

I shut my eyes, it shakes you when it is so close to home. Jared dragged over a chair, I went for a broom, listening to what they were saying as I cleared up the mess.

Runt was twisting the end of her scarf. "Yea, pretty harsh out there tonight. Doc and his lot got away OK and we were circling back to pick up some suppressant. How are you two doing?"

I looked at my watch, we still had ten minutes but it didn't hurt to be reminded. Jared looking over, looking at his watch. "Chrys, you OK?"

"Got ten, might as well go for it now."

He reached into his top pocket and pulled out a silver tube. "Come here then."

I hated this so much, I mean really hated it. If it wasn't bad enough having Helix Diane in the first place, it was the suppressant shots every six hours that really got me down. Not that we slept all that well anyway but it was a real pain to actually set an alarm and wake up for that. Jared was on twelve hours, he didn't have to do the early morning shot but he usually woke up when I did. It wasn't that it really hurt or anything. It was more that it was a constant reminder. I hate drugs, always have one and to have to take drugs so regularly. Oh well, no point going on about it.

Chuckles pulled out a glass bottle. "You two might as well have this little lot." Jared took the supply and pocketed it.

"Thanks, Chrystal, get over here."

I wandered over and he clipped the bottle he had in his other hand onto the metal tube. I didn't pull back my hair to help him because I just loved the way he did it. Runt looked at me and grinned, I think we had a long conversation about that sort of thing once. Girl talk."

Maverick had slipped a tape into the deck. The words drifted around us as we stood there.

> We will not die
> We will not be forgotten
> We will stand as our fathers have stood
> To wield the sword of our humanity
>
> They cannot crush us with their force
> They cannot crush a heart that beats true
> The cannot put out the fire with a thimble of water
> For it's fire passes from one to another
>
> Our words will carry through their wires
> Our message will find the true hearts
> Our beliefs are ingrained in humanity
> And our brother will awaken in the domes
>
> One day we will stand together
> One day all men will be free
> One day there will be peace
> One day…

9

The street seemed to change after the night of the barcode. I think when people have been treated like animals they started to react in a very basic way. Civilisation seemed to seep away in the days that followed. I guess it was more to do with us having an identity in not having a number, an individuality. There was more to standing against those who conformed than the number but that was a very basic symbol of the differences between us. The territory wasn't so black and white anymore. Being forced to conform just made me bitter and if I am typical of the street then I suppose there were others that felt the same way. Those wo were still alive of course, the price of not conforming was high. The street had once teemed with life, it was so different now.

I'd been so depressed after the time at the Coop and the GA had really pulled me down. So much so that I hadn't really noticed the decline. It wasn't overnight, thought the people that had gone were noticeable. It was slow and insipid. People moving on, people that just weren't there any more, people moving on because there was nobody to trade with, that sort of thing. I'd gone to Dynas Emrys in a haze and come back to what I can only describe as a fantasy. I still could not believe it, in the middle of all this. A mixture of emotions of course, the drug pulled me down, Jared pulling me up but there was no doubt who was the stronger. Confused, like this crazy bitch of a world. I still worked the streets, what was left of them, even though I knew I was pregnant. I think Jared understood, not that I ever asked him of course. I'd promised him that I'd back off but there was so much I had to do first.

I had to set up venues for the band for one thing. That took a while. Public meetings were illegal now and the curfew on the streets was enforced with prejudice. That made it difficult to find anyone wo was willing to loan space for this sort of thing. Then an idea hits me. I'd use the ones that had agreed, but there were so many empty buildings that the rest were scheduled there. Vortex was great, he managed to send encrypted messages to safe zones and we had our dates and venues. All I had to do was get the information to the band.

I left the bar in the early morning, before anyone was awake and made my way down empty streets. Nothing moved, the stillness was unnerving, unnatural. I could feel eyes watching me but then people were too scared to leave their homes these days. I don't know why but I didn't feel the same fear. The street was my home and it could kill me any time it wanted to. Somehow I knew that now was not the time to die. I was almost enjoying the solitude, the air smelt different. Still clogged with all the effluent of the Dome but it had a vague freshness that somehow made me smile. I'd given up on the respirator by then, no point, the pollution was too fine and the filter had become so clogged it couldn't be cleaned anymore. And still it rained, chilling drizzle but the pavements shone in the early morning haze.

It took about an hour to get to where I was going. Not new territory, a tenement building. I had a flat number and a time to be there. Time enough to catch Eve when she got home at the end of her shift before she went on somewhere else. No lift, the doors torn off long ago, the dark hole of the shaft echoing with an unnerving echo of guttural sounds from below. Snoring I hope. I climbed the stairs, ten flights later I stepped onto the landing, out of breath and glad to have made it.

The walls were covered with street art and signatures. Thing was that It was seriously talented work. I stopped for a while and just let the colours wash over me. Every inch of the stairwell and the landing was covered in chunky bulbous signatures and comic style figures. Somehow the crumbling plaster was held together with such a beauty that it took your breath away.

Look for the green door she had said. That was easy to find. Someone had painted leaves around the door, the word "jungle" emblazoned over it in blues and greens. I knocked, I waited.

A small panel in the door opened and I could see movement in the darkness beyond. Click, thunk, thump, click, enough security and bolts to keep out an army and the door was open and Eve stood there. Black leather and spiky black hair were pretty much her trade mark look. Heavy black make up giving definition to an alabaster white face. Long red fingernails and stunningly white hands, she opened the door and stepped back, letting me pass inside quickly. In a flash of movement she shut the door and bolted it, flicked on the light and I was dazzled.

"Good to see you Chrystal." Her voice, so deep and resonating in the narrow hall. She was one large and strong lady, very imposing, standing at about six foot, her hair making her taller. Her long elegant legs were encased in fish net stockings and a black leather bodice showed off her incredibly large assets. A tight leather mini skirt finished off the ensemble. She was stunningly attractive as well which was what I had first noticed when I had been looking for a lead for the band. Memorable, which had its good side, and its bad. She wasn't going to be able to do a gig and then just melt into the crowd and everyone was going to remember. She knew the risks, she knew the downfalls, but she was prepared to take them. Then she had begun to sing and that had blown me away the first time I had heard it. She had the strength and grit I her voice of Tina Turner but the melody of Enya. She was perfect and already an active member of the BFA so we knew we could trust her. Her and her boys knew how to survive and between us we had come up with a plan. It was the best way they could help to get the message across. We'd discussed it, they knew the risks.

She opened a door to my right and there were the five lads, three large biker types, black leather, studs and skulls, and two "Goth" types, tall, thin, pale and remarkably beautiful for men. Still, they came together to make such a sound. From rock to ballads, they could do them all. I hardly knew them but something had drawn us together. They made room for me on the battered red sofa and we sat down to chat, Eve disappearing to get some coffee.

The room was an incredible collection of old movie posters, ornate mirrors, old pictures and all kinds of glittery gold ornamental junk perched on other pieces. All had seen better days. Twisted around the piles of golden wood and metal ornaments there were long lengths of black lace giving it an abandoned attic feel. Treasures lost for centuries, that was what came to mind. In other times Eve would probably have been some famous rock star living in absolute luxury without a care for the world. But, she did care so she was here, with us and by what I'd gathered from our initial conversation she was glad to be. There was something Domeside about her but she didn't volunteer the information and I wasn't going to ask.

I pulled out a disc and put it on the rather grand glass topped, gold legged coffee table amongst the empty beer cans and overfull ashtrays.

"There are the dates and locations of the first five bookings. There's some lyrics that I've been given for you that you might like to look into putting to music and some other stuff that might be of use. I've paid over the booking fees for the venues that need it and all the basic financial stuff is covered. All you have to do is turn up, play the sounds and get away afterwards. Don't hang around, more than an hour and a half and you could get the PLEX on your tail."

Grif, the largest of the bikers piped in. "No encores then lads."

They laughed.

Serif, the most talkative of the Goths pulled out a tape. His gloves hiding most of his hand but where the fingers had been cut away his pale skin almost glowed. It was such a contrast to the stark matt black of the gloves. His nails caught my attention, fairly long and immaculately manicured. "We got a recording studio for the afternoon yesterday, got some of the sounds on tape. Can you do anything with it?"

Amazing, I felt my heart leap, this was just what I'd been hoping for. "Sure, I'll get it copied and get it available at the venues. We'll get it on the street as well, I'll see what I can do. If I play my cards right, might even be able to get it into the Domes." Well if Vortex played the ice right was more what I meant. Where would I be without him!

Eve came in with the coffee. "Hey, I see Serif has shown you our little surprise. Gets better and better doesn't it." She smiled that warm smile that really put you at your ease and made you believe that just possibly it was getting better.

"Sure does sweetheart." Piped in Elim, the tallest of the Goths and Eve's partner. He smiled and she smiled back. You could feel the connection between them.

She passed round the coffees and found a seat and once the initial pleasantries and the how are you's were over they were sitting and looking at me. I think they were expecting something. What the hell, I had to tell them. "Look, I've got a bit of news to tell you. It's not going to alter anything but I've got to let you in on it because it concerns you and I don't want you to doubt that what we are doing is at least going to get carried through from our end. I'm going to have to create a cover for a while and work through that which shouldn't really alter things from your point of view. I won't be able to physically be on the streets for much longer. I'd like to tell you why and I'd like to introduce you to Spirit. She's around quite a bit and has been seen around as well. She's not a lot different to me other than she's pretty nifty in the net. Hopefully she can get around quite a bit. I'm creating her as a multi user icon, a shared icon. Should make her fairly difficult to trace." I pulled out a folded piece of paper from my pocket and showed them the print of the angel icon I was planning to use. They sat in silence, listening. "Well she will arrange your venues but it will all be done by phone and message. You can contact her through me and all the usual channels."

Eve raised an eyebrow and then half smiled. "There's something else you want to tell us isn't there? There's a reason for all this?"

I smiled and nodded. "Yes, I've had it confirmed, I'm pregnant."

Eve's expression changed, it was as if she glowed. "Good on you Chrystal. A little bit of hope. Something worth fighting for."

She and the others like many on the streets were those discarded from the Domes. Children there were no problem and sometimes more than what was needed. There was a strict rule of a maximum of two children for a family so if others were conceived and the parents couldn't face termination they were dumped on the streets. Most of the people of the street were either abandoned children or people who had abandoned the Dome living for something a bit more real.

Actual physically born children on the street were more than rare.

Something worth fighting for, too right. It was like all those hard bikers and stand-offish Goths just melted. Grif reached for a box of beer and handed them round. Following the snap of the ring pulls we toasted the future and hope. I guess it was then that it all sunk in. This wasn't just for Jared and me, this was for everyone. From being a couple we had suddenly become part of everyone else's family, our hopes were their hopes and although they won't be around to see it I think part of them lives on in you.

We talked for about an hour about lyrics, sounds and equipment. They gave me a list of what they wanted and on a quick initial scan it was all possible. They had kept it to essentials so it didn't look too impossible, just very difficult.

I walked down the stairs, feeling more confident about the plans I had laid down and what I'd set in motion. It had to work, the band had to work. If the Original Sin was knowledge, then let OriginalSIN bring the wisdom which tempers knowledge to the street and beyond. Strangely enough when I was playing an old Meatloaf track it came to me. We needed an original idea, something that would make a difference.

And yea while I walk through the valley of the serpent I shall fear no evil for evil if evil be within it is sure as heck without. PLEXCops everywhere on the streets. The clean-up crew.

I slipped unnoticed into a side street and watched. They were driving very slowly down the street in convoy taking pot shots at anyone they saw moving. The curfew was still in force until 7am. I had at least an hour before then so it was going to be an interesting journey home. I scuttled up a fire escape and flipped up onto the roof. It was precarious, there was precious little to hold onto and the slates and roofing material was badly decayed. One false move and I could be dropping in on someone for breakfast.

Fortunately I was very lucky and I didn't get spotted or fall though a roof. I pretty much fell into the bar and slammed the door behind me, pulling across the bolt. Jared was sitting at one of the tables nursing a cup of coffee. I guess it occurred to me then how he still dressed in the same way. Same white shirt, he had a few of them, same waistcoat, he had a couple, same jeans or casual trousers. Same smile that was worth coming home to. He got up and fetched me a cup and I sat with him, in silence. There are times when words are just not necessary.

A stray round bouncing off of the bullet proof glass broke the silence. We both looked up. Jared shook his head, there was that smile. That tired, why can't they leave us alone smile. I walked to the stereo, chose something ambient and turned the volume down so it was just gently in the background. Jared lit up another cigarette, the tiny wisp of smoke rising gently. Quiet moments, moments to remember.

The time passed and I got bigger, and bigger and less able to get about.

The venues worked out and the guys were doing really well. They enjoyed it, all of it from the music to the thrill of the chase. I'd pretty much set up Spirit to do all the things I would have done and I gently bowed out of society. All that time, all that mattered was getting you here safely.

There was some reason to go to a place called the "Oubliette". I had to let Jared go on his own. He'd be with the usual suspects so for once I stayed at home and took care of the bar.

I gather that tempers got a bit heated there. I was given some paperwork afterwards and from that I understand that Julius P Madrid made his feelings felt. I don't know, I guess we all sound off from time to time but he did it in style and to a lot of people on a subject that was dear to our hearts. There had been talk for a long time that the UN had set up some master plan but to be quite honest I can't remember what it was. I remember writing to Gildae about it trying to smooth over the situation and I don't think there was anything too serious. Well not too long term anyway. Well he turned up again and nobody seemed to be too keen to shoot him so it must have been OK.

I was a bit busy anyway as while Jared was away at the Oubliette I went to stay with the Sisters of the Perpetual Railgun. I had been looking after the bar but I'd started having some pains so it seemed sensible to go there. After all they had enough firepower to hold off a large army. So, amidst their devotions and daily duties a small person came into the world, someone who was going to completely disrupt their daily life.

The Sisters were terrific although it did seem a strange sight to see those male nuns with you. Then I guess they were pretty used to children. They looked after a lot of orphans and even Jared had grown up with them. They picked up the children who were discarded from the Dome. The kids had fluffy handguns instead of teddy bears. I could imagine that. They got me into a routine of nappy changing and I was beginning to get really used to being there.

Jared must have got a bit of a shock when he got back to the bar and found me not there but I hope someone gave him the message. When he found out he was around as fast as he could and he couldn't wait to bring us both home.

I was sitting in a side room with you when he arrived. The door opened and he just stood there, silhouetted in the doorway. He just smiled and I could almost see the weight of the world lifting off his shoulders for a while. He held out his arms and I handed you over to him. Ex Cop, Ex Android Retirer, Barman and now Father and there was no doubt which he preferred. The hands that had taken so much life had now given something back. I couldn't help but feel warm when I saw him holding you. I knew you would always be safe with him and that he would die rather than see anything happen to you. We are a family at last, a real family.

Later that morning Vortex came into the bar and came over to where I was sitting. He never really looked worried, he was beginning to look very ill but then so would you if you had a head full of rotting cyberware. That is what the doctors had described. He was still functioning but the decay was obvious. He personally was as sharp but it was his life in the net that was being threatened. He was worried about Shade as he hadn't heard from him for a while. Guess that pretty much confirmed my worries about him. If he had full net access then he would have found him easily with no problems. Hardly surprising that Shade had taken a break. The destruction of Japan had shocked a lot of us, it was the complete desolation in moments, the thought of all those voices silenced in a moment. Worse for him, the poor lad had lost his parents. Saul his brother was back and trying to get him to re-join the Retirement Unit and his sister was addicted to Crystal Mist. I think anyone would be down with that lot to deal with. Still, if Vortex was worried I'd put the word around and see what I could find. I left Vortex in the bar and slipped out back to make a few calls. Credit I couldn't really afford to use but what the hell, friends are friends.

A message came back later that day. Not that it as good, he was pretty much backing out of doing anything at all. The response to my question wasn't much more reassuring but after a few messages he got the message back that he was working with Azrael on recovering something important. The connection was something to do with lottery balls. Vortex was instantly interested and so I gave him a method of contacting Shade direct and left them to it. Shade was still very cut up. He was slipping into some darkness that he wouldn't het out of but somehow I think that with something to work with he was coming around.

It didn't take long, not that we knew anything about what they were up to and it was days later that Jared and I got a message that we were needed to help recover a piece of equipment. I really felt at the time that I needed it. I had been a bit worried about Jared. He was spending far too much time just hanging around the bar. There was far too many mentions of Jeslyn as well, Jared's ex-wife.

I knew he was still in contact with her and I suppose that worried me a little. You know sometimes when he stood at that bar he looked so tired and I wondered if somewhere, deep down if he was regretting coming to the street. The constant raids, the depression, the lack of sleep on occasion, th lack of time for anything on occasion. It was taking its toll. I suppose I sill hadn't got used to the idea that he actually wanted to be wit me and somewhere in this whole crazy world there was something that was actually glad that I was alive. Then of course that time of the month when the payments were due to Jezlyn would come around again and for all his bluster about having to pay up I think there was still something there and by making the payments he knew that she was still alive. Then I suppose he must have really cared about her once and perhaps that never quite dies.

Highrise came into the bar, his face like thunder. He'd been hanging around right from that night I'd come to the bar on occasion but somehow he'd been off doing his own thing. I think he was some sort of hard EuroSolo and as such probably had a lot of business to attend to that I really didn't want to know about. He came in and went straight over to Jared. I didn't know what to do, whether to keep my distance or go see what was up. I just figured that Jared needed his space on this one and he'd call if he needed me. Still…

Highrise sat down, as they talked I could see Jared's expression change. Something really bad had happened. From the conversation I caught on the way over I worked it out. Jezlyn was dead. She had been shot in the back after she had met up with Highrise. A high price ot pay for what she had for us. The answer to one of our questions. Why the Domers didn't have any forms of the plague. The answer was simple. How often had I seen a bottle of PLEXMax and had it said on the label, that it "gives you life". Too right, the suppressant was in the PLEXMax. Drink it and you were fine. So all our theories that it had been in the water system or in the air conditioning weren't too far off. We just hadn't got the right medium. Same the poor bitch had to give her life to tell us and what it meant I don't know. Just another piece in the puzzle. Jared was pretty cut up about it though and that worried me. I backed off and disappeared upstairs, leave him to his grief. This was their moment, that was his past. I was his future and I was going to keep it that way. That was a part of his life I didn't want to think about, the thought of him in a family situation with someone else was upsetting.

The days passed in their usual way. The time came to go do this little job that was supposedly so very important and then the package arrived. I opened it with great trepidation. Black, that was alright, well cut, that was even better, but a suit! Now come on they had to be reasonable, it had been a long time since I had dressed up in one of these. It brought back memories. I slipped upstairs. Jared was busy looking at his rather smart suit and investigating how many pockets it had and probably where he was going to hide his shotgun.

I stood in front of the mirror, the hair could be made right, the suit was right but it was going to take a lot of make up to cover the tattoos. Then I opened a little packet with the suit, They had thought of everything. Fake skin. With make up it would cover the tattoos flawlessly. Oh well, I guess my last excuse just went out of the window.

There we were wandering about some PLEX organised museum on our way to stealing a commode. Yep, you have read that right, a china pot that they use dot use as a toilet in the old days. Apparently they used to keep it under the bed and now we were going to break into their display and steal one. I won't go into the details as it is all too embarrassing but what I will say is that it cost us dearly. Lady H was one of the cooks I had met at the Coop. She and her friend had started hanging around the bar and some of the things they were writing were amazing. I was really hoping that they would write some stuff for the band. Then Lady H's friend goes and gets herself killed trying to save a small child when it all went a bit wrong. Life just isn't fair sometimes. We get out of some pretty serious scrapes and then get caught up in something which at the time seemed so remarkably stupid. Fortunately the prize was worth the sacrifice, sort of, if you look at it all long term. Pretty harsh on those who had to pay it though.

We had our bit of the puzzle and duly handed it over to Vortex who apparently had the whole of the plan and needed the pieces. I'd leave it to him, I was sure he could handle it, that was what I thought. Handle it alright, he certainly did. Soon enough we were loaded in vans and cars and heading towards Portland Down, an old disused nuclear missile bunker.

I can't tell you what I thought as we rumbled through the streets. I don't think I noticed the street very much that day. I was tired and fell asleep on Jared's shoulder. I wasn't to know that was the last time I would see my home. The last time any of us would see it.

It wasn't too long a drive, we were lucky as well, there weren't too many riots and we managed to take a pretty direct route. I'll spare you the details, it was pretty quiet.

We arrived late afternoon on a dull overcast Friday but remarkably it wasn't raining. Everything was grey in a sea of dull green-yellow. Sickly looking grass that was more yellow than green clung desperately to what soil it could find and everywhere there were signs of past conflicts. Cracks in the stonework, craters, bullet holes, burnt out cars. A concrete wasteland in a perimeter fence, low stone buildings that had born the brunt of several serious attacks and nobody moving about.

I stayed in the van while Jared and some others did their stuff. I was best always to check a place out first and it would be easier to get away if most of us were in the van. So we waited and waited and then our intrepid explorers came back. Apparently it had checked out and what was more, Candyman was there. Leon Court's crew had got there first. How had they known? Then again when you have the sort of money that Leon Court's crew and got there first. How had they known? Then again when you have the sort of money that Leon Court has you are going to know quite a bit if you really want to.

I suppose as I didn't really know why we were there I couldn't speculate on Mr Court's interest. He was a "businessman" who had been successful. We'd tried to get information on him before when he had been sticking his nose into our business on the Ho but there was little to be had other than he had a lot of money. He had a lot of people working for him. He was a manipulator and extremely strange.

Plain grey stone, small windows that had long ago been smashed. Some glass shards remained mingled with the general rubbish that was strewn about. Some of our group were already inside. Jared had come back to get us. He pulled open a heavy, rusting iron door which creaked painfully and fell off its hinges as soon as it left the support of its frame. He caught it and lifted it against the wall as we stepped cautiously into the dimly lit interior.

We were met by a long thin corridor which stretched off into the distance. White tile floor and a gully on the right hand side, white tiled walls with pipes running along just below the ceiling. The pipes had been smashed in places but the floor was swept clean. The dim light came from the occasional lightbulb, rigged up from what had once been long light fittings and hanging on bare wires. It gave the place a really eerie feeling which suited the smell of damp very well.

Metal shod boots made quite a noise on the tiled floor. The doors we passed were open, broken off of their hinges and the rooms beyond were bare and unlit. After searching the first couple we gave up. They had been picked clean. Then again this was someone else's home. The Brothers had taken over this place. A fanatical cult that followed their saint, Johnny Helix, the hero of the people and the one who might hold the clue to solving the riddle of the cure to the Red Plague. As to what they were like, I'd have to wait until we'd travelled what seemed to be unending tunnels.

The tunnel dipped down and seemed to go on forever. Then we saw a bright light in the distance and sped up. As we got close the light moved, it was a very bright torch, dazzlingly bright. Still we kept walking until abruptly Jared stopped. I ran into the back of him and those behind me ran into the back of me. Then I saw what had made him stop. Silhouetted with white-yellow light was a very tall man, well built, long curly hair falling over the shoulders of his white robe. A ghostly apparition that was very solid, very real and holding his hands out to greet us. Welcome to Portland Down.

Portland Down was surreal. The cult had been there for years by what I could see, holding their devotions outside the shrine to Johnny Helix. A huge picture of him hung over the piles of technology that made up their altar. Not that we could actually get into the room. Here was a television screen that was generating some sort of sub-sonic sound that caused anyone who went in there to go into some sort of a seizure. Cerberus seemed to be alright with it but to the rest of us it was a major problem.

The events of the next couple of days were very strange. There was a woman there, with her uncle who claimed to be Deesa Branson, the granddaughter of Richard Branson. Perhaps I had better explain why we were there as it was only when we got there that it was explained to us, for security purposes.

I guess it all showed how much his partners trusted Jared Matthews, even way back. In those early days of his rise to power his partners had got hold of Portland Down and used it as a hiding place for certain important pieces of equipment which were some sort of an insurance policy. I'm going to explain the full story here although at the time we didn't know it all and I may have mentioned certain bits before.

Jared Matthews must have decided that he needed a super-brain computer to help him with his plots and schemes. He was in the process of creating Danforth about the time that his partners, Richard Branson, Bill Gates and one other began to get really worried. Somewhere in this time they managed to slip in a sub program which would create a back door into a section of Danforth's brain. This could be used for information and to control the rest. This apparently was what we would be able to utilise when we activated the machinery. Trouble was that it was initially only able to be accessed by the direct descendants of these people. Ok, simple enough. Then there was another twist in this tale. One of the programmers working on the project found out that the back door was there and worked out what it would mean at some undefined time in the future. He was working on the program so he used his position and the access he had available and put a little failsafe in himself so that he would know when it was activated. The system would literally call him on his mobile phone. He worked for telecommunications so fiddling his bill so that it would be paid forever wasn't a problem either. Then he wandered out into the chaos and somehow lost his mind. In his ramblings he gathered a group of people in the chaos that was raising its head on the streets. These were people who believed that violence wold solve the problem. The formed an order known for all time as The Sisters of the Perpetual Railgun. The founder member's mobile phone becoming their holy icon and it was built into their cross. They had a prophecy that one day the phone would ring and when it did it would herald the summoning of the Antichrist and it was their mission to destroy it as soon as it was activated.

Not that we initially knew any of this. We just knew that there was a box of technology in a room we couldn't get into and a group of fanatical cultists who were certainly not going to let us defile their altar. So throughout the day we managed to find a way to shut off he sub-sonics and in our usual true and honest way we waited until the Brothers were asleep, entered their shrine and used the equipment to activate the Back Door Danforth. Azrael was one initial operator, Runt apparently was descended from Bill Gates so she was the second and Deesa Branson was the third. So up pops Danforth, besuited and sarcastic but forced to explain the whole story to us. Elegantly built, good looking with a serious expression, he was willing to obey our every command. Now if that wasn't a set up I don't now what it! Well it seemed that way as he reeled off all manner of information in an answer to our questions, provided printouts and generally spilled the beans on all manner of aspects of Jared Matthew's life.

Questions flooded to him. Everyone's personal questions had to be answered and it all became a little chaotic as there was no cohesion and the important questions sort of good overlooked.

I think it was about this time that the Sisters of the Perpetual Railgun turned up and turned their guns on us. They steamed in, guns and voices blazing proclaiming the destruction of the antichrist.

It has to be one of the worst moments of my life. I now that Jared felt it too, probably a lot more than I did. He had been brought up by them and I had only seen them as friends. We as a group had no alternative, they had left us with no choice and although I know that I just stood there in amazement and Jared dived under the table it was a fast and bloody exchange of fire which left all the Sisters dead and Doc Harley having taken a bullet in the chest.

I don't think that anyone believed it. We'd spent time with them. I know on occasion we had laughed at them but they honestly believed in giving their lives to stop us. It made me think that perhaps we weren't doing the right thing after all. What did they know that we didn't? I know that their philosophy was based on the ravings of someone who, in any sane world would be considered a madman. Then again in this crazy world who is to say that the insane don't hold the truth. How many people like that woman wandering around talking about a box had some inclination of what was to come. What is the truth anyway? At the time I know we questioned the sanity of what we were doing. What gave us the right to think that we could make a difference?

It was quiet for day, we argued it out, trying to come up with parameters that would protect us and give us a working relationship with Danforth. We came up with the parameters in the end and put them to him. He accepted them, but then again he had no choice. Then it came to appointing operators, we decided on appointing those who wanted the responsibility. That was a decision we all had to make and the option was open to all of us. I can understand your father's reasoning for standing back on that one. I gues none of us wanted to know the truth about ourselves and for some reason by putting your hand in the box Danforth was able to give us a reading on what and who we were. I say this because there were a few surprises.

Crisis turned out to be someone called Dr Gabriel and a that point I think he totally lost it and became Dr Gabriel. YumYum, having just received that shock also found out that she was an Android. It was turning out to be a really bad day. Tayl found out that he was someone as The Phoenix, prophesied to be some sort of a saviour. Doc Harley, well he turned out to be Arthur, heir to the throne of England and Gildae was Aztech. I don't know I suppose I'd been suspicious about that one for a while. It was a great cover for her and the way she could carry on helping the BFA.

I guess that her relationship with Doc Harley wasn't going too well at that point. She was pretty cut up about a lot of things, not least that she had given birth to a son and that he was on one of the orbitals. That was something they had to deal with as a couple and I don't think from the way she was reacting that Doc had handled it very well.

YumYum and Crisis had disappeared to an upstairs room. Voices were hushed around the door but the information that came out was not good. He was going to be Dr Gabriel from now on, the last of the Crisis CPO had run out. So he was gone, the man we had known as Crisis was no more. We were left with someone else, a stranger. I felt so sorry for YumYum. To love someone that much then in a second they become someone else. How could anyone deal with that? But, we had to, we all had to. We were on the verge of something so completely unbelievable. We had in our power the instrument by which we could make a difference and that had to be treated with the respect it deserved.

In those couple of days we had to come to terms with the fact that we held people's lives in the balance and the information we had to work with was not optimistic. The planet was devastated. At the current rate of production necessary to keep industry working and people living the planet would have five years before something known as the "Cascade" set in. From that point on it would be a nosedive to oblivion for everyone. Not something we really wanted to hear. Danforth had come up with a plan and he had been working towards it for years. This was where the information we had began to come together.

Aztech had been important. Not just because Jared Matthews' obsessive love for her but because she had been "specially bred" by Danforth to be a leader. Her gene pool was amazingly diverse, created by geneticists. Her public face was the one that people trusted and listened to so in a new world she would be able to say things and get people to listen. Then she had disappeared and that had caused devastation to that plan.

It was in an effort to get her back that the power had been shut down throughout Ho Street. Apparently they would have been able to have found her through the STIMrig in her head. That same STIMrig that Crisis had offered as a trade for Blue, the STIMrig he didn't have because it was still in Gildae's head. Of course he as Dr Gabriel now and had no memories of this so there was no point making an issue of it. So, all that devastation on the street had been caused because Jared Matthews wanted her back. More importantly Danforth would have been behind it because he wanted her back for the ALKAHIRA Project.

Over the time we had found out that they were breeding oxygen producing plants. We had been close in our suspicion that Jared Matthews was planning to blast himself and his Board of Directors into space, we just hadn't got the details right. It seemed a bit daft at that point that we had had this great theory that he was going to blast the Domes into space. Thinking about it they were so fragile and held together by so many repairs that they couldn't possibly move. Still, what were we to know, we aren't engineers.

Jared Matthews was psychotic and paranoid. That much we had expected but somehow being faced with having to make the same sort of decisions I have to admit it, I did have a certain sympathy. We weren't in a position at that point to know if our plans could work, we just had to try.

Questions led to answers. Cerberus, our genetically altered dog-man had been one of the projects. I'm not sure but they may have called it Greyhawk, or was that the Ratty Project? In any case, both were created to be the workers and protectors of the colonists. Both projects went wrong, as did the Robot and Android Projects. So all in all they went through project after project and every one failed and ended upon the street giving us trouble or joining our cause. All their waste and some wonderful creations that they could not appreciate had ended up with us to work against them.

Then the messages started coming in. Just increased raids at first. Not unusual on the Ho but worrying. Then events spiralled out of all proportion. Vortex had found out that his sister was in a maximum security prison and had done all he could to get her out. Then, either by co-incidence or design there had been a malfunction in the holding system at the prison and the convicts had been released onto the street. Initially if it had just been a release it would have repopulated the tenements and as most of them were probably just people who had spoken out against Jared Matthews and the PLEX, more people to join us. No, this was all the excuse that Jared Matthews needed and he unleashed all the force at his disposal to clean up the problem. We wer helpless as report after report came in of people dying and the buildings being flattened. This was just what he needed to finish his redevelopment, he flattened it. Shade and Yali were getting what they could from the net, reporting to us as the sad statistics that were real, once living people, grew. It was an impossible situation and getting worse all the time. How it must have felt to be the relay of all that, to listen to your family being annihilated and everyone you had known being wiped out in a matter of minutes. The minutes drifted on and realisation dawned. We had lost the Ho. When the Houn 4, Yali's people, fell we knew it was lost, they were the last defence. It was gone, forever and ever, amen. Jared grabbed the phone and called the bar. The line was dead. That haunting tone said al we didn't' want to hear.

In the chaos that followed we packed what we could. Disheartened, angry, devastated, what words do you use to convey such a feeling of loss, such a screaming tearing realisation of what it meant. There was no home to go back to, nothing. There was no way back but there had to be a way forwards. The PLEX could not succeed and Jared Matthews would have to be made to pay for what he had done.

We had arranged a time to reactivate Danforth and a location but we couldn't hang around. If there was the vaguest chance that the PLEX knew about us then they would level the area. I don't think I will ever be able to come to terms with it. Then again, I don't think I want to. Its not something you accept and forget. It is something you remember and feel for the rest of your life. All I had ever known, all I had ever cared about was dust and blood. Well not quite. I clung to Jared so tightly then, just following him in a haze. I don't even remember what I said to those around me. I was just so fucking angry.

Jared was all I had left. At that point I had no idea where you were but I could only hope that you were safe. I was glad I'd taken up Gildae's offer to send you somewhere safe. I needed some sort of hope to get me through those first hours. The faces haunted me, the ordinary people but who is ever ordinary? Who is ever unimportant? Whatever we did from that day on would be influenced by them, their lives and the memory of who they had been.

I sat in the van in a state of shock to start with and then I started writing this. It didn't seem much when I started it but over the days it has become my sanity. It is my hope that someone will remember us and why we have done what we had to do.

For five days I sat in the belly of that van. Then we arrived and to be quite honest everything moved so fast that I didn't get a chance to keep up with writing this. I'm now sitting in a Yakuza Safe House waiting to get on a shuttle up to one of the SAISH units. We have made our decisions, we have made our choices and may God forgive us.

We have ordered the death of Jared Matthews. He's just too dangerous to leave around and too much of a figurehead of what has to be destroyed if the world is to survive. Vengeance too, that man has to pay for what he did to the street. We checked out the statistics and it still is not good but we at least have a chance with the plan we have decided to follow.

We have ordered the elimination of the PLEX Board. This gives us time while they are in confusion to get things in place. So, on the day known as Day 1, Danforth is going to shut down all the power on the planet. Back to the Stone Age when it comes to technology. A bit harsh for the netrunners but we will all have to adapt.

Vortex has downloaded the information we need to start again and we are going to go up to SAISH 2 and wait out the time until it settles down a little.

Something I had forgotten to mention was the explanation of Leon Court. Candyman and Alex Court had been there when we arrived and had been there for some time keeping the area safe. Candyman was one of Leon's employees and I wouldn't want to cross him or make him angry. The most noticeable thing about him being his cyber hand that was apparently lethal and fired projectiles. Alex, well she was immaculate, deadly and a relative of Leon Court. By what I had heard they were an item. Then overnight something happens. Candyman wakes up in the morning and she is dead, just run out of time. What that did to Candyman I don't know but I can imagine. To have not known that she was an Android.

Two of Leon Court's employees turned up. Damocles and his female companion. Both of them wanted to be made operators and for our sins we allowed them. This became relevant later as Leon Court seemed to be taking over the show. For all our planning somehow we ended up under his protection or should that read under his control. He owned the SAISH unit and he was deciding who went on it and the guest list was strange to say the least.

The last couple of days were very strange. We took the shuttle up to the orbital and woke in the morning to an explosion. Leon Court was dead, blown into space and that had compromised the hull. Sections have been shut down and we have to live in the rest. Nick, the AI that runs the orbital is functioning on partial power and with partial information and yet again we are in trouble. We are losing atmosphere but hopefully with the help of sealant guns we have managed to seal some of the breaches and the windows.

I guess all we can do is wait. Then again, we are stuck here with no guns and that is not going to please most people. Somehow I just know that its going to go crazy. This many people in such a small place. Recipe for disaster.

I'm not sure of the order of events either. Yali disappeared. I'd had it explained to me before. Nick, who ran SAISH 2 was linked to Kelly who ran SAISH 3 or something. Yali was a clone of Kelly and had been created to be the physical part of Nick. Now she had disappeared, leaving behind all her fetishes and equipment. Something she would never do unless she was in real trouble. Runt was taking one party down the air vents and I was supposed to be going with them but for some reason Deuce, the leader of the Wild Cards didn't want me to go. So I sort of led my own expedition to find her. I know, she shouted at me and I suppose we hadn't got on on occasion but on others, well scampering down tunnels was what I had done for a living pretty much. I knew the underworld of the street and I'd been in air vents before. This was something I could do and I was totally fed up with people keeping me out of trouble.

Not that I was as fit as I used to be and climbing around those vents was quite unpleasant. Still, it was better than sitting around doing nothing. I was also quite curious as to who the other 300 guests were and what they were up to so should I have found a way into their section to have a look I wouldn't have been disappointed.

I was climbing down a horizontal shaft when I landed in front of Deuce. That made him jump! He was quick as a flash and had his knife up but I caught his hand before he could do any damage. Not that he was glad to see me at all and I wasn't particularly pleased at being ordered about. I volunteered to go at the back but Ash, the Medical Android was not going to let me. Fair point, I would have disappeared at the first junction. She he had brains as well as being good looking.

The vents were thankfully clear and somehow we came across a room that contained all the weapons, taken off of people so they didn't blow a hole in the hull by accident. Someone was going to be really pleased with us. No sign of Yali though. Well, we grabbed what we could and I must admit we made our way back pretty fast as there were definite scratching sounds and the thought of Ratty out there with us was enough to get the adrenaline pumping.

I think that Deuce was worried about what Jared would do to him for letting me go with them. I'd already spoken to Jared about it. He'd never stop me although I knew it would upset him. When I got back I calmly walked up to him and told him about the guns. I don't know which he was more pleased to hear, me back or his guns being downstairs. Well I hoped his guns were there. We had grabbed all the bags we could carry. I'd felt my gun in the bag as it was distinctive with the Velcro and though he'd put his in the same bag, I couldn't tell. Still he got his shotgun and that was enough to keep him happy. Cerberus had gone down and caught Yali's scent. They should have used him to start with but then it was explained that they had only been looking for the guns in the first place. I was fuming over that but still, we'd made a lot of people very happy.

We had robots at the door. That was all we needed and a group had gone off down the vents looking for Yali. Not just Robots, they were the personal guard of one Jared Matthews Junior, together with a hologram of his father, the one and only. There I was at one point standing beside the man. You know, talking to him it wasn't as if he had horns and a tail. He was rational, logical and a businessman. Then I suppose to get as far as he had he had to have a certain charisma. They had had a very serious Ratty problem in their part of the Orbital. Guess we really needed a copy of that guest list. Who else was out there we didn't know about? Anyway, it then struck me, Aztech! She was being kept in a side room where she could be protected. She came out and saw her son. Like any mother who cares for her child she wanted to get to him but his guards wouldn't let her. One of them came over and gave her some details. He was doing well with his studies and growing into a fine boy. He did look it.

I didn't know what to say to her. I think I could understand how she felt. I had you with me but I know how I felt when you were away. I agreed to give him a message. He agreed to speak to me but he was so cold. He listened, he was polite and said that it was not the time to talk about it because tempers were too frayed. He had a point. I related the message back and understandably she was not happy but what could we do.

All hell broke loose. There was a gunshot. There was movement. Scarecrow had shot Jared Junior. Scarecrow, he had joined us dirtside before we took the trip up to the orbital but what triggered him to kill the boy I don't know. Hatred I suppose. He was soon dispatched by a robot but it was too late, the damage was done.

I didn't know where to run first. I tried to stay near Gildae as they told her the news. I didn't want her to rush into the room as the robots were likely to go for her if she did. They carried him out and into the med bay but it didn't look good. We just had to wait and see if he had inherited his father's skills for being a survivor.

Doc Harley came back but only in time to hear that his son was dead. It was a personal moment for him and for Gildae so we gave them their space. They had been through a lot together and now they had lost something that would have brought them the hope that you brought to Jared and myself. I felt I had no right to even speak to her at that moment. What right? I had you, and hope, and then there she was standing in front of me. All I could think about was how I'd have felt if it was you who had died. I just hugged her. I didn't know what to say other than we all loved her. It was pathetic but I couldn't think of anything else to say.

The robots left but we knew it would mean trouble. We got ready to expect it. Then Danforth turned up and shouted at Nick that he had forgotten what he was designed for. The orbital juddered and we were all thrown to the floor. Who knows how much damage was done to the already weakened hull. We were off to Mars to accomplish ALKAHIRA. Azrael had abducted two other operators and got himself granted Super-User Status, under the code-name Archangel and he had initiated the project in as close to its original form as he could. We had delivered Aztech into their hands and now he was going to make sure that nobody stopped him. Hew had gained control of nuclear missile sites dirtside and he was about to blow up the planet. We had to do something fast. There was only one answer. We revoked his user status, we got Danforth to take control of the missile sites. He couldn't get them all so we used what we had to destroy the others and ordered the immediate termination of Azrael. Then with a bit of help from the more technically minded who had crawled back into the vents we managed to turn the SAISH unit and bring it back into earth's orbit, unfortunately in PLEXSpace's area.

We were just recovering from this when the image of Jared Matthews was beamed into the room. Danforth apologised to him and told him of our plans before explaining that he had administered poison, Jared Matthews had only moments to live. He stated that Danforth had exceeded all his expectations, finishing with "Aztech I…" then he fell dead at the feet of Aztech and Doc Harley. I don't know, I couldn't help but feel sorry for him in a way. I'd ordered his death, I knew it had to be done but he was a tired old man who if there was a hell was on the way there. Danforth just stood there. There was real emotion, after all Jared Matthews was as close to a father as he would ever have and somehow I couldn't help feeling that

Danforth really did care. I had to do it, it seemed important that someone who had made him do what he least wanted to do at least apologised. We were there out of choice, we had control over his free will and we were manipulating him like a puppet. Wasn't that what we were fighting against? The least we could do was appreciate the gravity of what we were doing and the effect it was having on everyone else.

Nick's voice cut through, we were being shelled from dirtside. We had no control over them. The missiles were coming from Turing. As if that wasn't enough, Jazza, a robot and employee of Leon Court announced that he had set a bomb on the Orbital which would blow up if we didn't find Leon Court's murderer. Great, so we had enough suspects, nobody liked the man. We set about testing to see if anyone had explosives on them.

Jazza came over to Jared and myself. He looked genuinely upset which for a robot was very, very strange. Still, I had seen a lot of strange things and as I've said before it is as if the artificial intelligence can gain emotions with the experiences as we seem to lose them. All he could say was that he did regret that you would be killed. I thanked him for that, Jared just told him to go and play with Ratty.

W scurried around and tried to find the culprit. Then as the time got near Jazza took Jared and myself into the back room and said that he would take us and you away to safety. What happened to us after that would be up to us. He was genuinely upset and he was having real problems. It was like he kept forgetting what he was saying. Faulty programming under stress was all I could assume. It gave me an idea. There was something in what he had said, he loved children. There were the orphans from Ho Street somewhere on the Orbital. I decided to bide my time and try really hard to find the murderer.

The time came and he was going to take us. I refused to go. There was no way that either Jared or I would leave our friends. Also, I'd fought for so long for what I believed in and I had stood with the others. I couldn't leave them now. I knew that as you were my daughter you would understand that. Of that I had no doubt. I'll ask you one day if I get the chance. Jazza looked stunned. When he asked me why I would stay and not go with my child I had to think fast. I've forgotten her name but the partnership of cooks had been invited to leave as well and they were trying to argue with Jazza. They had already worked out that children were his weakness so I compounded the situation by handing you to the lady cook and telling her to go. Then I said that I wouldn't leave the other children on board.

Jazza granted an extension and headed off to alter the timer on the bomb. Cerberus and others had found it by then and they threw it into the airlock and it exploded over the earth, in the vicinity of Turing who had been firing at us earlier. Then all we had to deal with was PLEXSpace!

They began to shell us hard and fast and minute by minute we lost more of the ship. There was only one chance, we initiated Day 1. If they did destroy us, what would it matter, we had initiated what we needed to. Our survival was not essential to the survival of the planet. As the countdown ran they started launching ships that made their way towards us. Yali turned as many away as she could but ship after ship landed. Their crews of robots wore us down. I didn't see your father get hurt. I looked around and he wasn't there. When I asked where he was they said he was seriously hurt and was in the MedBay. I couldn't believe it, seeing him there. It was like to come this far and possibly lose him, that was an impossible concept to grasp. No chance, he's tougher than that. Although they had to do a temporary patch up job on his leg. He was up again, gun in hand and I was there beside him as the clock was ticking and more ships landed. Their crews piled into the room intent on stopping us.

An end of an era. All that time I'd been a pacifist but I was angry. Jared was beside me and I wasn't going to risk losing him. I just emptied my gun into the next group of "visitors". All eight shots, the same eight bullets that Jared had given me on that day at the bar before we went out to attempt to rescue Blue. I'd waited all that time.

Pretty poor victory, it would mean the death of billions of people but life for the earth. For that we had fought for, for that we had to hold true to the plan. I just hugged your father, we had a chance now. It's up to us what we do with the months and years that follow. Many will die on the road to building the new Eden but at least we stand a chance.

"Our deepest fear is not that we are inadequate. Our deepest fear is that we are powerful beyond measure. It is our light, not out darkness, that most frightens us. We ask ourselves "who am I to be brilliant, gorgeous, talented, fabulous?" Actually, who are you not to be? You are a child of God. Your playing small doesn't serve the world. There's nothing enlightened about shrinking so that other people won't feel insecure around you. You are all meant to shine, as children do… And as we let our own light shine, we unconsciously give other people permission to do the same. As we're liberated from our own fear, our presence automatically liberates others." Nelson Mandella, inaugural address as President of South Agrica 1994.

What can I write, how can I ever tell you how I feel at this moment. I'm sitting at a table and looking around a room full of people. The walls are pitted by gunfire, fragile and in need of essential repairs. Somehow the hull of this orbital has held together. SAISH2 has seen us through the battle. Our survival is unimportant, what we have achieved is what matters. I never thought I would see this day, never in my wildest imaginings, I could never have ventured to have hoped. About an hour ago the last gunshot was fired in this room and as more shuttled drifted towards us the Orbital's AI Nick counted down. The seconds seemed like hours as the last wave of robots teamed into the room. The voice echoed hollow in the huge habitation room.

Battered by aftershocks of missiles that had blasted into the structure and exhausted from defending our space I don't think anyone could believe it when the countdown drifted into single figures and then ended "You've won".

The words echoed in the silence when none of us could speak. The miracle of the moment, silence, achievement and the orbital was still standing, albeit that it was very fragile and in need of serious attention.

Perhaps we were the right ones for the job. A crew of administrators, street kids, a DJ and assorted military types, scientists and Net Runners. What chance did we have? Simple, every chance in the world.

It was a moment to reflect on all those who had done so much but had fallen long ago. Somehow it was as if they stood with us, that they heard the countdown too. Time to think about all those who will die from what we have initiated. Tears for the dead and the dying. The earth revolves below us, a ball of gasses, blue and green. It looks pretty small and fragile from up here, but we know it has a heart of fire. We have done all we can, it is now up to Gaia to compete what we have begun and bring her children home. No longer cocooned, time for them to spread their wings, to be free to feel, to learn and to understand for themselves. Free to feel the wind on their faces. The circle is complete.

Asha, all I can hope is that your generation learns something from what we had to go through and that never again do so few have to watch the deaths of so many to defend our planet home.

So as it began, so shall it end. I'll leave the final words to Doc Harley.

A man and a woman sit in a forest
Everything around them is green
The earth provides their food and the are not hungry
They drink from the stream beside them,
And do not grow sick because of it.
They have no guns, because no one wishes to kill them.
They are not judged because of the way they were born,
Because of past actions, or because of what they own
Or whom they are owned by
They are judged by what they do now
By how they have lived and how they love
And the judgement is that they shall be absolutely FREE

One day they may choose to have children, to care for and to love
These children shall not be taken from them
When they are grown, they will have their own choices
And together with all the other people they will build a world
Where only truth and justice will rule…

This is not our past
This is the future
THIS IS OUR EDEN DREAM

For which we fight, for which we are prepared to die.
And it shall set us free.

AND IT HAS MADE US FREE

In love and in service
To the Mother Below, the Father Above,
and the Spirit that protects us all
Believe in dreams and you might just see them come true.
All my love
Chrytal

.

REAL SURVIVAL

MEDICINAL PLANTS

When I was small I found a plant on the path at my parents' house. I planted it and it grew. It was a weed. That was because it wasn't a cultivated flower in the right place, a wild flower.

In the past these "wild flowers" were our medicine and could be again. Many medicines have been derived from "wild flowers" but now there is a problem. With the millions of people who are turning to Herbal Medicine these plants are now under threat. It is illegal to pick them in many places and those in towns and cities can't just wander out back and pick what they want.

They are the forgotten resource by some that if gone would not be there if we ever need them.

A tiny plant will struggle to live, that is what living things do. If we can't help then we can at least not hinder. The "Grandmother Plant" is a great way to go if you are going to pick from the wild. Never pick the first plant you find. Then you will never pick the last one.

There are warnings about how wild plants are being wiped out. If everyone who was interested picked them this would be true. Many places have by-laws that do not permit you to pick what you may like to. This is to protect the plants. There are far too many people on this planet now, the resources can't cope, so we do have to be more careful than we would like.

So we are going to farm them as well as reintroduce them here. They should be available in 2019 by post but we would also encourage that these plants are protected in the wild.

There are so many books that list recipes and how to use these plants, I'll leave that to the experts. There are also many other uses for the plants and I'll be working on those on the web site www.edendream.co.uk I'm working on a list of the plants we are growing and what they are useful for.

REAL WORLD EDEN DREAM

We are guardians of this planet. We don't own it, we borrow it. Mankind has such a need to "own". I've worked very hard to be able protect one little part of this world, to make it a "New Eden" in the hope that others will follow.

Just because you can doesn't mean that you should and knowledge without wisdom is a loaded gun. That has always been a "mantra" I've lived by.

We have choices, we have information and that is what makes us free.

The goats have taught me a lot. I had to make choices there too. From the first kids born to the ones this year. Traditionally horns are taken off of goats, no they don't naturally look like that. They have amazing "head furniture" which they use to play and to scratch themselves. They are a hazard and no doubt more of a problem in a big commercial herd which is being milked daily. Handy to catch them though when you need to do hoofs and dose them.

I chose not to take them off and to let them develop naturally. It can be a hazard and I've had a few knocks over the years but a small price to pay. The goats look magnificent, particularly the bucks (boys) and they can have much more fun smacking heads (which is natural).

From this point on I am looking at natural worming and a more natural way of keeping them. I put the question on a Goaty Friends on Facebook and I found that many people can manage this. Just by planting the right plants around will keep them naturally wormed. There is a chemical in some plants which helps. It is another step down the road to a more natural way of living and stepping away from chemical dependence.

It does mean "breaking the traditional rules" and I'll do that for the sake of the animals.

I was recently accused of poor animal maintenance because I didn't take the lambs tails off and because the dogs howl sometimes.

The lambs was a choice, not poor maintenance. The field is not overgrazed, not muddy and they are chemically wormed well enough so they don't have the messy rear ends what cause the problem in the first place. So they can keep their tails, they can wag their tails and they can be as nature intended. If they have a problem, they will get a shampoo (a natural one which I plan to make).

My Children of the Night make sweet music sometimes (the dogs howl). It used to be every evening at roughly the same time. That is not a sign of a distressed dog. They now howl if they hear something they don't understand and to find out where the rest of the "pack" are. It is a beautiful wild sound, usually started by one of them, they howl and then they settle down. They are allowed to be a little wild. They are exercised free of leads and they are a pack although they don't live together. They howl to communicate and it is a beautiful sound. Obviously not to everyone.

Smallholder by accident, that was how it stated about twelve years ago. I had been working in London and had done for most of my life, except for a few years in Guildford and Hove and my partner at the time was a Forest Keeper. He had an accident and we were going to lose our tied cottage, a beautiful place in Epping Forest so we had to find alternative accommodation.

I saw the word "smallholder" and I thought that might be interesting so I put it into a search engine, "Smallholding" actually and a fascinating place came up. It was an old Mill with the Mill Owner's Cottage. We were in a hurry to find somewhere so we went to see it and put an offer in that weekend.

We didn't buy that place in the end but we did buy another and there we were with four acres and a smallholding. Hugh Fearnley Whittingstall and River Cottage were the staple diet, books and big, big hopes. I dug three quarters of an acre with a spade and planted the vegetables and we got a couple of goats. We got chickens, free! I got rid of all the nasty corrugated metal and I wanted a tidy farm, like the Britains ™ Farm of my childhood. It all had to be "just so". It didn't take long to take those rose coloured glasses and jump on them. Animals make a mess and grass turns to mud if walked on. The neat, pristinely clean place of shows doesn't reflect the work that goes into making those places tidy just before the camera crew arrives. Take a look at any working farm, or smallholding, reality dawns. You do the best you can of course but there are only so many hours in a day and the important jobs have to be done first.

The move to Fferm Castell Gwyrdd (then known as Old Castle) was a natural one. It was a place where I could try things out and learn with more than enough space to do it all. It was not a rush to finish, it was a gentle learning curve so nothing much happened for a while. The animals were fed and wandered and I learnt about the land and what would be right for it.

It is allegedly an old castle, there are legends that there was one here and if you look at the layout, it does look like one. The location is about right as well. Another responsibility as not only is it likely to be the castle it has an ancient spring as well. Of course this is used but it is also a beautiful place that we didn't want to spoil too much. There is a stream too but the water does come from the spring, one part of the poem, tick.

Growing has been something I set aside until other jobs were mastered. I did try a small test planting, in a couple of wardrobes. The idea had been to shut the "doors" (which had become lids) when there was a frost but as I found the doors shut I pulled them off so the plants couldn't be deprived of light again. The soil is good, the climate is good, this year, here we go!

Eden Dream was the poem but it was something I carried on as a mark of respect to those who had made me focus on what was important.

There was so much information which to me was normal but I realised that it wasn't available to everyone. So, despite working at a Solicitors Firm all day I opened up a shop in the evening in Essex back in 1998 where I could contact different organisations to make this information available to everyone. Some came in, many didn't but it was there all the same.

I was at a dinner with William Hague and he asked me if I could get actual facts from the organisations, something the Government could work with. He was not interested in ideals, he wanted facts. I agreed as I thought it would be an easy task. I therefore telephoned Friends of the Earth and asked for the information. Their response was to request that I joined the local group. I did so and paid my membership fees. I had hoped that the literature that arrived would be full of the facts that I needed and I was ready to forward them on to be acted on.

I received glossy magazine like brochures which had no real substance and my name was mis-spelled on the cover. It wasn't something I'd complain about other than just after that I started to receive junk mail with the same misspelling. I found it horrendous that an organisation dedicated to the planet was condoning and making money from Junk Mail!

Suffice to say I had nothing to report and despite the offer, there was nothing to be taken up. Through the years the party has supported Eden Dream by allowing me to put on a small stand at their events and latterly by reading my letters. I hope in some small way that Eden Dream has helped over the years just by being able to put forward ideas and latterly to be involved in farming and to be able to "report back". Not that I write letters anymore since my mother died, I'm not sure that without here being there they would bother to read them anymore either.

Just after that I opened a shop in the evening. I took up an annual rent on a shop and filled it with information and brochures from organisations as well as providing a place where people could come and discuss things.

Initially the "organisation" had been designed to provide therapy rooms and help for those who needed it. It continued as a Web Site and an ideal which is needed now more than ever. There was a time I thought it wouldn't be needed again and I could "retire". Solar panels had a feed in tariff and it looked like the world was going "greener". Stuff green, it is practical, money saving and right! Now, I worry again.

What is it for?

It was hard to say when I was working in London for Solicitors' firms (Private Client so the "gentle" side of Law) and latterly for a Patents and Trade Marks Attorneys (saw loads of great stuff being patented and couldn't tell anyone). My vehement avoidance of training as a solicitor was not understood by those around me but I always felt that something else was more important.

I would say that my time working for a Patent and Trade Mark Attorneys did give me a confidence about looking for new ideas that could make a difference. I've learnt a lot, mostly about keeping goats.

The Eden Dream, Letter to Asha, is a warning. This is NOT a world we went! The ideal world would have happy people living in towns and those who want to or are able to live in the countryside as it should be lived in and by that I mean co-habited with, the world gives and we are guardians and give back. In my opinion it is not a "monster to be tamed" into some back garden that gives neat lines of food and how dare a weed appear or it will be blasted to oblivion with weed killer. There is a place for that, and a place for wild. As I have found, some of the plants we blast could be the key to our survival!

If you are going to survive after an apocalypse then the sort of survival taught by Bear Grills etc will be useful initially but, think about it. If everyone has the same skills the trees aren't going to last very long. If you want long term survival then the way to the future could lay in the past. They may get some people through the initial days but if you think about it, resources would do that anyway. What would be needed would be the long term things like a form of community farming as there would be no flashy tractors. The ground will give its bounty, plants want to live and many like fruits are designed to be eaten so that their seeds can pass on to another area. To survive is one thing, to survive well is another.

I was told of a SAS mission where two groups went out. One group survived perfectly well on what they found. The other did better, they found wild herbs and had a far better dinner. If balanced with the right nutrients (which isn't as complicated as it sounds) then that also improves health. There is no point winning a battle and dying of starvation in the years to come. The basics have to be there, water, good soil, seed and enough people to keep the wild ones away (weeds and bugs) and to keep them to their own area. Mother Nature does know more than we do however smart we think we are. Learning to listen, learning to learn and to let the land tell you what you can have is a far less arrogant way of going about things and it will make for an easier life. Bend her to your sword at your peril.

A smallholding is a house with a big garden where you can keep animals and grow crops. You buy it like you buy any other property. Mostly they are bought with no equipment and no animals and you have to start from scratch with that sort of thing. There are plenty of books and information on the internet and groups who will give advice, sometime more than you can handle and sometimes conflicting.

What I would like to create here is something a bit different. Everything has to support everything else, well that was the plan.

Of course we had to go and get the neighbours from hell who decided they hated us before they even moved in! We are going to be doing things differently and as they obviously have their own issues this has been like a red rag to a bull. They have done all they can to get us to go. Still here…

I kept pigs and they cut the fence wire and set a line of apples into their garden after telling me that the pigs would escape. I can say that now as the son has been rather proud of. That is what we are up against. Much more had happened since and to be honest it has set things back a lot.

It is not uncommon. One in five people have neighbour disputes and if you are going to do something "outside the box" then you can expect the ignorant to be difficult.

Truth is stranger than fiction. I can't believe that people can be like that. I'm used to civilised people, both at work and in my private life. I am certainly not used to the bile that has come from a neighbour.

The choice here to give up the houses for a caravan may be odd to some people but after years of pouring money into old houses, I think it wise. When you have a whole world of things to do then DIY and housework comes far down the list. If you can't handle the problem, remove it!

To give the animals what they wanted and to be able to have this wonderful place I had to sacrifice the house. Living in a caravan is a lot warmer! After ten years of the old place with no heating or faulty heating believe me it is so cosy to sit on a sofa with the gas on and be as warm as can be! It is like being on holiday all the time. My grandparents had a couple of dozen caravans at Weymouth so it does have that holiday feel.

Living off grid is fine if you have enough to be able to generate the power that you need. I bought a caravan kit which was only temporary. The whole system was temporary as the National Grid was connected as soon as they had sorted out removing the poles from the land and taking the cables underground.

Water comes from the spring. We went to various companies and then did it ourselves. We had been planning to try to use a hydro ram but in the end we went with a powered system. We may well put a hydro ram in later as a second system for irrigation. We have a too much water problem, we also have 1000 litre tanks for the animals and it is hard to keep up with using it all.

In all cases it relies on not being afraid to do things and to make things work. If you want water then go and get water. If it isn't where you want it, move it. Syphon systems and other processes are useful and there is always a way, even if it is a bucket.

In a dark future world nobody would have pumped water. Without the hydro ram, that also includes us as it is powered. I'll sort out the hydro ram one day, it is "on the list" but the powered system was quicker as there were a few issues with the ram we built and we needed to get water sorted quickly.

Animals make manure, which makes plants which feeds people and animals. Nothing is "waste", it is all food for someone.

I love the wormery. I bought one off of Ebay and it has been very useful. I'm about to use the compost it has made and the pots are sitting there ready. The plants are all too small yet. It is a perfect way to use what it truly waste.

In a survival situation life would be a little different. Here we would be too close to the town and would be a target for raiding as soon as there was trouble.

MAGNETIC HYDRO RAM WATER WHEEL TURBINE

None of this is novel or inventive and thus cannot be patented. The principle is that magnets can also repel and that a hydro ram will provide the spurts of water constantly without a power source which overcomes the problem that there cannot be perpetual motion.

If you imagine a water wheel which is "overshot". Water comes into the wheel from a Hydro Ram from a water source. This is a constant "push, push" of water which would start the wheel and keep it going.

The magnetic repulsion takes this energy and magnifies it so that between the two you get a constant flow which can generate energy (as well as pumping water and providing a water source).

I believe it would work and I have seen both parts work in principle. There is a patent for the magnetic wheel which was initially discovered in the 1800s so it is nothing new.

If both of these principles were put together and either used on a multi wheel basis or larger wheel basis there would be a "free" source of power that doesn't need to be stored as it is constant.

If a turbine is attached to this you have free power which will never stop.

HOUSE MICRO GENERATION

Water falls all over the house. Down the down pipes outside the house, off the roof, out of the grey water system. Why isn't that run through micro turbines to power the house?

Any turbines that could feed batteries would provide that source of power from an energy that is just wasted.

Mini wind turbines could be fitted to houses. The high winds we have these days would provide a very good resource for this.

Solar panels are another way of gathering power. Progress is being made all the time to make these more efficient but until we can improve batteries there is still a limit to what they can do and only during the hours of daylight.

ABOUT THE AUTHOR

This is normally where the "About the Author" bit goes. But technically I'm not "the author" as the original story was a Live Roleplaying Game which was created by Teece Flemming, Alex Hill, Dave Phelan and Katie Player and others. It was played out and created as it went along and started twenty five years go. This publication is to mark the 25 Year Anniversary of its beginning.

This is unofficial and not endorsed by the referees.

Printed in Great Britain
by Amazon